Casting Shadows

R J SAMUEL

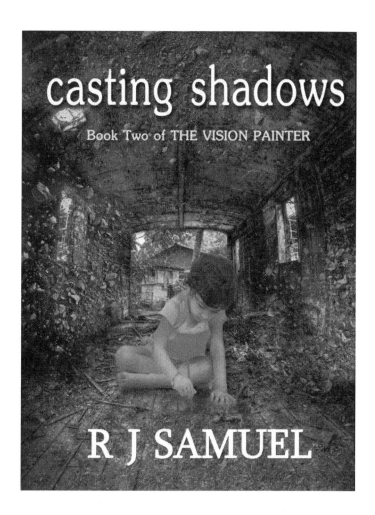

casting shadows

Book Two of THE VISION PAINTER

R J SAMUEL

Vision Ink Press

ISBN-13: 978-1482694833
ISBN-10: 1482694832

Cover Design
by
The Vision Painter Studio

Vision Ink Press

To Jesse, Hamish, Clio, and the rest of the menagerie, past and present. Love is not a strong enough word.

ACKNOWLEDGMENTS

Thank you to Helgs for putting the idea in my head of a sequel to Falling Colours and for encouraging me and reading every chapter of Casting Shadows as it was written. And to my beta readers, Max, Terry, Susan, Mary, and Lee, thank you so much for your help and your encouragement. Thank you to Lee for doing the proof reading as well as beta reading. I hope that we caught everything, but any errors left in are mine.

Thank you to all my readers for their continued support and interest. One of the best things about writing for me has been hearing from readers who have connected with my words and enjoyed my work.

PROLOGUE

Kerala, 1985

The shadow emerged from the blue and brown. The shape of a man took form on wood as coloured powder was slashed onto the makeshift canvas. Welts of raw sienna built up into the lines of a face drawn in a scream. The jaw-stretched anguish exposed the crimson pink of tongue and the stained yellow of teeth. Burnt umber shoulders rose and descended into thick knotted muscles of arms and forearms, fists clenched.

The powders mixed and swirled as they were ground onto the wooden board, the painter's howls drowned out by the music and chants that drifted in through the windows with the dense humid air. The *Holi* festival raged outside in the brightest of colours as the painter struggled on in the dimly lit room. Delicate fingers suffused with fury worked the pigments until the man-shaped collection of colours became a portrait of pain.

The sweat fell from the young painter's forehead onto the canvas and drew a streak down the vermillion-covered torso of the subject.

The painter paused before adding the final touch. The shaft of steel grey parted the red sea chest of the painted man.

CHAPTER ONE

The metal canister stared back at Kiran. The tape strapped around it proclaimed "Human Genetic Material" in bold red letters across an orange background. Kiran dragged the protesting container through her front door as quickly as she could, muttering about indelicate Danish sperm banks and smirking couriers.

"Ashley!" Kiran let the canister go and it settled onto the hallway floor with a clang.

There was silence from the study.

"Ashley! It's here." Kiran sat on the stairs. *That's what you get for living with a writer. Your potential child arrives at the door and she's still sitting at her desk contemplating the next words.*

"What's here?" The voice was distracted.

Kiran got up and pushed open the door to the study. She smiled. Ashley was obviously in the zone. She was sitting at her antique writing desk, scribbling on an A4 notepad, the keyboard to one side, her glasses lost in the sweep of red hair.

"Sarah or Jamie. Or both."

Ashley looked up. Her eyes were returning from whatever setting in which she had been immersed.

"Kiran, don't jinx it." Ashley felt for her glasses on her forehead.

"I am carrying out my own form of vision painting. Since I'm not allowed to paint for myself or now for you, surely I can put the words out there."

Ashley was now searching the desk for her glasses.

"The writing must be going well." Kiran walked over and slipped her hand through Ashley's hair. She leaned down and kissed Ashley on the nose, then retrieved the glasses and slipped them over Ashley's eyes.

"Not too bad. I should be able to email this out by deadline time." Ashley leant back and stretched out her fingers.

Ashley looked healthy and happy now, seven months later, but they still had the grief-wracked nights when the loss of her mother hit Ashley. When she woke up out of her sleep and got out of bed to stand by the window and stare at the trees that surrounded the house. She seemed to be drawn to those trees. Kiran often got up to find Ashley sitting outside in the dawn light, her back resting against a sturdy trunk. Kiran would sit with her; the two women snuggled under the blanket that Kiran brought, while the birds argued over who got to sing the next song to them.

Ashley got up from her chair. She squeezed Kiran's hand and smiled. "So, we have a date for tomorrow night?"

"Yes. And this time you're in charge of the 'Human Genetic Material' that was dumped on the porch. Can you believe the courier does that every time? God knows what they think at the depot."

"It isn't like there is that much of an audience out here in the wilds of Connemara." Ashley walked over to the canister in the hall.

Kiran followed her. "I know, I know. But what if Ron or Delilah call in? Or an actual vision painting client? Can you imagine? Not that I can remember what a client looks like."

"Dad will be fine with it. We do need to tell him soon, though."

"I wanted to wait until it worked. You know, present Ron with the news that he's going to be a granddad when there is actually a living thing in my belly and not just the stuff in a little straw out there and an egg clinging to hope. I still haven't figured out how to tell my parents I'm with you for keeps, not to mention, that we're trying to get me pregnant."

Kiran sank back down on the stairs.

Ashley frowned. "You *are* still okay with all of this, aren't you? It isn't moving too fast for you, is it?"

Kiran shook her head. "I know it's going very fast. But it feels right. Besides, it is my fault my stupid biological clock seems to have gone into overdrive." She clutched at the banister. "It feels like a river forcing its way through me, like I have no choice." Kiran raised an eyebrow as she asked, "You're the one I'm worried about. Are you still sure?"

Ashley hesitated, for just the slightest moment, and then smiled. "It would probably seem strange to everyone else. But I want you to be happy and this will make you happy."

"You're not just doing it for me though, are you? I thought you wanted a child as much as I did. Maybe not in the crazy ticking time bomb way, but, you know, in a sensible mature way."

Ashley sat down beside Kiran on the step. Kiran could feel the warmth where Ashley's shoulders rested against hers. "Kiran, so much has changed for me, for us, in the last seven months. Sometimes, I'm not the sensible, mature one. These days, I don't know what I am. I used to be so practical."

Kiran sighed. "Until you met me."

"Well, yes and no." Ashley smoothed a lock of red hair out of her eyes. "I'm used to being the one who did what she was expected to do. You didn't let anyone change who you were. I did. For so many years and now I don't know who I could have been."

"You're a writer. A good one. You're enjoying that, aren't you?"

Ashley nodded.

"You like living out here with the sheep and the stars...?"

Ashley smiled. "Yes. I love it. For other reasons too." She touched Kiran's cheek. "It would be nicer if you didn't have to live in Galway during the week though. If you could do what you love too."

Kiran held Ashley's fingers against her cheek. "I'm fine. I don't miss it. Really. I'm getting used to being the logical one. It suits me better than you anyway." She laughed at Ashley's face and stood up.

"I've got a good feeling about this one. Third time lucky." Kiran patted the canister. "Okay, come on. Let's get Eric the Dane ready."

"Kiran! You're not going to keep calling him that, are you?"

"No, I shall change it to 'your good-for-nothing sperm donor of a father' when the kid is misbehaving."

"Kiran!" Ashley laughed and Kiran's heart did its usual jump when she heard that sound.

∞ ∞ ∞

Kiran lay on the bed with her eyes closed and her legs up against the headboard and the wall. Myth or no myth, she wasn't taking chances with gravity. She struggled to keep her mind blank though the visions clamoured at the edges of her consciousness. She didn't know if she was allowed to visualise. She had not allowed herself after the last two attempts and after the events of the previous year, Kiran was scared. Scared of the gift she had been given and terrified of the unforeseen consequences of her every action.

She could hear Ashley discarding the empty straw and the used syringe. She opened her eyes to watch. The copper highlights in Ashley's hair glowed in the soft light of the bedside lamp and her face, paler after the winter, was peaceful as she concentrated on her task.

Ashley turned and caught her staring. She lay down beside Kiran and stroked away the hair that lay black and damp across Kiran's forehead. Kiran looked into those eyes that had captivated her from the moment she had seen them. And that still made her breath catch in her throat. She wasn't able to say it to Ashley but every day she fell a little deeper into her eyes, into her presence, her warmth, her strength.

Kiran murmured, "Even if it doesn't work, I'll still consider myself the luckiest vision painter in Ireland."

Ashley smiled. "You're the *only* vision painter in Ireland."

"Then *definitely* the luckiest one."

Ashley leant closer and whispered over Kiran's lips, "Do you ever take anything seriously, woman?"

"I'll have you know, I'm being very serious. Though I am beginning to think there aren't any vision painters left in Ireland. I can't be counted now considering I haven't done a painting in so long."

Ashley said, "It will come back. Give it time. What happened last year was bound to have an effect on you, even though you pretend everything is fine."

Kiran closed her eyes and let her body relax into the thick quilt. Images of Marge and Tony and Sean were the usual intruders in her head. She could feel Ashley's fingers tracing circles on her face.

Ashley's voice was gentle as it rustled through the hair around Kiran's ears. "Kiran, why is it so important to do this now? You don't talk about what happened and you're so anxious to have a baby now."

Kiran kept her eyes shut. The image of Tony's eyes as she'd last seen them, the tears glinting in the dim light of CCU, faded only to be replaced by the wreckage of Marge's body, the terror in her last panicked drive. Kiran's eyelids trembled as she tried to force the image off her eyeballs. She felt Ashley's fingers stroking and smoothing the wrinkling lids.

Kiran tried to keep her voice steady. It came out light and airy. "I'm getting old. Don't want to lose my last chance, do I?"

Ashley sighed. "You try and come across as this person who doesn't get hurt. Almost like you don't care. Kiran, this is me. We're in this together. You're going to have to start opening up."

"I can't explain it. It's like a craving, so strong and overpowering. Like I have to pass on my gift." Kiran opened her eyes. Her words had surprised her.

Ashley's fingers moved down Kiran's cheek. "Will you lose your gift?"

"I don't know. I hadn't actually thought of it."

"Did your father pass it on and then stop working? Is that how it works?"

Kiran shook her head. "He was in Ireland for a part of the time. He didn't work as a vision painter here. He was a businessman. He did a bit in the 90s when he moved back to India but he retired from the actual painting in 1996." She sat up. "That's when I started doing proper vision paintings here. I'd finished college. I did paintings for friends. It freaked them out a little, but it felt like the most natural thing in the world to me."

"Did your father retire because he couldn't paint anymore, because the gift had been passed on to you?"

Kiran tried to remember. She'd been busy in Ireland. Kerala and her parents had seemed so far away. She knew her father was very involved with building the retirement complex and with the Council work.

She'd told Ron that Ji couldn't paint for him because he'd passed on his gift. That had been the subliminal message she'd received and she hadn't questioned it.

Kiran felt the confusion crowding her mind. She didn't like to question her gift or the whole idea of vision painting. It had always felt normal to her. Now she was stuck.

"I don't know. I never talked to him about it. Not properly anyway."

She lay back down and closed her eyes.

An image of a baby crashed into her mind. Kiran hesitated, trying desperately to stop it but she couldn't. She let go and allowed the colours to develop. She pictured holding the baby boy and her arms encircled her chest as she lay in the vision. Her heart felt thick and heavy in every beat as the little body lay across it. She felt Ashley's lips brush hers and her weight move and settle on the bed beside her and Ashley's arms joined hers.

They slept with Kiran's legs still almost vertical until the pain from the lack of blood flow woke her up and she felt frantically for the baby, only to realise that she'd been visualising.

She woke Ashley and they crawled under the covers. As Kiran drifted off to sleep, she tried to ignore the vague feeling of guilt that tickled her mind.

∞ ∞ ∞

The sound of the telephone jangled through Kiran's whole body awakening her from a dream about being back at school. She lay there for a few moments wondering why the school bell sounded so wrong. From the pale light outside the window and the darkness in the bedroom she knew it was too early for anything but her father calling from India.

And too late for her to stop Ashley picking up the phone. *Great.*

Ashley held the handset out to her after only a few seconds. She buried her face in her pillow and Kiran could only hear a muttered "It's for your father's daughter," before she grabbed the handset.

"Dad?"

She didn't even bother to ask him if he knew what time it was. Not that it would have made a difference to him. When the notion took him to talk to his daughter, he called. Even at 3 a.m. Irish time. Kiran wondered how many times he had woken Ashley on a weeknight. He'd still not grasped the concept of Kiran staying at Ron's place in Galway during the week to be closer to the engineering firm where she was now working longer hours, and coming home to Ashley in Connemara for weekends.

"Kiran, is that woman always there?" Ji sounded distracted. He seemed to be going through the motions. Almost for her sake.

"Yes, Dad, she lives here. And I stay at her place. And her name is Ashley. Which you know very well."

"This is the doctor woman, right? The one who won't work as a doctor but has decided to be a writer."

"Yes, Dad. A writer for a medical journal. And she probably will go back to Medicine, don't worry."

"I'm not worried. Why should I worry? My only daughter is a lesbian. And she is now being kicked out of her own home by another lesbian. But, that is not why I called." He lowered his voice. "Kiran, your mother needs you."

Kiran sighed. "As in you want me to visit 'needs me'...?"

"No." Her father's voice cracked. "Amma needs you."

Kiran shot up in the bed. Ashley groaned and pulled back the quilt.

"Dad, what's going on?"

Ashley must have heard the panic in Kiran's voice. She sat up and reached over to switch on the bedside lamp.

Ji's voice was weaker than Kiran had ever heard it. "Kiran, she's in the medical centre. It was very sudden. They don't know what's wrong. I didn't want to worry you, but they are saying to call her family."

"I'll be there as soon as I can." Even as Kiran hung up, her legs were out from under the covers, her mind working on times of flights and calls to make. Anything to stop the screaming fear that was pounding at the door.

CHAPTER TWO

The jeep bounced and Kiran jerked awake from a fitful sleep. She raised her feet to peel her sweat-soaked thighs off the seat. Babu turned to grin at her, his teeth gleaming in the dark brown of his face and through the blackness of his moustache. She gave a smile that was more of a grimace hoping he would turn his attention back to the road as soon as possible.

Great. They were overtaking a bus. That would have been fine except for the fact that, while the road was wide, the bus was in the process of overtaking another car at the same time.

She held her breath as their jeep edged past the front of the bus and swerved back onto the correct lane, almost joining the carts and cows and pedestrians that thronged the dirt area that lined the tarmac road. She tried to think about anything but the screech of the brakes and the whoosh of the cars that they had narrowly missed hitting head-on. Tried to think about anything other than her mother.

It was 9 a.m. in India on the day after Saint Patrick's Day. There was no green bunting to welcome her on the road from Cochin International Airport to Pallata. There had been decorations in Heathrow airport. Shamrocks and green furry hats. Kiran had watched in bemusement from her makeshift bed on the plastic airport seating. Sleep had been cast aside after the phone call as Ashley had packed her a rucksack while Kiran searched online, grabbing one of the last tickets on a busy St. Patrick's weekend. The drive through Connemara had been a blur of mountains fogged by fear. Kiran had driven her car which Ashley would drive back.

They'd made the 7.45 a.m. flight to Heathrow where Kiran had a four hour layover. Grateful to find a few rows of seats without armrests, she had collapsed across the seats but couldn't sleep. She watched the legs parade through her vision, suitcases in tow. She counted shoes instead of sheep, but still the worry and exhaustion kept her awake for the wait before she could go to the gate for her flight. The stopover in Dubai barely registered. It was still baking hot at midnight there and she tried to prepare herself for the sweltering heat of Kerala. She found her connecting flight and landed in Cochin at 8 a.m. local time on Monday, 24 hours after the phone call from her father.

Babu had been waiting for her. He'd smiled and given the typical Malayalee shake of his head to welcome her. She couldn't remember any words in Malayalam to say hello and she found her head moving in a matching greeting. He was wearing a *mundu*, the cotton cloth wrapped around his waist, leaving bandy legs bare from the knees down. He held her pink rucksack awkwardly with its straps trailing along the shiny concrete. More used to suitcases with handles, she assumed.

The Jeep was waiting and she settled in for the journey she dreaded. Hurtling through the air in a tin can 30,000 feet above the ground would be safer than driving on the roads here. Especially the way Babu did it. Her mother had said he'd learnt to drive from his father who had worked as a driver for her grandparents. As the Jeep careered around the crowded roads, Kiran wondered who had taught the father to drive.

"How's Amma now?" Kiran tried in her broken Malayalam. It translated roughly as 'How's Amma sitting?'

She wouldn't be sitting, she'd be lying down. On a hospital bed. Kiran, stop.

Babu shrugged. It was a tired and slightly bewildered move of his shoulders.

The roads were busy with pedestrians, cattle and goats, scooters, rickshaws, cars, and buses; all trying to fight for their space on the road. Babu gestured when they approached the roadside restaurant where they usually stopped to eat her favourites of *dosai* and coconut chutney. But she shook her head. Not this time.

It was late morning as they approached the village. Kiran could feel the acid burning her empty stomach. They passed a few people near the temple. Some waved, recognising Kiran. She didn't have time to wave back as Babu swung around the bend and down the main street of the village. As they reached the next corner where the Vision Painting Training Centre was located, Kiran saw her father's best friend, Dinesh, at the window of his house. He held his hand up in greeting before disappearing from view.

The church came into view and Kiran started collecting herself. The retirement complex was built on the land behind the house where Elizabeth's grandparents, Kiran's great-grandparents, had lived. The simple gate and driveway to the old house that neighboured the church belied the sprawling complex behind, which boasted thirty self-contained houses built in an elongated oval around a park, a common dining hall, library, shop, meditation centre, and a state-of-the-art medical centre.

A few residents were standing on the road that started from the main house, her parents' home, and continued around the circle of houses. Babu didn't stop and as the Jeep sped past, the group ushered her on with worried smiles.

The medical centre was at the far end of the complex. Hidden away behind coconut and palm trees and shrubbery, nature planned to shield the residents from the clinical nature of the building. Ji had designed the complex to be a simple but comfortable retirement home for the residents, with its small patches of lawn and fiercely competitive flower beds. The twenty acre site was surrounded by coconut trees that leant into the sky waiting to drop their burdens. And beyond the skirting of trees lay the flooded paddy fields.

They pulled up in front of the medical centre and Kiran peeled herself off the seat and stepped out. Her clothes felt damp and heavy and completely wrong for the climate here. She hurried past the saris and *mundus*, barely able to acknowledge the greetings. It seemed like all the residents of the complex were either at her parents' house or at the medical centre. The humid air was heavy with their worry.

Kiran's sandals slapped down the polished stone floor of the corridor. The centre was air-conditioned with clean white walls. It looked completely different to the hospital in Galway, but all she could see was the corridor to the cardiac unit where she had gone to visit a man who had died because she'd done a painting.

This is because of Tony. Because I painted Marge. I did this. To my own mother. Kiran, stop!

There was a woman in a plain sari sitting outside one of the doors. She got up as Kiran approached and opened the door for her. Kiran hesitated, took a deep breath of antiseptic air, and stepped through into the room.

The room was shaded. The blinds pulled down to keep out the sun and noise. There was a bed with a chair pulled up beside it. The thin frame of her father was sprawled across the chair and her mother was lying on the bed. Ji had Elizabeth's hand in his and he moved his lips when he saw his daughter, but the smile was so full of fear that it hurt Kiran deep in her gut.

Elizabeth's eyes were closed and her body was still apart from the regular movement of her chest. Kiran let her breath out. At least her mother was breathing on her own. She didn't know what she had expected but she had been afraid there were going to be tubes and ventilators and drips and mechanical devices beeping every few seconds. Instead, there was just the rustle of the bamboo blinds and the breathing of her parents and a sole IV tube snaking its way into her mother's arm.

Kiran walked around the bed and took her mother's free hand. It felt dry and warm.

"What is going on?" her voice came out in a whisper.

Ji's voice was low as well. "She just collapsed. She was standing on the veranda yesterday or...what day is today?"

He took his eyes off Elizabeth and looked up at Kiran. She shook her head. He returned his gaze to his wife's face and continued after a pause, "She was standing on the veranda on Saturday morning waiting for the rest of the ladies. For the gin rummy. I was working on our autobiography in my study. I heard them shouting. I knew immediately. Kiran, I felt it like a pain in my chest. And I knew something had happened to her. When I got to her, she was like this. Very pale and in some sort of coma. She has not woken up since then." His voice got frustrated. "I don't know how long it is because I don't know what day of the week it is."

"Shalini!" Ji shouted the name and Kiran jumped. The woman who had been guarding the door popped her head into the room and Ji asked her in Malayalam what day it was. She replied in a hushed voice, Monday, and Ji looked guilty as he glanced back at the still-quiet face of his wife.

"She does not even hear me when I shout." He sounded like he was trying to reassure himself.

"She might be able to hear and she's probably storing up some special words for you if you don't stop shouting around her." Now Kiran was trying the reassurance. It wasn't working on either of them. "Why is she here? Why isn't she in a hospital?"

"She's been seen by the top doctor from Pallata Hospital. I had him brought here. He's a very busy man but he would do anything for me. I did a vision painting for him years ago. Top man in the hospital. Top in Kerala."

"And? What did he say about Amma?"

Ji said nothing. He just stared at the figure on the bed. His hair was whiter than she remembered from her visit last year when he had just been elected Leader of the Council of Vision Painters and was parading around the complex in full garb. Now he looked thin and old and rolled into himself like parchment paper. Her mother was 66 but she looked about 20 years younger, even though her black hair was liberally sprayed with gray. Her face was smooth and still beautiful.

"Dad, what did he say?" Kiran tried not to raise her voice. Her chest felt like it was being crushed in a vice.

Ji shook his head. "The man was totally lost. He said he did not know what was wrong with her. He said her vital signs are all fine and that there is nothing obvious on examination."

"But surely they should have taken her in and done a CT scan or something?"

"They will be doing that later today. They said Monday they could do it." He looked up at her. "I didn't want her moved until they were ready." He looked away at a dark speck lost in the whiteness of the wall.

"You're not telling me something, Dad?"

"The doctor didn't say anything else."

"Then why did you say that they were asking for her family to be called?"

Ji looked guilty again. He said in Malayalam, "It was not something he said."

"Then what? Dad, you're scaring me." Kiran gripped her mother's hand tighter.

He looked drained and fearful and exhausted. "I just thought you needed to be here. I might be a retired vision painter but that does not mean I do not still feel things." He was still speaking Malayalam and she struggled to translate the words.

"Did you have a vision? That something was going to happen to her?" The fear had gripped her by the throat and her voice stumbled as it crept out.

Ji shook his head. She could see his knuckles become more prominent. She hoped her mother couldn't feel pain. The same thought must have occurred to Ji as he gazed at his fist and slowly loosened his grip on his wife's hand. Ji pointed at the corner of the room before resting his forehead on the bed beside Elizabeth's hand.

Kiran looked around the room. There was another chair by the window. She dragged it over and sat down and laid her head against her mother's shoulder. She felt the exhaustion of the early morning dash from her house and the 24 hour trip pull at her eyelids. Kiran knew her father wouldn't answer any more questions. She rubbed her fingers gently over the tape holding the IV tube in place on her mother's forearm. Her father wouldn't admit if he was as lost as she was. She closed her eyes and held on to her mother's arm.

She heard the woman ask from the corridor if they wanted something to eat and her father grunt a no before she drifted off to sleep surrounded by the scent of cleaning fluid and talcum powder.

CHAPTER THREE

Kiran awoke to the sound of voices outside the room. For a moment, she couldn't figure out where she was. The feel of the shoulder against which she was resting and the softness of the arm, but mostly the scent of talcum powder brought the present back to her.

She raised her head and looked at her mother. There were no signs that she had moved. Her mouth was open and her skin looked pale in the dim light. Kiran rubbed the arm she was holding and watched the blood rush in and recede from the spot. Kiran had described Elizabeth's skin as the colour of Irish cream liquor while hers had a dash of Kahlua added. They used to joke about it and call each other 'Half-milk' and 'Quarter-milk'. The amount of Irish they were, amongst the Indian.

Elizabeth would tease her about her increased chances of bagging a Keralite husband with her fair skin. This was before Kiran had told them she was gay. After that, her mother said Kiran had lost any advantage she'd had with her fair skin as there were no lesbians in Kerala so she'd have to look in Ireland where she wouldn't be considered fair-skinned anyway. Kiran knew her mother had been joking and she'd been relieved that they could still joke around but she also knew the underlying worry that laced those words.

"I found someone I love, Amma." She whispered the words into Elizabeth's ear. "She's Whole-milk." Kiran smiled at her pathetic attempt at humour. She got up and neatened the already neat sheets around her mother's legs.

The door opened and Ji walked in. She didn't see the small frame of Dinesh behind him until Ji sat down.

"The prodigal daughter has returned. How are you, Kiran?" Dinesh's heavily-accented voice was loud in the stillness of the room.

"Fine, Uncle." Kiran found she lapsed into the old habit of calling everyone older Uncle or Aunty when she visited here. On a previous visit, she'd actually addressed a distant cousin as Aunty until she realised with horror that the woman was younger than she was. She would always address Dinesh as 'Uncle' though. She'd known him, and of him, since her earliest years.

Dinesh stood by the bedside. He was Kiran's height and she could see his scalp shining dark through the comb-over of gray hair on the top of his head as he bent it to look at Elizabeth. His white shirt was neatly pressed and he was wearing navy trousers instead of the customary cotton *mundu* worn by the other men. He was Ji's closest friend and had been the Leader of the Council of Vision Painters until Ji's election last year and he still ran the Vision Painting Training Centre.

"When is the CT scan?" Dinesh asked. He continued to speak in English to Ji, for Kiran's sake, she assumed.

"We are going to get the ambulance here at 1 p.m. I know the driver. He would do anything for me. I did a vision painting for him years ago. He will take us to Pallata for the scan at 2 p.m." Ji leaned back against the chair. He was wearing a *mundu* and a creased shirt over a singlet. Kiran could see the white hairs curling over the circular neck of the singlet and she realised with a jolt that for the first time her father actually looked 71.

"Ji, maybe you should take a break from here. Go and have a chai with the others. They are anxious for Elizabeth as well." Dinesh patted Ji's shoulder.

Dinesh turned to Kiran. "You can stay here with your mother. She would be very happy to see that you came to spend time with her."

His tone was neutral but Kiran felt the familiar drag of guilt.

"When your father comes back, I will take you to their house to unpack your...your...bag and to clean up. Were you able to fit a few saris in your bag?"

Kiran was acutely aware of the khaki trousers she had thrown on along with first top that she'd found. It was gray and rumpled and looked a bit how she felt after the travel and stress. Dinesh was examining her attire, her dishevelled hair, and she could almost see the mental shake of his head.

"I didn't really have time to pack properly." She tugged at the hemline of her top. "I completely forgot to pack a sari." *Not that I possess one, apart from the one I drape around the curtain rail as decoration.*

Kiran could see her father examining her as well. There was a look of disapproval in his eyes. He got up and stretched. The two men exchanged looks. Her father looked almost apologetic.

Ji said, "I'll stay with your mother while you go and clean up. Dinesh can take you to the house. Where is your suitcase?"

Kiran had no idea. "I assume Babu still has it."

Dinesh turned to leave. "Come, Kiran. Babu has taken your bag to the house. I'll take you in my car."

She leant over and kissed her mother's forehead. Elizabeth had not moved.

Kiran followed Dinesh out of the room, irritated by their need for her to appear presentable even at a time like this, but she was also curious. Her parents' house was well within walking distance of the medical centre.

There were still about twenty people outside the medical centre. A mixture of men and women, their eyes filled with worry that gave way to assessment and curiosity as Kiran walked with Dinesh to his car, an immaculately preserved black Ambassador. The driver jumped out and opened the back door for Dinesh before running around to open the other door for Kiran.

Dinesh just said "Ji" to the driver and turned to Kiran. "I have not seen you since last year when you came for your father's happiest hour." He smiled. She noticed he was missing a few teeth. He had always looked older than Ji despite them being exactly the same age.

"What age are you now?" He asked.

That was direct. As usual.

"Thirty-seven, Uncle."

"My goodness. Time flies, does it not?" He looked genuinely surprised and she could see him turning the number over in his mind. "I still remember that energetic little girl who used to play with Rishi. You were such a pretty little girl, even though you insisted on wearing his old clothes to climb the trees."

Kiran wasn't sure how to take his use of the past tense regarding her prettiness.

"How is Rishi? Is he still in England?"

"Yes." For a moment Kiran thought that was all he was going to say about his son but after a long pause, he continued, "He's arriving tomorrow for his holidays. He's divorced now."

Dinesh spat out the word 'divorced' as if it was a bug that had flown into his mouth.

"Is he still working at the same firm?"

Dinesh nodded. "He's a senior vice-president there now."

"That is such a good position. And in London too. You must be so proud."

Dinesh lifted his hand to pat her knee leaving five ovals of moisture on the plastic seat cover. "Yes, yes. Of course I am. Of course. Where are you working now? Ji said you gave up the Engineering for some time. What were you doing? He did not say."

He took out a handkerchief and wiped his forehead and barked at the driver to put on the air-conditioning. But they were already pulling in to her parents' house at the gate to the complex and Kiran clambered out grateful she didn't have to answer. She was sure her father would not be happy with her if she told Dinesh she'd been a waitress.

Babu was waiting by the Jeep in the courtyard of the house. Her rucksack was lying by his feet and he lifted it up and waited for Dinesh and Kiran to climb the steps to the house. The coolness of the shaded veranda was a relief from the direct glare of the sun but the humidity was still intense and Kiran longed for a cold shower.

Dinesh pulled back the gold-coloured levers on the ornately carved door and walked into the house. Kiran took off her sandals and followed, drawing coolness from the marble floor into her aching feet.

Babu laid her rucksack at the bottom of the marble staircase. He said, "Shalini is with Amma. When you are hungry, I can take you to get food in the hall or we can get something sent here." He only spoke Malayalam but he spoke slowly and clearly and with loads of gestures, knowing Kiran's difficulty with the language, especially in the first few days of her visits. She smiled and somehow got across the message that she would eat later, after Amma's return from the hospital.

Dinesh did not look like he was leaving. He wandered into the sitting room and Kiran sighed. She needed to get to her room and get away from the heat for a little while. Ji had only installed air-conditioning on the ground floor when he had modernised the old house but the upstairs bedrooms were naturally dark and cool.

Kiran went into the sitting room. Dinesh was sitting on the wicker couch.

"Babu, bring us some chai." Dinesh ordered as he waved Kiran towards a chair beside him.

They sat in silence for a few minutes. Dinesh pointed at a black and white photograph on the wall. "Your father and I think of each other like brothers. That photograph was taken in 1958 when we were 17. It was taken at the funeral of Ji's father, your grandfather. Ji came to live with us then."

The photograph showed two young men with sombre faces, both dressed in white. Ji was taller with a striking face and he seemed to take up more of the photo. She knew that the photo had been in the same spot on the wall for many years but she didn't remember seeing Dinesh in it.

"Your father and I have been talking."

Great, now what? What had they come up with this time? Some new renovation project or the latest idea to advance the ancient and venerable profession of Vision Painting?

"You know I said that Rishi is arriving tomorrow?" Dinesh looked awkward for a second. Kiran nodded and he continued, "Ji and I were talking about your positions."

"Our positions...?"

"Yes, you know, since he is *divorced*," This time there was an actual bubble of spit on his lips as he said the word, "and you are *unmarried.*" She hadn't thought he could say another word with as much distaste but he managed it. "We were thinking that, as you are of an age where there is not much chance of a match with an eligible man, that the natural order of things has revealed itself to be a match between the two of you."

"*What?*" Kiran couldn't help the word spilling out as her jaw dropped open. She wasn't sure she'd understood his convoluted argument. But it seemed as though Ji and Dinesh had agreed to a marriage between their 'disgraced' children.

Dinesh frowned. "This will be an excellent match. It would have been arranged a very long time ago when you were still young if that son of mine had not decided to shame me and leave behind his gift and his home and go to that foreign country to study software. I warned him but you see what happens when you ignore your elders. He ended up marrying a foreigner. Of course it would end in this way, what do those English girls know about the way things should be."

Kiran decided she had better stop doing an impression of a fish out of water. She closed her mouth. But in her mind she was still sitting staring at him with her mouth open.

"My *father* arranged this with you?" Her voice was dangerously close to a squeak. What was Ji playing at? He knew beyond a shadow of a doubt that she was gay and that she was happy.

"Yes, yes." He jiggled his head and the reflection of the window shimmered on the polished walnut of his scalp. "As I said, your father and I are like brothers."

So you want me to marry my cousin?! Kiran didn't want to be rude. She decided to save the tirade for her father when she saw him next and after her mother was better.

She asked, "Is there no younger woman? I'm sure someone like Rishi, being your son, could be matched with someone much more suitable. Or who lives in England maybe...?"

Dinesh looked puzzled. As if he had expected her to be delighted to be saved from her marriage-less state. Babu appeared at the door with two silver cups of chai.

Kiran felt a wave of exhaustion and jet lag sweep over her. "This is very sudden. And I am so tired and worried about Amma." She got up. "I need to clean up and be back at the centre before they come for her. They might let me go with her to Pallata."

Dinesh hitched up the leg of his trousers as he got up, like he would have if he was wearing a *mundu*. She got the feeling he had worn the trousers especially for her.

"Yes, yes. Of course. We will talk more. Tomorrow you will come to the training centre and meet Rishi."

"I would like to spend as much time with Amma as possible."

"Of course, of course." More head waggling. "The next day then. Your father is scheduled to give a talk to the students and the Council. He will want you to be there."

"But he will be with Amma." Kiran was starting to feel the anger at her father and the profession rise through her.

"Yes, yes. But it is a great honour for Ji. Elizabeth will be fine, I'm sure. She doesn't look like she is in any danger."

"We don't know that. I don't see any of you brilliant vision painters doing anything to help her!" Kiran covered her mouth. Dinesh was now staring at her in disbelief. And Babu, though he didn't understand a word they had said, wore a similar expression.

Dinesh said carefully, "You know that we cannot do anything for another vision painter or their family or loved ones. My ancestors and yours were the ones who made the rules that have guided us for more than a hundred years."

"What good is this gift if it cannot be used to help those we love?" Kiran tried not to let the bitter helplessness she was feeling show in her voice but Dinesh frowned as he took the chai from Babu.

"Kiran, you should not talk of my profession in such a disrespectful manner. The vision painters have a long and distinguished history." There was a slight smirk at the corner of his mouth. "I cannot allow you to attend the training, but you will learn a great deal about your father's and my profession if you come along to his talk. If you listen, that is."

Dinesh drank the chai in one long gulp and handed the empty cup back to Babu who gestured at Kiran with the full cup he still had in his hand. Kiran shook her head.

Dinesh said, "So, the day after tomorrow. The talk is at 10 a.m." He turned to leave. "I expect you to keep your Western opinions to yourself. The trainees are being taught the proper values. I do not know what your father has taught you." He turned and stared at Kiran and his dark brown eyes were hard. "There are no women vision painters, there cannot be, and there never will be."

He didn't wait for an answer. Babu held the front door open for him and Dinesh walked out leaving Kiran standing in the sitting room trying to decide whether to cry or scream.

CHAPTER FOUR

Kiran looked through the clothes spread out on the bed. Nothing suitable. They'd have to accept her in her jeans and a shirt. She smoothed out her hair which lay damp against her shoulders. It would dry into a fuzz around her head but she didn't have a hairdryer.

She pushed her things aside and lay down on the cool sheets. She wanted desperately to talk to Ashley, even just to hear her voice, but her mobile wasn't set up to work here. She decided to call from the house phone after the CT scan. She closed her eyes and pictured Ashley's face, the turbulent red hair, the dormant volcanoes in her eyes. The image was so clear that she could see every crease in the irises. She felt her heart jolt as it still did every time she saw Ashley in person or in her mind's eye.

She placed her hand against her navel. Was the race still on? Or had an outcome already been decided while she was travelling halfway across the world. It would have to be a resilient swimmer to make it through and succeed. Kiran felt the now familiar craving for a child surge through her. The craving familiar since the events of the previous year. Her mind flitted over the idea that she was trying to distance herself from her gift but it refused to settle on the thought.

The bedroom was an oasis and Kiran didn't want to leave to face the sight of her mother unmoving, unresponsive. So unlike the normal Elizabeth. Kiran had felt sympathy for Ashley as she'd struggled through the loss of Marge, but now she felt an empathy that hurt in its sharpness. She closed her eyes and shook the pain away. Her mother was still alive. Something could be done. If she couldn't find someone to help, she would do a vision painting herself.

Kiran sat up with a jerk. She had not done many vision paintings since painting Marge out and painting Ashley with Jennifer. She'd been busy for a short time before Ashley had painted Kiran onto her canvas. After that, after the events had found the time to seep into her, Kiran had not been able to face her gift or its power or the devastating consequences. She couldn't start again by breaking the rules.

Yet she couldn't stand idly by if her mother was in danger.

∞ ∞ ∞

Kiran didn't think she could get any warmer or sweatier, but the weight of the humid air pressed down through her head and pushed the moisture out of every pore. The waiting room was full so she stood outside the hospital and watched the air trudge despondently around the parked cars. There seemed to be so much more earth here than in Ireland. There was green too, but the shades were browner.

She heard her father call her name and she hurried back into the waiting room. The eyes of the sari-draped women were distracted from their worries by their curiosity as they stared at her. Kiran knew she didn't fit in here.

Her father was standing inside the door to the consultant's office and he gestured at her to come in. She took a seat beside him. There was a nameplate on the desk that read "Dr. Parinavashan Thangamma Vishan" under which were a string of capital letters which Kiran hoped were significant and useful for her mother. Dr. Vishan looked young, in his fifties, but experienced enough, with an air of authority. His suit jacket was slung over the back of his chair. Sweat stains made large circular patterns under his armpits, the white shirt showing brown skin stuck to it. He was writing in small neat writing on a sheet of paper. He looked up from his notes and nodded at her before addressing Ji.

"The CT scan shows nothing, Sir." Dr. Vishan straightened his tie and frowned.

Ji let out a sigh as he leant forward. "How is that possible? What does this mean? What is happening to Amma?"

Dr. Vishan shook his head. He spoke in Malayalam. "I thought we would have some news for you today but I have to admit I am puzzled. I have not seen anything like this before." He was tapping the pen against the desk, the sound hitting Kiran like a wasp trying to batter its way out through a glass door. "But she is comfortable and does not seem to be in any immediate danger."

"So isn't there anything you can do?" Kiran blurted out.

Dr. Vishan frowned again as he swivelled his head to look at Kiran. "I think we have done everything that can be done for the moment in the way of investigations. Every system in her body has been checked. There is no cause that we can ascertain for her present condition."

He turned back to Ji. "Do you want us to keep Elizabeth here? We will of course provide the best medical care for her, but if I am honest, I don't know if that is the best all-around solution."

Ji was shaking his head. "No, I want her at home. Kiran is here and can help look after her. I will get some of the women to watch her constantly." The fear in his voice was making Kiran's heart trip nervously.

Ji got up. His hand was shaking as he shook the consultant's hand. Dr. Vishan looked for a moment like he wanted to ask Ji a question but instead he got up as well and came around the desk to see them out.

"The nurse at the medical centre can come to the house and change the IV if necessary, can she?" Dr. Vishan asked as he opened the door.

Ji nodded. "Elizabeth will not be without medical care, Doctor. I want her at home with me. We will make sure she is watched." He put his hand on Kiran's shoulder and she felt him lean on her though he was trying to support her as they walked out through the waiting room.

∞ ∞ ∞

The worry stretched through the room between the seated figures of Ji and Kiran, bouncing off the walls and off the stillness of Elizabeth on the bed between them.

Ji broke the silence. "Do you want anything to eat? They will bring you anything you want. Maybe some *cappa* and fish curry?"

Kiran shook her head. Even her favourite foods would struggle to get past the tight knot in her throat.

Ji got up and paced, his tall frame casting a distorted shadow on the walls. He had showered and changed into a clean *mundu* and shirt and was looking more like his everyday self. He had even trimmed the stray white hairs of his moustache and beard that dared to grow in the wrong direction.

He stopped by the foot of the bed. "I am giving a talk day after tomorrow. At the Training Centre." He glanced at Kiran's expression and looked away just as quickly to examine a loose thread on his pressed shirt. "It is an annual day of events at which the Leader of the Council first gives a talk to the trainees and then a speech to all the Council Members and Vision Painters." He peeked again at Kiran's face. His voice had a note of pleading in it as he continued. "Kiran, I am the Leader of the Council. I am expected to hold up the traditions. Many people were surprised when I was elected last year. Some were against me."

Kiran still did not say anything.

"Amma will be fine for those hours. She has not moved. Her condition has not changed. Shalini will remain in the room with her until we get back."

"*We?!*"

The bushy white eyebrows rose. "Of course, we. You are here. You are my daughter. Do you not want to witness this historic event?"

"I want to witness my mother waking up, not a bunch of old men walking around congratulating themselves."

Kiran regretted her words almost as soon as they had emerged. Ji looked hurt, as usual, by her irreverence. "Uncle Dinesh has already told me about it. He asked me to attend. But he does not know I am a vision painter too. I am not allowed to say I am a vision painter just that I paint." She made a waving gesture in the air. "I paint pretty pictures." She looked her father straight in the eye and he dropped his gaze to the floor. She continued, this time adding Dinesh's singsong Malayalee accent and head wiggle, "Women cannot be vision painters. The whole world will just blow up."

Ji shot her a look. "That is not why women cannot be vision painters, Kiran. Why do you show such disrespect for our profession?"

Kiran said, "How can it show such disrespect for me? You know I have the gift too. Why can't I talk about it here? You would have had to tell the Council about Marge. They would have known about my gift. So why not now? Why do they insist that only men can be vision painters?"

Ji sighed. This discussion had been played out many times and she could see him slip into the usual words.

"The gift is passed from father to son. Vision Painters are only allowed to have sons. You should not even exist!"

"Yeah, I got that bit the first hundred times. Thanks again for reminding me."

Ji sat down heavily. "What do you want me to say? I left the profession for you. I took you away to Ireland. I should not even have let you paint but I begged Dinesh's father to let me help you express your gift. I gave up the best years with my gift so that you could be...so that you could have yours. And what do you do? You treat our profession like a joke. You paint dead women back to life. All I can say is, thankfully you stayed away from us here."

He saw her face change as the words flew across her mother's body and landed with a sting. His tone softened, as he said, "Come with me tomorrow. I want you there. You are my child. It is not your fault you are a girl."

"Wow, thanks. How could I refuse?" She turned away from him and looked at her mother's face. "I can wait with Amma now if you want to go and get your speech ready."

She could feel him staring at the top of her bowed head, but he didn't say anything. She heard him get up and leave the room.

CHAPTER FIVE

The Vision Painting Training Centre was based in Ji's old family home. It neighboured Dinesh's home and the dividing wall between the back of the two houses had been opened up to allow free passage. The houses were on the corner of the main street as it swept around to the eastern half of the village where the church and retirement complex were based.

Kiran moved awkwardly through the narrow passages as she followed her father and Dinesh to the room where the students were waiting. She was already starting to feel the familiar sense that she was out of place. They passed rooms where she could see stacks of uniformly sized canvases, easels, and walls covered with shelves of tubes of paint. She relaxed slightly as the stench of turpentine and oil pigments assaulted her nostrils with the familiarity of an old friend.

She felt slightly better that at least she was more appropriately dressed since one of the women working at the complex had dropped off a few saris at her parents' house. Kiran had struggled to work out how the seemingly eternal length of colour was supposed to be draped around her. She'd given up and begged Babu to get help. The woman had arrived back, grinning through the gaps in her teeth, and in minutes, had tut-tutted the sari around Kiran's waist, tucking it in at the top of her newly acquired floor length underskirt and pinning it to the shoulder of the equally new blouse.

The woman had reached around from behind her and pleated the material into straight lines that fell from her navel to the ground. Kiran had a sudden memory of her mother kneeling behind her, arms reaching around her waist, pausing in the shared task to squeeze Kiran's little fingers. Talcum powder memories that brought tears to her eyes.

She'd come downstairs carefully, trying not to step on the hem of the sari. This was like being wrapped up like a mummy but without any fastening holding the contraption in place. How did all those millions of women do it? But she had been relieved to see the pride in her father's eyes as he took in her appearance. He hadn't said anything but he was beaming as he had walked down the street in front of her.

On the 200 yard walk over to the Centre, Kiran had found herself rubbing at her midriff which was not used to this kind of exposure to public air not to mention the blazingly hot sun. She still had her arms across her stomach as she walked into the room that seemed to be a wall to wall display of eager young faces.

Kiran ignored the curious, and admiring, looks from the young men and took a seat at the side of the room, right at the back. Well, at least she would get to hear the formal history of her father's profession. *And yours, Kiran. Right. The chances of them accepting her were as slim as them holding a Pride parade for her.*

As Dinesh and Ji set up the front of the room, Kiran looked around at the men sitting waiting. There were about thirty of them sitting on rows of folded out wooden chairs. She could see mostly the backs of their heads, all with shiny black hair, and their side profiles. She caught an occasional sneaked look back at her.

One face stared back as she swept the room, and she paused her scan. He was sitting at the back as well, but at the other side of the room. He looked familiar, and he was older than the others. They were all in their late teens or early twenties; this man was in his forties. His black hair was starting to recede off his face and the skin of his slightly fleshy face was fairer in colour than the others and though he was fully Indian, he looked foreign in the room. His trousers and shirt were well-cut and European, his leather shoes shone amongst the dark-sandaled feet.

He was still staring at Kiran and as she met his eyes again, he smiled and nodded. She was used to the look of appreciation from men but there was an air of assurance and sense of familiarity from this man that unsettled her. And then she realised who he was—Rishi, Dinesh's son. He had a roundness to his face, the hint of the receding hairline, and the short stature, but he was handsome with it. He'd grown at about the same pace Kiran had. She would still fit into his clothes now. She smiled back at him.

A lectern had been set up at the front and Dinesh rapped on it and cleared his throat to get the attention of the room. The low hum of conversation ceased as the audience turned to face forward. Rishi raised one eyebrow and winked at her before turning to listen to his father.

Dinesh cleared his throat again. The lectern had obviously been set up for Ji and it came up to Dinesh's chest. He moved to stand beside it. Dinesh spoke in Malayalam and Kiran tried hard to concentrate and understand what he was saying. All the speeches today would be in Malayalam and while her ear had already improved, it was going to be a struggle.

"Trainees, as you all know, we are here to listen to the Leader of the Council of Vision Painters talk about the history of our great profession. We will be having the 200th Birthday celebrations for our Founder in 2016 and the preparations will be starting soon for that magnificent occasion. Today is a day we set aside every year to renew our spirits as we first immerse them in history here and later we look to the future at the Association meeting. So, without further talk, let me introduce our current Leader, Guru-Ji."

Ji had been sitting at the top table, nodding at Dinesh's words. He got up and went to the lectern. He was dressed in trousers and a shirt, the gowns would come later. He rested his arms on the lectern and raised one hand to halt the clapping.

"My dear students, it gives me great pleasure to see all of you here, so eager to learn, to experience the wonders of our great profession." He glanced at Kiran in the back and she wasn't sure if there was a twist of his lips before he looked back at the front row. "You will all be receiving the very able training of your tutors led by Dinesh, and this talk is a way to remind you of where all of this started."

Ji paused and took a sip of water from a glass on the table at which Dinesh was now sitting. He went back to the lectern and continued.

"In 1816, a man was born in a small village in Kerala. He grew up with no idea of the great gift he possessed. Until, at the age of 25, he became aware. He was a quiet man, a painter, an artist, and a wonderful listener. The people of the village went to him when they needed help. He was not rich, but he gave them more than they ever got from their landowners. He absorbed their stories, he felt their pain, and one night, after a particularly harrowing story told to him by a young farmer, he had a vision. And in that vision, the farmer told him what he needed. The painter woke up the next day and filled a canvas with this farmer's hopes and dreams. He did not keep the painting. He gave it to the young farmer who, while appreciative, I am sure, did not see the value of this art but he put it in his hut. Within a few months, the young farmer's life matched the painting. *But no one realised.*"

Ji paused. He looked around at his audience. All the young men were leaning forward slightly, waiting for him.

Kiran glanced at Rishi. He was focused on Ji as well. She turned back and caught Dinesh staring at her. He looked away quickly, at Ji who was taking up the story again.

"The painter continued in his normal way. But then, it happened again. This time with an older man, a tax collector. And this time, the thoughts were starting to come together in the painter's mind. But he did not trust what was happening. So he tried it again. A woman, a housewife. A young boy. An old man. And it happened each time. And people began to notice. And they came to him more now for help. And when he just listened as usual, they would ask him, 'Sir, can you paint for me?' And he did as they asked."

Ji wore an expression that Kiran knew very well. She called it his "Indian Swami" look. The tiredness and worry of the last few days seemed to have slipped away, at least temporarily.

"Soon, the word spread through the villages and people would come from near and far to see this painter who could make their dreams come true. He was of Christian origin but the people called him Guru. He was a thoughtful man and he had never been concerned with worldly possessions so when the people asked him what he wanted in return for his paintings, he would smile at them, and knowing that they did not have much and they did not paint, he would say, 'Paint me into whatever you would like me to have.'"

Ji took another sip of water. Kiran wished she had a glass too; the heat in the crowded room was stifling. "The painter was a widower and he had a 5 year old boy when he started to recognise his gift. The boy would sit and watch his father paint, and of course, when children respect their fathers, they wish to imitate them." Ji looked over at Kiran again, and she sighed. "So this boy also started to paint. But he was not painting the dreams and aspirations of people, he was painting what little boys paint. What they see around them. And nothing happened, of course, because there is no point painting what is already there. Not in vision painting anyway, maybe in modern art." Ji smiled at himself. There was a quiet laugh from the back of the audience and Kiran looked around to see Rishi covering his mouth. She noticed a tiny furrowing of Dinesh's brow when she looked back at the front of the room.

"The painter decided to try training his son. The boy struggled to understand the adult issues that affected the people whose stories were being told to him by his father. The paintings were getting technically good but the visions were not materialising. But the painter knew that his son had the same gift so he persisted. And when the boy reached the age of 17, there was a breakthrough. His first vision painting was for a young woman who did not want to be forced into an arranged marriage and the boy painted her wish which was to be married to another young man in her village. When this vision came to pass, the painter knew he had been right all along, and that his son had become a vision painter, like his father. The painter continued to train his son and his thoughts turned to the future for his son and for this gift."

"Our Founder, the first Guru, continued to work with his son and they helped many people and people believed in them. As I said, Guru was a thoughtful man and he thought about the gift he had discovered in him and his son and he wrote down his experiences. He started to formulate reasons and ways to develop the gift. He took the milestones from his life and set them down as guides. These are the original guides for the way we live now. Guru made sure that his son had a son before he was 25 and that son was trained from the age of 5 and in that way the line continued. But when he was 55, and his grandson, the third Guru, was 5 years old, Guru himself started to go out to the other villages and he searched for a certain type of man, and he took the 5 year old son, and trained them too. That group of boys included my great-grandfather and Dinesh's as well. So the group was widened. And the codebook was started based on the guidelines developed by our Founder. This work was continued by the second Guru. It was in the time of the third Guru, in 1921, that the first Council was formed as there was a need for strong leadership. My great-grandfather was the first Leader of the Council. This role was passed on to my grandfather and would have been to my father. Over the years, the guidelines have been refined, and rules and punishments have been added but the basic principles remain the same. And that is the codebook that you study in this training centre. Those are the rules you will agree to live by every day. And those are the punishments you face if you break any of the rules. All are there for a reason."

Ji looked across at Dinesh, who looked at his watch and nodded. "I hope you will all realise what a great tradition you are a part of. Your fathers were vision painters, your sons will be vision painters, I hope you will be worthy of your place in the chain of our great profession."

Ji smiled at the young men who clapped enthusiastically.

His eyes sought out Kiran, and she was very tempted to ask why he hadn't mentioned the fact that there were no women in the profession and the reason for their omission but it felt like completely the wrong thing and the wrong place, so she smiled back and clapped as well.

CHAPTER SIX

The students had left the room and Kiran stayed seated wondering what she was supposed to do next. Dinesh and Ji were talking at the front. The only other people in the room were Rishi, who had also remained seated through the exodus of bodies, and a man sitting in the second row.

Rishi got up and approached her with a smile. She stood as well and he leant forward and kissed her on both cheeks. She could feel the graze of his skin even though he was smooth-shaven.

As he leaned back she said, "Hi Rishi, I thought you lived in London not Paris."

His smile widened. "Was that too French for a first greeting? Hi Kiran. My, you have grown out of that little tomboy look, haven't you?" He looked vaguely surprised and grateful.

"I'll have you know I can still beat you at tree-climbing. In fact, we could find a coconut tree now and see. Might have to change out of this thing, though it might come in useful as a harness." She tugged at the pleats of the sari.

She immediately regretted doing that when his eyes moved down and slowly back up to her face, lingering over the bare skin that showed between the top of her skirt and the bottom edge of her blouse. He didn't seem in the mood to climb trees. She clasped her hands in front of her, her arms covering her midriff.

"Rishi. Kiran. Come, come." Dinesh gestured them over. He and Ji had been joined by the other man.

Rishi moved back a foot to let her out but Kiran had to brush by him to get out to the aisle between the chairs. She could feel his gaze on her back as they walked towards the others. She was very conscious of the damp blouse sticking to her skin under the curtain of her hair.

Both Dinesh and Ji were grinning as their offspring walked up the aisle. The man standing beside them didn't look like a student either; he was also in his forties and dressed in black trousers and a white shirt with faint blue stripes.

Dinesh said, "Kiran, this is Vijay. I very much wanted you to meet him before he left tomorrow. He is going to work in Ireland and we were hoping you might help him settle in when you get back."

Ji was nodding. "Of course she will help him. We must all stick together. She is working in a very good job there and she has a house. Kiran, you remember Rishi, Dinesh's boy. Of course you remember him, you two were so close. He is working in England. Excellent job in a very good company. Isn't that right, Rishi? What are you now, senior president?"

Rishi nodded. "Actually, senior vice-president but I might as well be senior president. I make all the tough decisions there." He laughed.

Kiran smiled politely and turned and nodded at Vijay. "Yes, of course, please feel free to ask me anything you need to know and I will try to answer. Where are you going to be working in Ireland?"

Vijay smiled at her and said in a voice that was accented but not heavily so, "I will be joining a software company in Galway city. That is where you are, are you not? I would of course appreciate any local knowledge as your venerable father has said."

His face was gentle even though it was firmer than Rishi's and his eyes were respectful while appreciative in a distant way. She had a vague sense of knowing him from somewhere and wondered if she had climbed trees with him as well in her early years in the village. He and Rishi seemed to be the same age. What had Rishi been when they'd played together, six or seven years older than her?

Rishi moved forward very slightly but in such a way that he was separating her from Vijay. His arm snaked around her shoulders and he laughed and said to Vijay,

"We will both be able to introduce you to the European ways, I'm sure Kiran can show us the sights when she is back."

He turned her towards him; she could smell his soap and aftershave underlaid with the faint smell of sweat. "It will be great to catch up with you as well. How long has it been, 30 years?"

Kiran nodded, her cheek chafing against his damp shirt. She could feel Dinesh and Ji's eyes on them. She saw a look of what seemed like pity in Vijay's eyes before he replaced it quickly with a smile.

Kiran said, "Vijay, I'll give you a friend's details and you can call on him when you get to Galway. I'm sure he wouldn't mind. He's fascinated by vision painting and I'm sure he would love to meet you. I don't know when I'll be back, it all depends on Amma." She moved out of the circle of Rishi's arm. "I really need to get back to her, if you will all excuse me."

Dinesh said, "We will see you later at the Assembly then. It is a big day for your father."

She nodded and walked through the door, trying not to trip on the sari in her haste.

∞ ∞ ∞

There was no change in Elizabeth's condition. She was now in her own bed in the main bedroom of the house. There were two women in the room with her at all times when Kiran or Ji were not there. One of the women was Shalini. She and the other woman sat on the floor outside the door when Kiran went in to be with her mother.

Elizabeth's face was peaceful in the shadowed oasis of her bedroom. Kiran sat on the chair beside the bed. She had a sudden overpowering urge to see her mother's eyes, to hear her laugh, to just hear her voice. She reached over and gently raised one of Elizabeth's eyelids. The normally vibrant blue-green iris was now a circle of calm in the white. Kiran felt the fear trickle down her spine with the sweat. But at least there seemed to be no pain. Wherever Elizabeth was, she did not seem to be suffering.

She smoothed the eyelid back, almost guiltily. Her fear was screaming at her that her mother would not come back if she didn't do something. Kiran jumped up and the chair crashed backwards and clattered on the marble floor. She rushed to the door as it opened and Shalini looked in, her dark face curious. Kiran ran past her and down the staircase. She headed for the room where Ji's old vision painting equipment was stored.

The studio was at the back of the house, its single window displaying a small garden with a pond surrounded by bamboo, green leaves sweeping down into greener water. Beyond that the banana trees waved their fronds and the outline of an old shed leant against the fence. Kiran rushed in and locked the door behind her. The familiar smell of paints and turpentine still clung to the air though the room hadn't been used as a studio for years.

Kiran's hand shook as she felt the bottles on the shelf, pushing some aside, taking some down. She was operating on remote control, her hands finding the right tubes of paint, the right brushes, the canvas. She set up the easel and placed the canvas on it. Her movements were slowing. She could hear her father's voice in the hallway asking for her followed by a female voice and Ji's footsteps approaching the door.

"Kiran!" Her father's voice was anxious. Not angry.

She placed her forehead against the door, feeling the ridges of the carving. She could hear him breathing on the other side. The handle shook on her side as he tried it.

"Kiran! What are you doing in there?"

She didn't answer.

"Kiran, you know you cannot paint for your family or loved ones. Please do not break the rules again. Kiran, you do not know what the consequences will be for Amma."

There was still no anger in his voice, just anxiety laced with understanding.

"Kiran, I have to go and get ready for the Assembly. Amma is fine. Amma will be fine. I trust you will do the right thing this time."

She heard his footsteps as he walked away down the hall and climbed the steps, his sandals flapping in an uneven rhythm.

There was a wicker chair in the corner of the studio, its undercarriage cobwebbed. She sat into it, and stared at the canvas that mocked her in its blankness.

∞ ∞ ∞

Kiran awoke to the sound of banging on the door. She jumped up trying to get her bearings. Her father's voice had lost its anxiety, it was now impatient.

"Kiran, we have to leave for the Hall now. The assembly starts soon and I cannot be late."

She rushed to the door and unlocked it. He tried to poke his head in but her body was blocking the canvas from his view. She edged him out and closed the door behind her.

She shook her head and he nodded. The relief on his face was obvious but fleeting as he nudged her towards the stairs.

"Go quick. Get ready."

Ji was dressed in the full ceremonial garb that the Leader of the Council wore. His tall frame seemed even more imposing in the black gown with a red and gold band at the waist and a covering robe of pinks and reds and cream. Despite its beautiful blue colour, her sari looked plain beside his outfit.

Kiran hurried back to the bedroom in which she was staying. Someone had placed one of Elizabeth's saris on the bed and the gold threads shimmered on the red background in the light through the slatted blinds. Kiran showered quickly and didn't even attempt to put on the sari on her own. Shalini smiled and clucked through the ritual, finally standing back to beam at Kiran and nod in approval.

The trip down the staircase was even harder this time with the sari weighted down with gold embroidery. Ji hurried her out of the house and into the Jeep and Babu backed out of the driveway and drove down the road to the reception hall that dominated the grassy area at the centre of the circle of houses.

There were residents on the verandas of the houses, watching the procession of cars that wound their way slowly to the Hall. Most were old black Ambassador cars and the men in them were a variety of ages from fifties to late seventies. Kiran counted 11 cars as they pulled up in front of the large grey building that was used for various occasions for the complex. More cars were parked at the side of the hall and she presumed these were owned by the ordinary members of the association.

Rishi and Dinesh were getting out of the back of one of the Ambassadors and Vijay climbed out of the front. Dinesh was wearing the ceremonial garb of a Council member which comprised a white robe with a band of blue and gold around the waist which in Dinesh's case made him look even shorter.

Kiran tried to get herself out of the Jeep without the sari falling off. She was collecting the various trailing pieces when her nostrils were filled with the scent of Rishi's aftershave and she felt his hand on her arm.

"Do you need assistance, my fair lady?"

She gathered the last errant piece of the sari and shook her head. "I think I'm good. Not used to these contraptions, as you can see."

Kiran walked gingerly over the packed-earth area towards the front doors of the Hall where Vijay was standing watching them with the hint of a grin on his face. She could feel Rishi's full palm against her bare back. She tried to walk faster but he kept up with her pace and the hand stayed in place. Her father had disappeared with Dinesh around the side of the building.

The chatter in the Hall from the sixty or so men harmonised with the buzzing of the overhead fans which were fighting a losing battle against the humid air. And sixty pairs of male eyes turned to stare when Kiran walked in with Rishi and Vijay on either side of her.

The eyes bore varying degrees of curiosity, interest, and downright hostility. None were friendly. Kiran sank down in a chair in the back row and waited for the audience to turn back and face the front. Rishi and Vijay took the seats on either side of her.

There seemed to be three age groups of men in the audience, one small set right at the front were in their 70s or 80s, the middle most numerous group were in the 50s, and the rows at the back were filled with the late teens to early twenties age group who had been at the training centre.

Someone at the top of the room rang a hand bell and the audience stood with a scraping of chairs and a rustle of cloth.

The Members of the Council filed in and took their seats on either side of a chair at the long table which dominated the front of the hall. The audience remained standing and erupted in applause as Ji strode in to take the central chair.

Despite her antipathy to the group and the trappings of the profession, Kiran could not help the feeling of pride that swept through her when she saw her father. Not for the robes and the colour as much as for the strength that emanated from him. He looked like he had been born for this role, he seemed more comfortable there than at home with his family.

Her positive feelings were starting to wane a few hours later as the speeches dragged on and the afternoon sun slammed the building and seeped through the walls. She sat slumped in her chair and let the self-congratulatory words wash over her, their hot air breath bringing no relief.

Finally it was the turn of the Leader of the Council and Kiran straightened up as Ji stood and addressed the crowd. He spoke of the facilities they were building, the encouraging trend towards a wider recognition in the community, and the need for constant vigilance and adherence to the rules. There were nods of agreement from the Council Members and she could mostly see the shine of black hair bobbing in the back rows in the gradient of black through gray to white at in the front rows.

Ji was stern as he reiterated the necessity for rules and the absolute harshness of the punishments for breaking those rules. His eyes swept over Kiran and she could see, even at that distance, that they were filled with concern. And she felt like a child again, caught in the spotlight of his stare. A guilty child, though she had done nothing wrong.

The assembly ended after Ji's speech and chairs were moved to line the walls as folding banquet tables were set up with trays of food. Kiran needed some fresh air, the heat outside had to be better, even in the full glare of the afternoon sun, than the thickness inside the hall. She had reached the large doors when Babu came racing in and collided with her, knocking the breath out of her lungs. He was gesticulating and speaking in Malayalam but she understood the message clearly.

Amma was awake.

CHAPTER SEVEN

Kiran ran into the bedroom and stopped just inside the door. Ji, who had delayed only to tear off the heavy robe, collided into her back. They both stared at Elizabeth who was sitting up in the bed being fussed over by Shalini.

Elizabeth looked as peaceful awake as she had in her earlier state. Her turquoise eyes were calm, her hair combed straight, the streaks of silver highlighting the deep black. A smile broke out on her face when she saw Kiran.

"Kiran, what are you doing here? You didn't tell us you were coming." She turned to Shalini and said in Irish-accented Malayalam, "Why didn't you tell me my Kiran was here? Why just comb my hair and let me lie here?"

Shalini grimaced at Ji and Kiran. She didn't seem able to speak. Her face creased and she started crying.

Elizabeth frowned, "It is fine. Everything is okay, I wasn't scolding you." She looked bewildered.

Kiran took her mother's hand, dropped it, and hugged her tight instead.

"You scared us, Amma. How do you feel?" Kiran leant back and examined her mother's face. There were fine lines but her face looked years younger than her 66 years. Elizabeth frowned again. She tugged gently at the IV tube that snaked out of her arm.

"I feel fine, why shouldn't I? Ji, what have you been doing?" Elizabeth looked over Kiran's shoulder at her husband, who was rooted to a spot just inside their bedroom. Then she noticed what Kiran was wearing.

"Kiran, is that my best sari? You agreed to wear a sari? I don't know why you didn't before, you look very good."

Kiran just nodded. She was trembling with relief. Ji walked over to the bed and took Elizabeth's other hand. Kiran had never seen her father cry and she was shocked to see the tears rolling down his cheeks and into the white beard. There was a clatter of footsteps ascending the stairs and Dinesh and Rishi appeared at the door of the bedroom. Elizabeth glanced down at what she was wearing, which was respectable enough, a plain cotton house gown that covered her up.

"Is there a party going on? That has just moved to my room? Welcome, Dinesh. Do come in. Ah, Rishi. Is that you?" She snuck a quick look at her daughter and Kiran could see a shade of guilt in her mother's eyes. *So had she been in on this crazy marriage proposal too?*

Kiran shook her head. She would deal with that later. She knew her mother hated to be kept in the dark, about anything. Her father seemed unable to talk.

"Amma, you have been in some kind of sleep for a few days. We were very worried."

The expression in Elizabeth's eyes changed, very subtly but Kiran was so close, she noticed it. It seemed to be confusion, laced with fear.

Kiran asked, "What is the last thing you remember?"

"I was waiting for the girls to play gin rummy." Elizabeth seemed very certain.

"And nothing after?" Dinesh asked.

Elizabeth shook her head.

"And how do you feel now?" Dinesh moved up to the foot of the bed.

"Perfect." Elizabeth sat up straighter in the bed. "In fact, I would like to get up and have a bath and put some nicer clothes on." She examined the bandage covering the IV. "And take this thing out. Ji, perhaps we could move this gathering to a more appropriate venue?" Her voice was firm.

Ji found his voice, "Amma, don't you think you should stay in bed. The nurse will come and sort out the tubes. I will call the doctor. He's the top man. He's a very busy man but he would do anything for me. I did a vision painting for him years ago."

Elizabeth squeezed his hand and smiled. "I'm perfectly alright. I don't need the doctor, however indebted he is to you. Have you done any paintings for a cook? I'm starving."

Kiran got up and Elizabeth swung her legs over the side of the bed.

Ji jumped to his feet. "Shalini, go to the Hall with Babu and bring some of the banquet back here."

The woman hurried out.

Elizabeth looked pointedly at Dinesh and Rishi, and Ji turned to them and said. "Let us go and talk in my study." He looked at Kiran, who was helping Elizabeth to her feet. "You too. Mala can help Amma." He waved the other woman over from her hovering post at the bedroom door.

Kiran felt guilt wash through her again as she followed the stern figure of her father.

∞ ∞ ∞

Ji led the two men and Kiran down the stairs but he walked past his study and towards the studio. He pushed the door open and held it as the others filed in. Kiran could feel the trail of curiosity left in Dinesh and Rishi's wake.

The men looked around the studio. It was exactly as Kiran had left it earlier that afternoon. Tubes of paint lying out alongside paintbrushes. The canvas sitting on the easel, its white surface mocking their suspicions.

Kiran turned to her father. "See! I told you I did nothing."

Dinesh cleared his throat. He said in a heavy measured tone, "But you seem to have thought of painting something." He walked over to the table and picked up a paintbrush and slowly flicked its tip between his fingers.

She could hear Rishi behind her whisper, "Uh oh..." but he was careful not to let Ji or his father hear him.

Kiran turned and glared at Rishi and then at Dinesh. She said the words one by one spelling them out as if trying to convince herself as well, "I did not do a painting of Amma."

They still did not look convinced.

She said, "Dad, you know I would not do that. Not now."

Dinesh butted in, "Not ever, I hope."

Ji turned away from them. He touched the blank and dry canvas and said, "She did not paint anything."

Dinesh raised his head and shoulders, trying to stretch himself to his full height, which was still only at Kiran's level. "I believe that. But only because I don't think anything painted by her could materialize. You two can play at the thought of her vision painting but we know she cannot."

Rishi whispered again behind her, "And another strike for Women's Lib." His breath tickled her neck and she tried not to rub the area.

She stopped her anger from making her say anything more. She had broken those rules once before, even though only Ji knew that, so she was hardly in a position to dispute their suspicions now. And there was definitely no way she was bringing up the fact that she actually had an extremely strong gift, she wasn't going to be able to prove it anyway.

Dinesh had turned to stare at her and she tried to keep her face calm and unruffled. He flicked his eyes behind her to Rishi and nodded his head at the door before snorting and walking out. Rishi patted her on the shoulder before following his father.

Ji's head was bowed and he was facing away from her. His voice was quiet. "Kiran, this time I will not forgive you if you painted for Amma." He turned and left the studio, brushing past her protestations of innocence.

∞ ∞ ∞

Kiran sat back and sighed. She couldn't fit in any more food. Every one of her favourite home-cooked Indian dishes lay partially eaten, nestling in banana leaves on the table. Shalini and Mala had carried out aluminium tiffin containers laden with the brightly coloured tastes and textures of her childhood. They had brought the banana leaves for Kiran knowing that they added to her enjoyment. Elizabeth and Ji had plates.

Elizabeth smiled and ladled more of the *cappa* onto the fish curry, the yellow cassava mash sinking into the chunks of fish in red spicy liquid pooled on the dark-green shiny leaves.

"Eat, Kiran. You are not going to get this in Ireland. What do you eat there? Are you eating properly?"

"Yes Amma, Ashley is actually a great cook, and I eat like a pig all weekend and starve all week with her father." She laughed at her mother's expression. "No, it's fine. Ron cooks as well. Between father and daughter, they're actually teaching me some cool things about cooking."

Ji snorted as he wiped his plate clean with a piece of *chapatti*. "He cooks?" He held out his plate and Elizabeth pushed a container of curry towards him. Kiran grinned as he had to help himself, throwing another *chapatti* onto his plate and covering it with curry.

Elizabeth said, "Some men actually make themselves useful. This Ron sounds wonderful. Though Irish men are as bad as Indian men. They first expect their mothers to do everything for them and then they think their wives will just step in. Ron is a widower?"

Kiran nodded. She couldn't meet Ji's eyes.

Elizabeth waggled a finger at Ji. "See, that is why he has had to learn to do things for himself. I don't know what would happen to you if something happened to me?"

Ji's expression froze and Elizabeth reached across and rubbed his hand. "Ji, it is okay. I am fine. I was just joking. I'll be around a lot longer than you, don't worry." She laughed at him and turned to her daughter. "So, what do you think of Rishi?"

Kiran stopped with her hand in mid-air, the *cappa* sliding off her fingers and back on the leaf, splashing curry onto the table.

She stared at her father. "Yes, I meant to bring that up, Dad. What is this I hear that I am to be married off to a man? As arranged by my father and his friends."

Ji wriggled in his skin. "Not just any friends. In fact, just one friend. He's like a brother to me. Dinesh and I did discuss something about Rishi. You know he is senior president of a very good company in London? And I know you really like him. You practically grew up together. It really is an auspicious match. This would have happened when you were still eligible if he hadn't married that English girl."

Elizabeth and Kiran were both staring at him and his voice mumbled off into silence.

Kiran said, "Dad, you know I'm gay. I am also with Ashley and I hope to spend the rest of my life with her."

Ji said, "Yes, you say that some woman is living in the same house with you, but we are serious now. You are still unmarried at your age. That is really not acceptable, Kiran."

He looked at Elizabeth as if to encourage her to join in but she remained silent. He continued in an impatient tone, "We have been patient with you, Kiran. Let you live in Ireland. Let you talk about these crazy Western things. But you are an adult now. And I am an important figure in this community. I am tired of the whispering, 'Oh look, Ji's daughter cannot find a husband', or 'Oh look, Ji cannot even manage to marry off his one daughter'. I cannot have that any longer."

Kiran cleared her throat and addressed them both. "Ashley and I are very serious. We love each other." She tried not to mumble, but the next words came out reluctantly. "And we are trying to get me pregnant. In fact, I might actually be pregnant right now."

Kiran swung her eyes from her father's stricken face but was met by a similar expression on her mother's face.

"I know Ashley is the right person for me. It is like my soul knew it, from the first moment I saw her and every minute since. Surely, you two, of all people, understand. You broke all the rules to be together. How can you not understand? And I really want this child, Amma. It is like a craving deep in me. Why should we not have a child just because we are gay?"

She willed her mother to nod, or smile, or in some small way acknowledge that she had heard and understood Kiran's plea. But Elizabeth stayed motionless and silent, her eyes fixed on the remnants of their feast, and Ji got up and slammed his fist down on the table. The plates clinked back down, the leaves just flapped gently. He gestured at Elizabeth as if to say 'See what you've done', turned and walked out of the room, slamming the half-doors behind him. The creak of their hinges covered the silence that had followed his exit as the wooden flaps waved forlornly after him.

CHAPTER EIGHT

Kiran sat on the veranda and watched the evening chatter and movement of the residents around the oval of green at the centre of the complex. They strolled in grey-haired couples, the men with one corner of their patterned *mundu* tucked in at the waist, their cream casual shirts, the women in white cotton saris draped over blouses in orange or blue or yellow, the bright flashes of colour blending in with the flower beds that they stopped to examine.

The air was heavy with the promise of rain and Kiran wished for the drenching that would come as a relief to the incessant pressure of the humidity. She could hear her parents arguing in Ji's study, their voices low murmurs of anger and irritation.

Kiran could see the residents making their way back to their verandas, looking up at the sky. She was startled at the sound of the first crack of thunder. The rain started almost immediately, streaming down in wavering sheets of grey on an invisible clothesline. She reached out and held her hand under the pounding drops, their warmth a delightful surprise on her skin after the cold drizzle of Ireland.

An arm reached out beside hers, cream skin pale against brown as mother and daughter watched the water bounce on their arms and drip off their elbows. Elizabeth pulled her arm back in and wiped her wet hand on Kiran's hair and face. Kiran gave an involuntary laugh and pushed her away.

"Are you trying to soften me up now that you've joined him in marrying me off to a man?" She said it jokingly but she couldn't hide the hurt in her eyes.

Elizabeth put her wet arm around Kiran's waist and pulled her in to rest her head on her daughter's shoulder. She rested her other hand gently on Kiran's stomach.

"So, I am going to be a granny even though my only daughter doesn't like men. We live in interesting times. Who's the father? Do we get to meet him?"

"Unless you want to search for him donating at some bank in Copenhagen, I think that is highly unlikely."

Elizabeth chuckled. "I don't think I want to try that. So, when do we get to meet your soul mate? She sounds very nice. And you seem to have moved very fast. How long have you known her?"

Elizabeth's tone was light but Kiran knew her mother.

"I don't know if we'll be able to come here to visit. It might be too much for Dad. But, we would love you, both of you, to come to Ireland. Maybe if this try works, you could come and stay for a while?"

"Ah, Instant Granny Babysitting Services I see. I guess I only had to put up with raising you, I deserve to have to go through all of that again." Elizabeth laughed.

"You would love Ashley. She's kind and funny and intelligent. She thinks and cares deeply about things. And she's beautiful."

Elizabeth straightened up. Her face got serious. "And she's from a different culture, Kiran. As you said, you couldn't bring her here. That will cause a rift, in time. She's not going to understand the pressures. She's not going to fit in here." She gestured around her.

"Amma, I don't fit here. I know I don't really fit there either but at least Ashley and I can live together openly." Kiran said. "You didn't fit here when you first came back, did you? But you stayed for Dad. And you're happy, aren't you?"

Elizabeth nodded. "But, I felt a strong connection to this place even before I met Ji. I am home here. When we lived in Ireland, I knew that Ji would never be considered Irish. How could he be? He is fully Indian. He never wanted to be anything but Indian. He gave up so much for us, Kiran. Try and be gentler with him, with the paltry dreams about you that he is left with." She sighed and turned to go back in. "He gave up his dreams for us. I lived with that knowledge for a very long time. He is happy now but he lost so many years. I don't wish that for you. I want you to live your dreams, but all I'm asking is that you understand what this is doing to your father, and what he gave up for you."

Kiran put her hand on her mother's shoulder. "Amma, you've never told me what happened. You and Dad won't tell me anything. Why we left here in the middle of the night." She nodded when Elizabeth turned back to her with a look of surprise. "Yes, I remember. Not the details, but I remember it was night and I remember being afraid. And you being afraid. And the rush. Having to leave my toys here. Wondering why I couldn't see Rishi and the others again. And why we had to live in such a cold place."

Elizabeth said in a gentle voice, "It wasn't like that. It was just not as well planned a move as it should have been. Ji got a job in Ireland which he had to start right away. That's all." She turned away again quickly and Kiran got the feeling that for the first time ever her mother had lied to her.

"Why did there have to be special permission to let me paint?" Kiran called after her. "And why the hell can't women be vision painters? We can do it better!" But her mother had gone and Kiran was talking to the empty chairs on the veranda.

∞ ∞ ∞

Ji was sitting at his desk his hand gripping a pen over a notepad, but the pen was still and he was gazing out of the window which in the daytime would provide a view of the complex he had designed and built. There were papers on every surface of the study. The door to the room was open and the light of the lamp on his desk spilt into the dark hallway. Kiran watched him from the door for a few minutes before knocking gently and entering. He ignored her and straightened up in his chair, scribbling on the pad with a frown of concentration.

She stood at the window and blocked his view of the yellow haze of streetlamps and the fronded silhouettes of leaning coconut trees. "So, how is the autobiography going?"

He grunted and kept writing.

She tried again. "Is that what you are working on? Is it nearly finished?"

He looked up, the light from the lamp glinted off his glasses, his eyes magnified through the bottom of the lenses. "I am a very busy man. I'm writing the autobiography for me and for your mother. I have the edited Codebook to check. And I am writing a book about the history of the profession."

"Wow, that's a lot. Have you got someone to type it all out for you?"

He snorted. "What do you think that we are heathens? That we cannot type. I have an excellent typist who will do the work for me. A busy man, but he would do anything for me. I did a vision painting for him years ago."

Ji looked up and caught the white of Kiran's smile in the shadows. He glared at her. "See, you do not take anything seriously. This book will be the first description of our origins, our profession. It has taken years to collect all the material." He gestured at the papers all around him. "Years to find. And it is so precious. It took days just to make the copies. Our history to be written out. It will be a legacy fitting for the fourth Leader of the Council to have come from the same family. But what do you know or care for our traditions. You and your Western," his voice dropped to a whisper and he sneaked a look at the open door, "lesbian," his voice rose again to a normal volume, "crazy, disrespectful ways."

"I'm sure it will be an amazing book. I would love to read it when you are finished. Ashley is a writer, maybe she could help."

Ji looked stunned. "No. You cannot read it. Neither of you. It is only for members of the Association. The real Vision Painters. You can only read the autobiography and the Codebook. You might understand the sacrifices then, and the guidelines that you should be following if you were a real vision painter."

His fingers were twisting the pen and his eyes were wide. Kiran held up her hand and said quickly, "It's fine, Dad. Sorry, I thought it was for the general public." His shoulders dropped back down. "Though, you do know that there was some stuff on the internet about vision painters. Written by somebody who seemed to have a grudge against you. That's how Ron found out a bit about the profession."

Ji laughed as he leant back in the chair. "I am highly respected, Kiran, if not by you, by all the vision painters. They know what I have done for the profession in the short time I have been in charge. And even before that. You may not think it of your father, but I was a progressive and forward-thinking man who brought this profession forward."

He got up and stood beside her at the window and made an expansive gesture towards the complex slumbering outside. "As I did for this village and for many senior citizens in Kerala. Is this not such a well-designed retirement place for our elders? They are happy here. I am happy with what I have achieved, even if you think I am nothing. Even if you completely disregard my wishes despite the sacrifices I made for you."

Kiran said, "You've told me enough times. But I can't change how I feel because of those sacrifices. I'm grateful, but this is just the way I am. And it would mean so much if you accepted that. If you could be happy for me." She put her hand on her stomach. "Dad, what if it worked? Will you accept our child as your grandchild? Whether it is a boy or girl?"

"So, you will not consider the proposal from Dinesh and Rishi?" He turned to look at her and his eyes were harsh.

Kiran shook her head. Her throat felt tight and painful.

Ji turned back to the window and addressed the glass, "Then, please stay in Ireland. Don't bring any woman here and don't bring your...your...offspring...here either."

"Dad!"

He turned and she felt the warmth of his hand as he rested it on her shoulder for just a moment, before nudging her towards the door. His voice was as strangled as hers had been. "Go and spend some time with your mother. She misses you. Babu will be ready at midnight to take you to Cochin for your flight."

CHAPTER NINE

Kiran scanned the meeting area at the Arrivals Hall in Shannon which was packed with people, suitcases toppling off their wheels, prams, and trolleys. Her eyes were red with tiredness, her clothes stuck to her, and she was still smarting from the irritation at the usual questioning she received at Immigration. Two bored Immigration officers sat in their booths, sieving through the long lines of tired passengers. The suspicion in the man's eyes, even when she handed over the purple EU passport, which showed she was Irish. She made a joke with him, putting on even more of an Irish accent, and he nodded her through with a laugh. The usual pattern of her travels through the borders of home. The tiredness this time just adding to the hurt.

Kiran shifted the rucksack on her back. It was heavier now than when she'd gone to Kerala. There were a few treats, a bag of banana chips, the bright orange honey-soaked rings of *jilabi*, even a Tupperware container with the thick syrup and almond balls of *gulab jamun*. Kiran hoped the syrup wouldn't leak out onto the papers she had taken from her father's study. They were copies, she knew, but the guilt she felt was bad enough. The last thing she wanted was to drown the paper in syrup.

She forgot everything in her eagerness to see Ashley. It had only been a week but she had only had a chance to hear Ashley's voice twice. The conversation stilted by the location of the phone within earshot of Kiran's parents. The ache of

77

missing her made Kiran realise how much Ashley had become a part of her life.

She saw the mane of red hair first and then Ashley's eyes searching as well. Kiran dragged her rucksack behind and tried to act casual as she sauntered over but she rushed the last few feet to Ashley and, despite her reserve about public displays of affection, she grabbed Ashley and kissed her. A long full kiss that forgot the people swarming around, the curious eyes, and the long journey from a place that would never be home if they could not be there together.

When Kiran finally stepped back, Ashley's eyes were unfocused as she smiled and leaned forward and kissed Kiran again before reaching around her to pick up the rucksack. They walked towards the parking pay machines.

"How is your mother?"

"Almost back to normal. Dad won't let her do anything so she's chomping at the bit. I'd give it a few more days and the natural order will be restored."

"What do they think it was?" Ashley dropped the coins into the machine and retrieved the ticket. They walked out into the cloudy evening, Ashley carrying the rucksack, Kiran holding her hand.

Kiran shivered. "They have no idea. Maybe it was exhaustion or heat stroke or something. She's acclimatised after being back there for twenty years but maybe the heat just got to her. You wouldn't believe the heat and humidity there. I was sweating just thinking about it." She stroked Ashley's arm, which was a creamy bronze colour, much more tanned than it had been the previous week. "Despite this effort, you would struggle there. I see there has been some sunshine here in my absence?"

Ashley laughed. "Yes, you missed what will probably be our whole summer. It was glorious. I'm afraid I lay out in it the entire time." They found the parking space where Ashley had left her car, and Ashley put the rucksack in the back seat. Her voice turned serious. "I wish we could go back to the house and not have to stay in Galway tonight." She leaned and whispered into Kiran's ear, her breath tickling and teasing, "I missed you."

Kiran stopped and kissed her again, pushing her gently against the car. She whispered against Ashley's mouth, "I know. But I have to work in the morning. They were really good to give me the week off with no notice. We could be really quiet; Ron is in his own world on his side of the house." She groaned as Ashley stroked her lips before pulling away with a smile.

"Well, there will be no hanky panky tonight at the house. You seem to have sent a package that has ended up staying." Ashley got in and started the engine.

Kiran hurried around to the passenger seat. "What package?"

"Some guy called Vijay?"

"He's *staying*?"

Ashley nodded. "Yup. My dad offered him a room. Temporarily of course. Just until he finds somewhere."

"You're kidding me. I gave him Ron's number just to say hi. I was going to meet up with him when I got back. Show him around and stuff."

Ashley pulled out of the parking space. "He doesn't seem to be any trouble. He's a nice guy. But he's staying in the room next to ours." She smiled. "You must be exhausted and you're going to be jetlagged. I'll be happy just to hold you all night."

Kiran slumped back in the seat. "Actually, to be honest, I might damage my reputation as a lover of some skill if I were to attempt anything in this state." She pushed Ashley's arm at the snort of laughter from her. "Hey! You could at least pretend!" She smiled at Ashley who was trying to keep a straight face and snuggled down in the seat to sleep, her hand resting on Ashley's thigh.

∞ ∞ ∞

It was strange to see Vijay again in such a different setting. His skin was darker than hers but seemed so much browner and Kiran realised she was getting used to the paleness around her. Kerala had been an intense palette of humidity and colour, an oil painting of heavy richness. Ireland was a watercolour of greens washed through with pale blue and grey.

Vijay had been embarrassed as he explained how Ron had insisted on him staying at the house. He couldn't seem to get over the warmth of welcome or the coolness of the climate. Kiran and Ashley had stayed in Ron's living room with Ron and Vijay for an hour, after which the jerking back of Kiran's tired head every few minutes prompted her to finally give up on any semblance of hospitality.

She was glad Ashley and Ron sensed that Kiran didn't want Vijay to know about their relationship. Kiran made her excuses and went upstairs to her bedroom on her own. She knew Ashley would give it a respectable length of time before following her up.

She had unpacked and was stretched out on top of the covers when Ashley came in. Kiran sat up with her back against the headboard and Ashley sat on the bed, holding her hand, playing with her fingers.

Ashley said, "You must have been so worried about your mum."

Kiran nodded. "She's always been the strong one. Well, dad is too. But she has this energy. It was so strange to see her lying there, but not there." She gripped Ashley's fingers. "I'm so sorry about your mother. I knew it at the time, how hard it would be, but when I felt that fear, that pain, seeing her there so helpless, even letting the thought enter my head that something could happen to her, that I might lose her..." The rush of words stalled in the bottleneck of tightness in Kiran's throat.

Ashley reached out and put her arms around Kiran. Her voice was soft. "She is fine now, Kiran. She will be fine. Maybe they could come here and visit for a while. Maybe that would be good for her. Has she visited Ireland since she moved back to India?"

Kiran shook her head against Ashley's shoulder. She nestled against the warmth and softness. "Maybe when the baby comes."

The tiredness was catching up and she lay back against the pillows.

Ashley said, "I have some news. I'm not sure if you will like it." She had her eyes fixed on their intertwined fingers.

"Go on."

"I got a job in Galway."

Kiran sat up. "That's great! Wow, Ashley! You don't have to go back to Dublin...Why would you think I wouldn't like that?"

Ashley looked up and met her gaze. "I would be working with Jenny."

Great! Kiran tried not to let her expression change but her muscles tightened at the mention of Ashley's ex. *Jennifer the Perfect. The Greek or Roman doctor goddess.*

"Kiran?"

Kiran retained her smile as best as she could. She tried widening it, but that mustn't have worked because Ashley did not look convinced by the effort at a smile.

"Kiran, I chose to be with you. Not Jenny. *Dammit*, woman, we are trying to have a child together. Why do you have that look in your eyes? Like I've already left you for her or something?"

"I don't. I'm happy for you. For us. No, really, I am." Kiran leaned back and closed her eyes. "I'm just exhausted. When do you start?"

"April 1st, Fool's Day. Good day to restart my career as a doctor."

Kiran squinted at her through barely open eyelids. "You are a great doctor. You couldn't help but be. You're the most caring person I know. And the most intelligent. And the most beautiful."

Ashley laughed. "Okay, okay. Enough. Get some sleep. You can barely keep your eyes open."

Kiran moved to let Ashley in beside her. She wanted to tell Ashley about the proposal that her father had tried to push on her but she couldn't keep her eyes open any longer. As Kiran drifted off, her arms wrapped around Ashley's waist, she felt the unease course through her as she realised that one of the last vision paintings she had done was of Ashley with Jennifer.

CHAPTER TEN

Kiran groaned as the alarm clock blared through the haze of her exhausted sleep. She reached over and punched the buttons on her phone until the noise stopped. She swung back her arm meaning to wrap it around Ashley and try and sneak a few extra minutes in bed. The space beside her was empty.

Kiran sat up. Her body clock was trying to wind itself up. She was alone in the bedroom. She checked the time. It was still early, the clocks hadn't sprung forward yet, and it was dark outside at 7.30a.m.

Kiran got ready and wandered downstairs for breakfast, assuming Ashley was up early and having breakfast with her father. But Ron was on his own in his kitchen. He had an apron wrapped around his thin frame and his silver hair was neatly brushed.

Ron examined her face. "You look like you've been chased all night by the hounds of hell. Here, sit. Have some breakfast before you go." He took some scones out of the oven and cut them open, spreading butter that melted into the crevices of the warm pastry.

Kiran shook her head. The thought of eating didn't appeal. "Where's Ashley? Is she not having some?"

"She has already headed back to Connemara. She wants to get as much writing done before she starts her new job. And she needs to brush up for work as well. She didn't want to wake you. She said you were in such a deep sleep she was surprised you could still snore." He laughed at Kiran's expression.

Kiran pulled up a stool at the counter. Ron's kitchen was warm and bright, the ceiling halogen lamps casting round spotlights on the surface in front of her. She gratefully accepted a cup of coffee.

There was a light knock at the door and Vijay came in. He was dressed in a navy suit, with a white shirt and a navy tie. He smiled and nodded when he saw Kiran and gestured to the suit with a quizzical expression on his face.

Kiran smiled. "Looking good, Vijay. But I think you might be a little bit overdressed for a software company in Galway. However, I can't be sure. You'll know after the first day anyway."

Vijay sighed. "It is difficult to know what to wear and do on your first day."

Ron pushed the buttered scone towards him and pulled up another stool. "Don't worry about it. Before you know it, you'll be right at home."

Vijay sat and helped himself to a coffee to go with the scone.

"Where were you working before this? IT? In India?" Kiran asked.

Vijay nodded. "But also in Europe and the Middle East, and a time in the United States."

Kiran got up. "You'll be fine. The Irish are very friendly. I've got to go to work. Do you need a lift?"

Vijay said, "That would be very good. Thank you. I need to find a place to stay, maybe somewhere near the company, so I could take a bus to work. I'm not sure I want to start driving here yet. I will take a taxi back this evening."

He finished his scone and drank down a big gulp of coffee. He turned to Ron. "I am very grateful for your hospitality, Sir."

Ron laughed. "Please, you're very welcome. And I feel really old when addressed as Sir. As I said before, please call me Ron."

Vijay smiled. "Thank you, Ron. I need to find a place very soon because my friend is visiting this week." He turned to Kiran. "Your friend, really. Rishi has decided to spend the last week of his vacation here in Galway helping me to settle in."

Kiran's heart sank. "He hasn't."

Vijay wiggled his head. "Yes. He has. But he has booked into the best hotel in town. The G or some letter like that?"

Of course he would. *Great.* She would definitely have to tell Ashley now.

Ron frowned. "Kiran, are you okay?"

She gave a weak smile. "It's a long story. And I'll be late. Come, Vijay, we'd better go. Traffic is going to be bad."

∞ ∞ ∞

Kiran sat and fumed at the jam of evening traffic that she could see stretched in front of her on the Quincentennial Bridge. Her body had given up trying to figure out what day of the week or what time of the day it was. It just knew that she was on her way home and a line of cars a mile long at least, stood between it and a soft, warm bed.

Her eyelids drooped and she turned the radio up. The newsreader's voice was cut off mid-word when the Bluetooth kicked in as her phone rang. She glanced at the radio display and was startled to see that it was an Indian number. Her father never called her on her mobile and not at a reasonable time like this; he usually saved his calls for her house phone at 3 or 4 a.m. in the morning. The volume was still on high so Ji's voice blared through the car speakers and surrounded her.

"Kiran? Is that you, Kiran?"

"Yes, Dad, That's usually what happens when you dial my number."

"I have no time for joking round. Your mother is sick again. Not in the same way. She is awake this time. But she cannot get up." His voice was stiff with fear, but also a lot of restrained anger.

Kiran felt a wave of nausea hit her. The sweat broke out on her forehead and her chest hurt. She needed to pull the car over but she was stuck on the outside lane and no cars were moving.

Her father continued, "We found something in the studio, Kiran." He stopped.

"What? What did you find?"

"Don't act like you don't know. Kiran, I cannot believe this of you."

"I have no idea what you are talking about, Dad. Please tell me what is going on." Her fingers hurt and she realised she was gripping the steering wheel. She loosened her hands and wiped them on her trousers.

Ji lapsed into Malayalam. His anger was still radiating out of the speakers. "We found a painting, Kiran. A painting of your mother. In the studio, leaning against the wall. But it was not a positive picture. No, it was of your mother lying sick in her bed."

"What?! Who would do that? How could anyone do that? To her?" The cars moved forward a few yards and the driver behind her hooted the horn, the blare cutting through the confused babble in her head. She glared at the driver in her mirror, but edged the car forward.

"You were the only one there. Kiran, I told you not to paint. Now, look at what has happened."

The traffic inched forward. Kiran felt like screaming through the airwaves at her father but she kept her voice calm. "Dad, I did not paint. Yes, I was tempted to paint her better. Why would I paint her sick?"

He was silent. The air in the car was still and dense. "I don't know. But the painting is from your hand. The strokes, the use of colour, I am your father, I taught you. I would know your paintings anywhere."

Tears of frustration welled up in her eyes. "You have to believe me, Dad. I promise you. I did not, I would not, paint Amma like that."

"Then who did?" Ji's voice was breaking up under the weight of stress.

Kiran had no answer. The honking of the car horn behind her startled her. She turned and glared at the woman in the car behind. The woman looked as stressed as Kiran felt. She was mouthing words, alternating between directing them at Kiran and at the child in the car seat in the back who was obviously screaming at the top of its lungs.

"Why would anyone want to hurt Amma?" Kiran asked the air.

Her father answered, "Everyone loves her here, Kiran. Everyone loves her. She is special."

"I'll try and get a flight. As soon as possible." Kiran was trying to figure out how she could ask for another period of time off after the last week.

"No." The word dropped out of the speakers and landed with a thud.

Kiran said, "I need to see that she is okay. I need to be there."

"No, Kiran. I don't want you coming here. Stay away."

"I thought you believed me. That I didn't paint anything." Her voice was high and strained.

He said in Malayalam, "I do not know what is going on. But I don't think you should come here. I will keep you

87

informed." The line went dead with a click that resounded in the car.

For a second, Kiran felt a shot of pure fear slice through her. She shook her head. She had not painted. She had fallen asleep on the chair in the studio. The canvas had been as innocent as when she had picked it up and put it on the easel. *This could not be happening.* Nobody would paint somebody in a worse way than how they were. That was negative. Vision Painters did not do negative.

Kiran managed to avoid the wrath of the mother behind her by moving in some kind of unison with the rest of the traffic. But her mind and her heart were with her mother in Kerala, lying there, sick, *dying?* A victim of one of Kiran's kind, another vision painter?

CHAPTER ELEVEN

Rainclouds were spreading grey fingers over the tops of the mountains and Kiran felt sorry for the lambs huddled under their mothers' spindly legs. Connemara was ready for spring, but the season stubbornly refused to settle on sunshine or rain.

She had hesitated at the turn to Ron's house. She'd put her foot down and passed it as her urge to see Ashley won out against the more sensible need to stay in Galway for work the next day. Another early morning would do her no harm, whereas not seeing Ashley was hurting.

The hour-long drive on roads that bent through mountains and bogs kept her mind busy though she barely noticed the hulking shapes on the horizon or the shadowed depths in the ground. While her head tried to work out what was happening, her heart was crying in fear. More than most people, she knew the potential power of a vision painter's gift. She had painted a dead woman to appear again. Kiran knew it hadn't just been the physical painting. It must have been the confluence of Ron's desperation and Kiran's immersion in that loss, her ability to empathise to the extent that she felt the physical pain of the separation. The nine nights of extreme pain that she had suffered as her mind let itself loose into the deepest well of Ron's soul.

In the months after Marge's departure, Kiran had tried to avoid analysing what had happened. To forget as much as possible that she had brought Marge back, that a man had died as a result, and that another was paralysed for life. The gift that she had enjoyed all her teenage and adult life without really questioning had felt like a curse for the last few months.

She had not admitted, even to Ashley, that she could not paint now because she could not bear to listen, to feel, to empathise. She was still haunted by the pain she had caused, whether the souls who suffered had been right or wrong, good or bad. Now her own mother was in danger. Kiran knew that. She felt it deep in the echoes of her own mistakes, of the strength of her own gift. If someone had painted Elizabeth into sickness, how much more could they choose to do to her.

A sheep, its wool drying into twisted curls below its belly, raised it head from its chewing and threatened to move into her path. Kiran looped around the sheep bringing her focus back to the car and the road. She reached the edge of the trees surrounding her house and eased into the driveway, trying not to race, not to let the need to be home and with Ashley, take over.

There was a black sports car parked at the front of her house. Kiran braked and the pebbles moved around the wheels in protest.

Jennifer?

Kiran sat in her car and stared at her house. The trees were shaking their heads, and the shadows of the leaves trembled on the roof. There was a light on in Ashley's study. The rest of the house sulked in darkness. Kiran slowly reversed the car back onto the road, the wheels dripping stones that lay crushed on the asphalt as she drove away.

∞ ∞ ∞

Kiran walked through the main house meaning to avoid Ron and Vijay and head straight upstairs to her room. The drive back had been a blur. Her mind was aching to go blank. She passed the open door to the dining room and was surprised to see Vijay in there, setting the table. He looked very casual in brown slacks and a cream jumper.

He smiled when he saw her and gestured at the oak surface of the table that was partially covered with napkins and placemats. "I'm no use at this. Please don't tell Ron, but I would appreciate some help."

Kiran smiled back though it was an effort she had hoped to avoid. She found the light switch and the central chandelier blossomed into light. She wandered over to the antique French sideboard and took out the silver and china.

She paused in her task. "What's all this for. Surely not for just the three of us?"

Vijay shook his head. His deep brown, almost black, eyes reflected a multitude of tiny beams from the chandelier. He seemed to be trying to suppress a laugh.

"Ron has very kindly decided to cook to welcome Rishi to Galway."

"Rishi is here? Already?"

Vijay nodded. "Yes, apparently he feels a very strong urge to help me settle." He grinned and Kiran realised that he was actually very handsome, especially when he smiled.

It's not you Rishi wants to settle! Kiran frowned. She looked down at her attire which was fine for a day at work but was definitely going to look out of place in the formal dining room. She definitely wasn't in the mood for this. Not tonight. Actually, not any night.

She helped Vijay with the formal table settings, her movements tight with annoyance. She knew she should phone Ashley but she didn't. She dropped a knife onto the table and it clanged off the fork. She could see Vijay looking at her hands as she tried to straighten the cutlery.

Her voice shook as well as she said, "Amma is sick again."

His hand stopped, and the glass he was holding, hung in the air between them. "But you said she was fine when you left."

"She was." Kiran sank down onto one of the chairs, the back of it holding her upright.

"I am so sorry to hear that. Is it the same as before? If so, maybe she will recover in the same way." He was standing beside her and she could feel him awkwardly patting the curved wood at the top of the chair, close to her shoulder.

"It is not the same. She's awake this time. She cannot walk. My father won't tell me much more than that." She put her head in her hands, her hair falling forward in a black veil over the white of the china plate. "He doesn't want me to go there."

"You have just arrived back from India. He does not want to bring you all the way back, I'm sure."

She wanted to tell him that she knew otherwise. Her own father believed the worst of her. But she would have to explain why Ji would think that. So she just nodded.

Ron said from the doorway, "Kiran, is everything alright?" He was holding a vase with orange lilies. Vijay stepped back and Kiran took her face out of her hands and nodded.

She shook her head. "No, it isn't alright. My mother is sick again."

And someone painted her into sickness, my father believes it was me, and my Ashley is with her ex-girlfriend at this very moment.

Ron placed the vase on the table and sat down in the chair beside her. He took her hand. "I'm sure she will be fine, like last time. Do you need to arrange the ticket? Use my computer in the study."

Kiran shook her head again. The kindness in his voice broke through her reluctance to tell them. "A vision painter has done a negative painting of my mother." As the words came out, Kiran felt the fear of saying them out loud.

Ron tightened his grip on her hand. "That's not possible. Is it? I thought vision painters only painted the positive. Surely it would not work. The client would not ask for something negative for himself, and third parties cannot be affected."

Kiran looked him straight in the eyes and saw the understanding creep into them. If she could do it for him to affect Marge, and if painting had been so powerfully effective, then they were dealing with something that was as powerful and that broke the rules. But not just the rules. What Kiran had done had still been positive and had been rooted in a desire to help, whatever the unforeseen consequences. This was different.

∞ ∞ ∞

Ron had immediately offered to cancel the dinner but Kiran knew there was no point hiding away in her room which is where she wanted to be. She sat on the bed and spread out the material she had taken from her father's study before she'd left his house. She'd passed the study on her way out to Babu waiting in the Jeep. Her father had left the lamp on and she'd stepped in to the empty room meaning to switch the light off.

Kiran had stared at the open safe, at the two bundles of papers held together with elastic bands. She knew they were the copies of the material her father had found. Their ornate Malayalam script and the outline of smaller pages were dark against the white of the more modern paper. They were lying in amongst a few copies of the codebook and a stack of papers covered with handwriting. Her heart was pounding in her chest and her hands shook as she transferred one of the bundles, a codebook, and some of the loose scribble-covered papers into her rucksack. She had switched off the light and hurried out to Babu for the midnight trip to Cochin.

The material looked foreign on the pastel cover on her bed. She took the elastic off the bundle of papers and examined the top sheet. The words made no sense to her, she could understand the spoken words of the language to some extent, but the script might as well have been ancient Egyptian hieroglyphics it was Greek to her. Maybe Vijay would understand it. He had been present at the training centre. He must have some background in the profession. She would show it to him later. She checked her watch and sighed. Rishi was due in half an hour.

Kiran showered and changed into a pair of black trousers and a turquoise blouse with a Nehru collar. She sat at the mirror and brushed her hair in long strokes that transported her back to the comfort of a childhood memory. The bruised skin under them shadowed the blue-green of her eyes and reminded her that she was a darker version of her mother. Her skin, her hair, her eyes, all were just a darker shade of the woman who lit up their hearts for as long as Kiran could remember.

The doorbell cut through her memories and she groaned. She didn't have the strength for Rishi. But, she needed to know whether, through Dinesh, Rishi had been allowed more access than she had been to the inner sanctum of the profession.

∞ ∞ ∞

Kiran could hear Ron in his kitchen as she went down the stairs. Rishi was waiting with Vijay in the salon. Rishi perched on the end of the chaise-longue; Vijay standing by the fireplace. Rishi's eyes appraised her as she walked in to the room.

Might as well have not bothered with clothes, and these aren't even revealing! Kiran adjusted the high-cut collar of the blouse, leaving her arm covering her chest as she rested her fingers on the turquoise pendant that hung from the silver necklace she had put on. She seemed to be trying to cover herself up every time she met Rishi.

Rishi sprang up from his seat and approached her, his smile flashing white teeth. He held her by the shoulders and said, "Another French kiss?" and without waiting for an answer, leaned across and kissed her on both cheeks. Her toes curled in rebellion but she smiled back.

"Hi Rishi. When did you leave Kerala?" She didn't know if he had heard about Elizabeth. He must have left the village shortly after Kiran had.

"Just this morning. That's why I am so late. And I look so rough." He smiled again as she took in the suit he was wearing, its grey surface as smooth as the uncreased white shirt with faint pink stripes. He must have stopped at the hotel on the way, or he had travelled in First Class. After the same journey she had looked like she had just emerged from a tumble dryer.

She raised an eyebrow. "A week is a very short holiday in India. Did Uncle not mind?"

Rishi shook his head. "He encouraged me to come and help Vijay find his feet here."

Out of the corner of her eye, Kiran could see Vijay's quick smile.

She said, "You haven't heard then that Amma is sick again."

Rishi's eyes widened. "No. I am so sorry. I haven't been in contact with my father after I left. Here I am, chatting away, imposing on you all. What is the matter with her?" He seemed genuinely disturbed.

"I don't know," Kiran said, "And it is difficult to find out."

Ron came in to the living room with a bottle of wine. There were four glasses on the coffee table beside a corkscrew. "A good year, I think. My late wife, Marge, was the one for picking the right wine for any occasion." He paused, and held the bottle out for them to see.

Kiran shook her head. She wasn't going to risk it.

Rishi took the bottle and examined the label. "You're right, an excellent wine. A very good choice, I'm sure your wife would have approved."

Yes, just before she drank the whole thing. Kiran suddenly missed Marge, as annoying as she had been. She wondered what Marge would have made of Rishi, who was presenting the bottle back to Ron with a flourish.

Ron opened the bottle and poured out the wine.

∞ ∞ ∞

Rishi and Vijay had helped clear the table and the four moved back into the living room. Dinner had been a slightly stilted affair but the food had been delicious. Ron opened another bottle of wine and Kiran got a glass of juice for herself.

Ron couldn't contain himself any longer. "As Kiran knows, I am fascinated with the idea of vision painting. I studied what I could find on it but there is nothing like meeting people who have firsthand knowledge and who are steeped in the history of that ancient profession."

Rishi leaned back on the chaise-longue and sighed. "It was a sore disappointment to my father that I did not stay in Kerala and follow the path that he had chosen. Especially when he became Leader of the Council in 1991 when *his* father retired as Leader." He took a sip of his wine and examined the red liquid, "Pop felt it especially then, I think. The bloodline of leadership ending with him."

"At least you got a chance. No one answers me when I ask why women cannot even be vision painters, not to mention Members of the Council, or Leaders. My father must be holding on to the leadership position now wondering what the hell to do," Kiran said.

Vijay was sitting upright in the armchair. "Did you know your two families have held the leadership of the Council since the first Council was formed in 1921?"

Rishi and Kiran shook their heads and Vijay continued, reciting as if it was information he had recently studied, "The first Council was formed under the leadership of Kiran's father's great grandfather and he held that role until he retired in 1941 at which point his son, Kiran's great grandfather, Ji's grandfather, took over." Kiran quirked an eyebrow as she tried to work out all the grandfathers.

"Tragedy struck in 1958 when the assumed successor to the role, Ji's father, died at the age of 42. Ji's grandfather retired early, they say due to a broken heart, and Dinesh's father took over the leadership."

"Is that when my father moved in with Dinesh's family?" Kiran remembered the photo on the wall, the two young men with sombre faces.

Vijay nodded. "Dinesh's father, Manoj, took on the role of Leader but he also took on the role of father and mentor to Ji who was 17 at the time, like Dinesh. He raised the two boys as his sons."

"So that's why they keep talking like they are brothers." Kiran turned to Rishi and said, "See, we are cousins. Did you realise that? Almost practically brother and sister."

There was a little frown on Rishi's smooth forehead. "I don't think that is how they see us." He smiled in a tight movement of his lips. "I think they see us as a hope for a generation they have lost. There are other vision painters, yes, but none from the two greatest families."

Ron had been listening quietly. He seemed to be drinking it all in with the little sips of wine he was taking. He broke in,

"What will happen to the leadership if there are no active sons from either line to take over?"

Kiran and Rishi both looked at Vijay. He shrugged. "That is of course a worry that they have for the future. There are other members of the Council but it would be the first time since 1921 that the Council was led by someone outside of either of the two families."

Rishi grinned. "What is needed is an amalgamation of the two great families, isn't it?"

Ron and Kiran exchanged looks and she could see the realisation in his eyes. Rishi leaned forward and his eyes lit up. Kiran glanced at the glass in his hand. It was empty.

Rishi's voice took on a grandiose note. "That would be something that would obviously please my father and Ji very much. If you think about it, this could never have happened before. There has been no female offspring before. The lines have always continued with the addition of genes from outside. This would be merging of two of the great families, and in addition, the possible production of a vision painter of incredible purity and power."

Kiran glanced down at her hand which had automatically covered her abdomen. Rishi hadn't noticed but as she looked back up she saw Vijay's eyebrow rise before he looked away.

Kiran wanted to ask more but she felt trapped in the room. She cleared her throat and got up. "I'm sorry but I've another early start tomorrow."

The three men got up immediately and she held up her hand. "Don't mind me, please stay and chat."

Rishi took her hand and kissed it with a flourish. "I hope we will get to spend some time with you tomorrow. Perhaps after you finish work, I could take you all out to dinner?" He turned to include Ron in the invitation. "I really would like that. It would give me a chance to show my appreciation for your wonderful generosity."

Kiran groaned inside, but nodded her head joining Ron in accepting the invitation.

CHAPTER TWELVE

"We don't take coloureds here."

The woman's voice was just clear enough to carry behind Ron and drift onto Vijay. The woman ignored Kiran who had been delayed squeezing out of the back of Ron's Jaguar which he had pulled in very close to the wall in front of the house.

Kiran felt the blood rush to her face. She stepped up beside Ron and put her hand on his arm to stop him. He seemed like he was about to launch into an attack.

The woman continued addressing Ron. "I thought it was for you." Her eyes flicked past his shocked angry face and examined Vijay. She wiped her hands on her apron and backed up slightly behind the glass walls of her porch.

Ron said in a voice that struggled to remain civil, "Do you realise how many laws you are breaking right now?"

"What law says I have to rent my room to someone like him?" The woman was still talking as though Vijay and Kiran were not present, or did not understand English. She leaned towards Ron and her breath was a damp break in the white cloud reflections on the glass. "These days you cannot be too careful." She backed away and disappeared through her front door. They heard the lock clicking into place.

Ron turned around slowly and Kiran could see him struggling to meet Vijay's eyes. He said, "I am so sorry. I cannot believe what just happened. I am so sorry."

Vijay shook his head. "Ron, it is not your fault. I probably look like a terrorist to her. After all, am I not just another brown man?"

Kiran was used to the occasional remark that highlighted her difference, her lack of belonging, but this was the first blatant act she had experienced.

She turned to him. "Vijay, I'm sorry. I don't know what to say. We should probably have just stuck to the apartments. It was my stupid idea that you were better off lodging and having company."

Vijay said, "Really, it is fine. It was a nice idea. And you are both very generous to spend your time off looking for a nice place for me." He smoothed down the jacket of his suit. His tie was at an angle and he straightened it and smiled. "I didn't realise it was crooked, must have been what persuaded her."

Kiran laughed and Ron gave a grudging smile. He said, "I still have a good mind to report her. In this day and age."

Kiran moved towards the car. "No point. What good would it do? Let's go and find a real estate agent."

Ron and Vijay followed. They were silent as they got back in and Ron drove away from the housing estate.

Ron slung the Jaguar around a roundabout and burst out, "That's it, Vijay. You are staying in my house. At least until you are properly settled in Galway. It is a big place and we rattle around in it, don't we, Kiran?"

Kiran nodded from the back seat. This would be awkward with Vijay not knowing about her and Ashley.

Vijay hesitated, and said in a subdued voice, "That is very good of you, Ron. I really appreciate it."

Ron changed direction and headed for his house. He parked the car at the top of the driveway and turned around in his seat. "Kiran, Ashley called again. She's coming to

Galway this evening. I asked her and Rishi and she's going to come to dinner as well."

Great. This was going to be fun, hiding from Rishi and Vijay. They went in to the house and Vijay went up to his bedroom. Ron gestured at Kiran to come in to his living room. He poured them a coffee and patted the couch.

His eyes were kind and concerned. "Why did Ashley not know about your mother being ill again?"

She sat down.

"Kiran? Did you two have a fight?"

She shook her head. "No. But things are going to be very difficult with Vijay here. And while Rishi is here."

"Do your parents not know already? About Ashley?"

She nodded. "But the rest of the village doesn't know. For my father's sake, they cannot find out. Dinesh, Rishi's father, my dad's best friend, he doesn't know. And he is a big man in the Vision Painting Council. Rishi doesn't know. They are trying to arrange a match between us."

Ron said, "I got that impression last night. But that is just talk by this Dinesh and Rishi, isn't it? Surely you have had other marriage proposals before? Can you not just ignore this one like the others?"

"Those other proposals were just people trying to get in with my father, or there was some spare single or divorced man around who couldn't be matched with any young eligible women."

Ron smiled. "I hardly think that is the case. They would have seen a photo."

"Thanks. But this time my father is involved too."

"In putting forward the proposal?" His eyebrows shot up.

"Yes. And yes, he knows I'm gay. And yes, he knows about Ashley. He now even knows about our possible child..." Her voice trailed off as she realised what she had said. Ron's eyebrows were still stuck in two silver curves. They curved down into a frown.

"Child...?" His voice was tight.

Kiran squirmed on the couch. She rubbed her palms on the ribbed fabric.

"What child? What are you two talking about?" Ashley's voice was light as she strolled in. She put her bag down on the counter. "Any coffee going, Dad?"

Ron turned to his daughter. "Supposedly your child. Which no one could be bothered to tell me about. I am just your father."

Kiran couldn't meet Ashley's eyes. She knew the look that would be in them. She could feel the glare through the back of her head.

"I didn't know I had a child. Pray, fill us in, Kiran." Ashley's voice stretched out gently and Kiran felt it like a gentle smack.

"I might have mentioned to Ron that I might have mentioned to my parents that we were trying for a baby."

"You two are trying for a baby and you didn't think I might like to know. I mean I understand how you might want to keep it from everyone until it worked but telling Kiran's parents..." Ron sounded so hurt.

"Yes, Kiran. Telling your parents...?"

"Look, it just came out when they told me about their proposal for me to marry Rishi."

Great. Kiran, just stop talking. Father and daughter were looking equally shocked now.

"For you to marry who?" Ashley's voice had reached another level.

Kiran turned to face her and turned back quickly. Redheads sometimes were just as hot-headed as reputed. Kiran took a deep breath and stood up and faced them. "My parents, well, no, my dad and his best friend, well, his kind of brother, got together and thought that it would be a good match between Dinesh, that's my father's best brother, well, his son, that's Rishi, and Ji's daughter, that's me, obviously."

Ashley looked confused.

Ron nodded. "Yes, her father knows she is gay and you are together. And he apparently now knows more than I do. That you are trying for a child."

Ashley shook her head. The red shimmered.

"Dad. I'm sorry. I would have picked a better time to tell you. If there was anything to tell." She glared at Kiran. "There isn't any more, is there? Like you haven't already done the test and told your parents the good news, have you?"

Kiran shook her head.

"Well, at least that's something." Ashley poured out a coffee and took a sip before placing the mug down on the counter with an angry click. "So, this Rishi person, is he the one who is taking us all out to dinner?"

Kiran gave a little nod.

"And what part am I supposed to play in this little charade?" Ashley's eyes were angry behind the steam coming from the coffee cup. But the hurt in them was worse to see.

Kiran said, "I can't have them all find out. Ashley, you have to understand. My father is not able to deal with the fact that I am gay. Not really. He will talk about it but he can't understand it. It is not in their culture. If you were there, you would see it too."

Ashley said, "Somehow I don't think I'll ever get invited there, do you?"

Kiran lowered her eyes.

Ashley continued, "I'm supposed to be your life partner. We're trying to have a child together. But you are too ashamed of me to take me to where you're from, to let your parents see me. What about our child, Kiran? Will your parents be grandparents to our child? Will I have to wait here while you take our child to see his or her grandparents?"

Kiran could feel the hurt in each word that cut into her heart. It mirrored the pain she felt when her father had dismissed her and the child she might be bearing.

She looked up at Ashley. "I am very proud of you. And I would be very happy for you to meet my parents. My mother would love to meet you and if we have a child I am sure they will both like to visit here." She took a deep breath and continued, "But my father does not want to see any of us if we have a child. So, I won't have to make that decision. I have lost the right to even visit them. And now my mother is sick again, I can't even go and see her because my father doesn't trust me after I painted your mother."

She stopped as she saw the shock in Ashley's eyes.

"Your mother is sick again? When did that happen?" Ashley put down the mug and came around the counter.

Kiran said, "My dad called yesterday evening."

Ashley stopped. Her voice crept out. "Yesterday?"

Kiran nodded.

"And you didn't call me?"

Kiran said, "I drove out to you straight away." She waited for Ashley to show some sign. Ashley just looked puzzled.

"Around 7.30...?"

Ashley frowned. "You didn't."

"I didn't want to disturb anything."

"Like what? I would have stopped writing immediately. Kiran, what is going on?"

"Jennifer's car was parked outside. I didn't want to disturb anything."

Ashley's eyes widened. She looked at Ron who had frowned at the mention of Jennifer. She picked up her bag and placed the strap over her shoulder. Her movements were tight, as if she was holding in words that were trying to jump through her skin. She picked up her keys and turned to Kiran. "You didn't trust me enough to come in. And you actually thought I would be with Jenny in our home."

Kiran said, the words rushing and jostling each other to get out, "I didn't know. Her car was there. I know you still feel guilty for leaving her to be with me. Remember that I painted the two of you together."

Ashley turned and walked towards the door. "Enjoy your dinner."

"Ashley. Please. Just tell me. Why was she there?"

Ashley had her hand on the door handle. She spoke to the door. "Jennifer wasn't there. It was Delilah. She decided to buy my car and came round to show me."

Ashley turned around to Kiran's shocked face. "Yes, Kiran, I still feel guilty about Jenny. I hurt her badly when I chose to be with you. Right now, I'm wondering why."

She pulled the door open and Vijay was standing with his hand raised to knock. She gave him a tight smile and walked past him and down the hall. Vijay stared after her and at Kiran who was standing with her mouth open.

Vijay said, "Sorry, I didn't mean to interrupt. I just wanted to let you know that Rishi is waiting at the restaurant."

Kiran nodded and rushed into the hall. She ran to the front door but she could hear the engine racing and she saw the back of Ashley's car disappear through the gate.

CHAPTER THIRTEEN

The ground floor of the 'g' Hotel was sumptuously laid out in moods that varied from cream chandeliered splendour to hazy pink and dark chocolates. Kiran was not in the mood for any of them as they walked through to the bar at the far end. She wanted to be in Connemara with Ashley sorting out the mess. She wanted to be in Kerala watching over her mother. She wanted to be anywhere but here, talking to a pompous man about their non-existent future. But, she couldn't seem to get past the anxiety, the urge to smooth things over for her dad, to make sure that being Kiran didn't wreck his standing any more.

Rishi was resting against the bar, his face almost hidden in the dimness but the strip lighting glowed off his face in shades of pinks and blues. His clothes were casually expensive, cashmere and silk. He smiled when he saw the three of them and Kiran knew there was another French gesture on the way. He held both her hands and examined her cream blouse before moving up to her face. He leaned in to kiss her cheeks, whispering, "You look wonderful, little kitten."

Little kitten! He was the same height as her! She realised he was calling her by her nickname when she'd been five and running around the village barefoot after him, pulling up the sleeves of his shirts because she wouldn't wear the dresses the ammas had laid out for her. She smiled at the memories. Rishi's eyes lit up as he took in her smile.

"Not so little anymore." She pulled back gently.

Rishi squeezed her hands and released them. He turned to Ron, who was watching them with the hint of a frown on his face.

Rishi said, "I still cannot get over the fact that this beautiful young woman used to chase me around the village dressed in my clothes. Isn't it funny how we don't realise what is just under our noses."

Kiran turned towards them, her cheeks getting hot. Ron nodded and gave a tight smile. Vijay was smiling and she glared at him. His grin got wider.

"Drinks anyone? Or should we go right in?" Rishi's hand rested on the small of her back and Kiran leapt forward towards the restaurant door not caring whether she appeared too eager for dinner. There was a pause behind her before the three men hurried forward and Rishi leant in front of her to open the door to the dining room.

She was seated directly across from Rishi and through the dinner she caught him watching her, over the rim of his wine glass, as he withdrew the silver fork from between his lips, as he licked the cream off his dessert spoon.

Kiran sipped at her coffee. The conversation had been light and general so far: Vijay's new job, his previous jobs, Kiran's work. They were all relaxed as Vijay told them stories of his travels. Tension had surfaced for only an instant when Ron mentioned that Vijay would be staying at the house for a longer period than they had initially thought. Rishi had continued the conversation but Kiran had seen the narrowing of his eyes.

When they were having their coffees, she asked, "Why did you decide not to be a vision painter, Rishi? Surely as the son of the Leader, there would have been so much pressure on you?"

Rishi nodded. "I escaped the pressure by leaving early." He leant back in his chair and patted his belly. "Ah, that was delicious. Yes, I wasn't yet in training and my mother ran to England with me in 1980 when I was 14."

He smiled at the look of shock on Kiran's face. "You didn't know that?"

She shook her head. She was trying to remember what age they had been when they'd played in the village.

"You were only five when you used to follow me around. I think your family must have left shortly after that. I didn't have contact with my father for a while but, didn't you also leave in 1980?"

Kiran frowned. She only had vague memories of that time but she remembered the rush of their departure. She remembered it was dark, and she was frightened. She remembered her mother's soothing voice, but even at that age she sensed the difference in that voice, the threads of fear in every breath. She nodded at Rishi.

"We went to London. That is where we lived from then on. My mother was a remarkable woman but thankfully she also had family there. Otherwise, we would never have managed. I got to go to an excellent university. And I got a foot in the door of an upcoming software company and worked my way up. I am almost at the top now," Rishi said.

Ron was running his fingers through his hair and the silver strands stood in confusion. He asked, "How did you father react to your departure? I thought vision painters did not marry? How did your mother manage to get away?"

"Yes, they don't marry. They breed a son." Rishi's lips twisted. "Just one. The great white hope of the family line."

Kiran asked, her breathing tight, "But what if they have a girl?"

Rishi shook his head. His voice seemed to fill out as he waved his wine glass like a wand. "That is one of the wonders of their lives. It is almost like it has been decreed that things will happen in a certain way, at prescribed times in the lives of the vision painters. They are born to a vision painter, they start training early, between 17 and 25 they have an arranged assignation with a chosen girl, usually a young girl, and then a boy is born. At 25 the vision painters are ready and start their lives as fully fledged vision painters, and the line, the wonderful cycle continues. There has been no fault in that line in 200 years."

There was a silence as they absorbed what he had said. Rishi looked at Kiran and his eyes were like hard black pebbles gleaming under a stream. He said, "Until you."

She sat back. The hard cushioned back of the chair felt solid as she leaned against it. The fear she had felt as a five year old pushed its memory into her mind crowding out the questions she had for Rishi.

Rishi said, "And me. In that I didn't follow that path."

Ron asked, "So, do you have the gift? Have you ever tried to do a vision painting?"

Rishi nodded. "But, I am untrained. Rather, I have no formal training. I looked at the profession and the rulebook. When I got back in contact with my father, he tried to train me. I have the gift but it is not focused. He says my strokes are like that of a gifted child, undisciplined, but wild and effective."

Ron said, slowly, "So, the gift is innate, and is focused by the training. And it happens whether the child is a girl or a boy."

Rishi snorted. "No. Well, yes, you are right about the gift and the training. But a woman cannot be a vision painter."

Kiran found her voice. "Why is that? Do you know?"

Rishi looked surprised at the question. "Well, it would never have come up before. And as you heard from our history talk, the first Guru laid out the gift, its powers, the training for the boys. The rules were added later. It just never came up." He leaned forward and tapped his finger on the table, pointing it in her direction. "See, in this unique case, you, where a girl was born to a vision painter, you have not got the gift. Even though you were born to one of the strongest and greatest vision painters. In fact, your father lost his way in the profession after that. How could anyone believe in him anymore?"

Kiran shook her head. "How could they stop believing in him just because of that? Didn't he go on to prove his gift?"

Vijay said, "That was much later, Kiran. Your father did not get a chance until much later."

Kiran felt the weight of two centuries of tradition and blame pressing down on her. She had hounded her father to let her paint, spoken to him with disregard about his profession, his dreams. She cringed at the thoughts of the arguments that had raged in her teenage years. And she had blithely continued on her own path. The silence was stretching into uncomfortable.

Ron took a sip of his brandy. He asked Rishi, "So when you painted, did the visions materialize?"

Rishi laughed but the smile didn't reach his eyes, which were full of a hurt he couldn't disguise. "Small stuff, Ron, small stuff. To be honest, I didn't do any more than try to please and impress my father."

Vijay said, "Dinesh is very happy that you are in contact again. He talks about you all the time."

Rishi laughed again, a harsh sound this time. "He can barely mention my name! Especially now that I am divorced." Rishi played with the word on his lips as he repeated it. Kiran could see his lips curl as if it tasted bitter. "Divorced from an English girl, a foreigner no less." His eyes caressed Kiran's face as he examined her. "Like you, I am an outcast. You do not fit in with their plans. My future is blank to my father right now. But, he has great hopes for it." The tiny beads of sweat on his forehead nodded in agreement. "As I have."

Kiran bent her head away from his gaze and shivered inside.

Ron said, "Should we retire to one of the beautiful bars?" He looked around the room. "Haven't they done such a wonderful job of decorating this place? My late wife had it booked for a family occasion this year."

Kiran kept her head down. Rishi and Vijay looked at Ron and he said, "My daughter, Ashley, was supposed to get married and the reception was booked here."

Kiran didn't know whether he was trying to remind her that she needed to go and sort things out with Ashley or whether he was trying to lighten the weight of Rishi's stare. The first option worked. She felt her stomach tighten at the thought of Ashley and Jennifer. The second option didn't work

Rishi said, "This would be a wonderful place for a reception!" He sat up and looked around.

Vijay asked Ron, "What happened? With Ashley and the wedding?"

Ron smiled. "Since then, Ashley met the right person for her. They haven't decided what they are doing about it but I hope they do not mess it up."

Vijay said in a gentle voice, "She is lucky. They both are. Even if it means you don't get to be the proud father giving her away right now. And she is very lucky to have a father like you. You seem to be happy for her just because she is happy now."

Ron nodded. "I come from a different generation, but I've always thought everyone deserves to make their choices and have a chance at happiness. Families can put too much pressure to force their children into a mold that is really only a reflection of what they would have liked to be."

Kiran looked up at him. She sighed. "Do you know how many times I've wished my father would think like that? I got tired of being shaped, not that he had much to play with considering the one huge defect."

Rishi said, "We have a chance to put everything right. To make our fathers very happy and very proud." There was a note of desperation in his voice and it jangled on Kiran's stretched nerves.

The waiter came over and the conversation changed into a gentle argument over settling the bill.

∞ ∞ ∞

She could imagine the phone ringing, the handset on the bedside locker beside Ashley. Hopefully not startling her awake. But there was no answer and the dial tone buzzed before settling into empty noise. Kiran dialled the number again. She was lying on her bed, the mobile pressed hot to her ear, and she watched the darkness outside as it clung to the window pane.

"Yes?" The voice was Ashley's but the tone was not loving.

"Sorry, did I wake you?"

"No, I wasn't asleep."

"You know it is 2 a.m., right?"

"Kiran, surely that should be my question for you? Though it seems to be another thing that runs in your family."

"Sorry. I wasn't able to sleep either."

"Good."

Kiran took a deep breath. "Ashley, I am so sorry. About that thing with Jennifer."

"I can't believe that you wouldn't trust me."

"Ashley, I'm sorry. It is just that I know what my paintings have caused. And I can't wipe away the words you wrote for her. The word I used to create the vision of the two of you. I mean, I was insecure before that, considering she is so perfect, but those words will always remain with me."

Ashley didn't say anything. Kiran waited.

"And? What else are you sorry for?" There was a slight thaw in Ashley's voice.

"Telling my parents about us trying for a baby."

"And?"

"And not wanting my dad's world to be messed up even more than I seem to have managed without even knowing."

There was silence on the other end of the line.

After a few long seconds, Ashley said, "I don't know what you mean. How have you messed up his world? He seems to be doing fine. He is leading that Council which is what you said he always wanted. His only problem seems to be that he cannot accept that you are gay and you're not going to conform to what he wants you to be."

"It is more complicated than that. There are so many things I don't know about what went on. And I have to find out. Surely you understand. I'm terrified, Ashley. That something worse is going to happen to my mother." Her voice dropped. "And that I might be responsible."

There was a sound of movement and Ashley's voice came out stronger. "Why would you think that? Your mother is sick again. Why would you be responsible?"

"They found a painting. It was of my mother, lying sick."

"What? No. But I thought that couldn't happen. You told me all vision painters paint for good only." Ashley paused. "Why would you think you were responsible?"

Kiran whispered, "I was in the studio there. I got everything together to paint. I knew it would be breaking the rules but I was desperate for my mother to wake up. I was going to try and paint her better. But I didn't. At least, I think I didn't. I fell asleep and when I woke up the canvas was still blank. But my father said the painting was in my style. Ashley, I don't know what to think. But I would never have painted my mother sick. Not even in any unconscious guilt over last year." Her voice dropped even lower. "At least, I don't think so."

The silence at the other end of the line was longer this time. "Your father thinks you painted it, doesn't he? Because you painted my mother. Does he not realise you haven't been able to paint since? Does he realise what you are doing to yourself because of that?"

"Do *you* think I painted my mother?" Kiran held her breath.

"Of course you didn't." Ashley's voice was strong and sure.

Kiran let out the breath.

"Kiran, call him. Talk to your mother. She probably cannot understand why you're not there or why you haven't contacted her. You haven't, have you?"

"He won't let me. He is furious and upset and he must be terrified as well."

"Who would do something like that? Somebody must hate your mother or your father very much."

Kiran felt a sob catch in her throat. "Nobody could hate my mother. And if it is targeted at my dad, she's in trouble. None of us can paint for her. My dad will not break the rules. And I don't know what will happen if I paint again. I can't take the risk."

Ashley's voice was gentle. "Kiran, you can't imagine anyone ever thinking badly of your mother. But you don't know your parents' past. You don't see them as human beings with faults and who might have made mistakes. You told me before that vision painters imagine and paint the good in the hopes of their clients. How could someone paint the opposite if there wasn't something bad to focus on?"

Kiran said slowly, "I know things happened when I was young that they won't talk about."

Kiran raised herself up in the bed. She had shoved the papers under her pillow and they rustled under the cloth. She pulled them out and gazed at the squiggles. At least, the handwritten sheets were in English.

"Ashley, are we okay?"

"Kiran, you need to get some sleep and then call your parents. Everything will look better in the morning. If you have another half day tomorrow, come home for the afternoon and we can talk."

"I do. And we've sorted Vijay's accommodation out. He's staying here by the way. For the next while."

"Oh great. More hiding."

"For a little while."

"See you tomorrow, Kiran." Ashley had switched off the phone before Kiran could tell her she loved her. She said it to her mobile anyway.

The house was quiet. Vijay was asleep in the next room. She would ask him tomorrow about the Malayalam writing. But for tonight she had some reading to do.

CHAPTER FOURTEEN

Kerala, 1958

There was a time when Ji was too young to remember his place in the world; as the son of a vision painter, the grandson of the Leader of the Council of Vision Painters, the great-grandson of the first ever leader of that esteemed Council. But Ji could not recall that time when he did not know.

And from this moment on, everything would change. As he watched his father's coffin being lowered into the depths of the stone-sided hole, he knew that things would change. He was now a 17 year old vision painter-to-be, with no father, no mentor, and no mantle to cover his shoulders.

Ji moved those thin broad shoulders as he shivered in the sun and watched the heavy cover being slid over, sealing in the gentle man who would now never bring his brand of quiet strength to the leadership of the Council. Who would never be able to teach his son in the way all vision painters did.

The grave lay in the grandeur of the family vault that absorbed and spilled the sunlight off its sculptured stone whorls. The vault bore the bodies of his great-great-grandfather, his great-grandfather, and now, his father, a break in the chain, in the natural order of things. The missing one, his grandfather, looked like he was ready to take his place as well. He looked a broken man, his grey hair, full and strong, had turned white overnight. The current leader of the Council was sitting in a chair that had been carried hurriedly across the road for a once strong man.

Ji felt a hand on his arm and looked down at Dinesh who had been standing with the other vision painters. Dinesh was also dressed in white, his face stretched, his round glasses magnifying shock and grief.

Dinesh whispered, "They have set up the room in your father's house for mourners. My father said we should go there and wait."

Ji stumbled on the stone kerbing as he turned and allowed himself to be led away from his old life to an unexpectedly uncertain future.

∞ ∞ ∞

Ji slipped away after four hours of grief-soaked bewilderment. The waves of mourning were threatening to drown him, the whispers deafening in his ears.

His father was dead.

His grandfather did not seem able to speak.

Ji walked out of the house and turned left down the main track through the village. He did not want to turn right, to walk past his new home with Dinesh and Dinesh's father, Manoj. His new family. He walked towards the church.

Manoj had spoken to him in Ji's father's studio. Reassured him that all would be fine. But they had both known that those were just words to numb the change. The leadership had passed in the last few hours, not formally, but by tacit acceptance that the white-haired man who could not speak, the broken figure of their leader, would not be able to continue.

The Church looked deserted. The new priest had not arrived yet after the previous priest had left without notice to return to Ireland. There had been no masses for a few Sundays. Ji just wanted a place to sit in quiet, to think. He wandered through the church grounds and tried the side door that led to the vestry. It was locked.

The house next to the Church looked empty as well. The couple who lived in the house were in their forties but they had not ventured out of their house much after the scandal that had rocked the village over a dozen years previously. Ji had only heard the rumours. He'd been too young, only four years old.

Ji walked by the side of the house, down the dirt road lined with coconut trees. He could see the shape of an old shack, through the curling edges of the fronds of banana trees that crowded into the garden of the house. He reached across the wood-slatted fence and plucked a short fat banana from its bunch. He hadn't eaten for three days, ever since the last breath of air and blood escaped the confines of his father's chest.

The flesh of the banana was sweet and he forced himself to eat it as he pushed through the humid air. He would need strength to continue. He was still a vision painter, however far removed now from his line. Manoj was a good man, a solid man. All Ji's life, Manoj had been like a favourite uncle; Ji wondered what he would be like as a father.

The eyes that studied him through the fence were tortured, but the pain was an old wound not the freshness reflected back from Ji's.

"I am sorry. I should not have taken the banana from your tree." Ji tried not to stammer as he faced the grey-lined man across the bristled top of the fence.

The man just nodded and turned away.

"Please allow me to do a vision painting for you when I have finished my training."

The man stopped but did not turn around. "I thought you could not even take a banana in payment."

Ji stammered as he replied. "Yes. I mean, No. I cannot accept any payment. But it will be a few years."

Ji could hear a faint trace of a smile in the man's voice. "Maybe the years will reduce the memory of wrong-doing. Until what is left is just emptiness. Not even a banana."

Ji said, "I might not be trained yet but I have the gift. And you carry so much pain. I could try if you would let me."

The man turned. His eyes were dark in the grey brown of his face. "You must have heard the stories about us. What do you think you can do to help? Bring back my daughter? Re-awaken a desire to live in me? Or in my wife?"

Ji felt his nerves tingle but he spoke anyway, his voice trembling. "Your granddaughter. She is innocent. Why is she suffering for that man's sins? What do they say? The sins of the father...?"

Ji felt his heart jump at the sudden rage in the man's eyes.

"You are a young boy. You know nothing, vision painter or not." The voice darted through the wooden slats.

Ji pressed on despite the fear. "Her life and your lives should not be filled with so much pain."

"How do you know she is in pain?"

Ji's voice grew stronger. "How can she not be? I am not too far from a time when I could remember such suffering. To be torn from everything you know. To lose it all in an instant. Even if she was only a child, an innocent baby."

The man shouted, "What do you know? What do you know? You are a boy!" He turned away, his voice choking in his throat as he ran from the fence and Ji could hear his cries through the flapping of the green-veined leaves.

CHAPTER FIFTEEN

The painter flexed fingers that were stained with the colours of sickness and pain, mixed in with beauty. Bilious yellow and harsh red crept into the creases blotting out softer hues. Hands gripped and discarded brushes in bursts, between breaths that wrenched through airways, heated and damp.

The touches were delicate when they landed on the canvas. The fury of the preparation calmed to a smooth stroke as the painter shaped the outline of a woman, lovingly curved the bristles around the bends of the body, the silence in the room broken only by hisses of breath.

The movements turned fluid as long hair was worked around creamy bronze skin, a smooth face, eyes closed, mouth open in painful painted gasps.

Tears fell from the painter's eyes, reluctantly dropping from lashes that longed to close. The painter took the guilt from the woman, the hurt from her heart, took them in, felt every drop of pain, and mixed it into the pigment until the portrait of the woman was complete.

The painter slumped onto the ground as the final drops landed on the canvas. The woman in the painting was beautiful even as she screamed her guilt to an empty room.

CHAPTER SIXTEEN

Kiran's hands moved through Ashley's hair, holding, stroking, gripping. Her lips roamed over Ashley's face, the tip of her tongue touching, tasting, hungering for the familiar, searching for the new, the millimetre of smoothness undiscovered, unexplored. Kiran's breaths echoed in her chest before escaping, matching Ashley's moans, pulsing between their bodies, shortening, gasping, held, and finally released.

Ashley's eyes were closed and her cheeks flushed in the afternoon sun through the window. Kiran raised herself onto one elbow. She stroked the tint of red, the shade of her lips, and ran her finger gently over Ashley's eyelids. Ashley smiled, a slow crease of cherry across the paleness of her skin.

Ashley opened her eyes. Kiran felt her heart move and her breath catch again, as she felt herself drown in the depths of Ashley's eyes. She waited for the customary fear that followed. For the panicked second when she considered life without this woman. For the realisation that she had fallen so far, so deep, that she would never be able to haul herself back without leaving most of herself behind. When the fear came, she knew it was reflected in her eyes.

Ashley was looking at her.

Kiran shook her head and her thoughts away and said, "Lucky we're at home and not at Ron's house. Vijay would definitely have suspected something if he heard the sounds you just made."

Ashley's blush grew redder. "Look who's talking." She stretched her arms out and grabbed Kiran and rolled over her.

Kiran laughed as the red waves of hair tumbled over her face. "Someone thinks she's strong, does she?"

Ashley nodded.

Kiran whispered, "Well, you might want to be gentle with me, you never know, there could be a teeny life trying to take hold in there and you're just shaking it loose."

She laughed again at Ashley's face, and held her tight as Ashley tried to roll off.

"Woman, you're a doctor."

Ashley sighed. "I know, I know. I'm just nervous." She lifted herself off Kiran and lay down beside her putting her hand over Kiran's belly. "Go on. Do the test. I can't take the waiting."

Kiran squeezed Ashley's hand and took a deep breath. She got up and retrieved the pregnancy testing kit from the chest of drawers. The bathroom was across the hall and she left both doors open as she carried out a normally mundane task with her heart battering its way through her chest.

The minutes were silent, pacing between them as they sat on the bed and waited.

The strip bore a cross of blue.

Kiran stared at it for a moment before handing it to Ashley without a word. She felt the tremble in Ashley's fingers as they grazed hers over the innocuous white plastic. They sat with the stick between them. It perched on a fold in the bed cover and peered at them, the answering line on its back pointing at the two dazed women.

Finally Kiran spoke. "I hope Eric the Dane didn't lie about the shade of his hair. I'm hoping our kid has hair like yours not Ronald McDonald's."

A snort of laughter escaped from Ashley. "I should have known you couldn't be serious even at a time like this."

"It is a serious matter. How is the poor child going to manage, looking like that clown?"

"Kiran, I love you," Ashley said, "You know that, don't you?"

Kiran smiled and nodded. She reached over the stick and took Ashley in her arms and they held on to each other. Kiran could feel their hearts thumping through their chests and hers was filled with wonder laced with fear. Someone else to love, to worry about, to try and protect, to lose. She couldn't even protect her own mother, now she was going to be one.

∞ ∞ ∞

The house was mostly dark, just the hallway light left on for her. Kiran sneaked up the stairs and into her bedroom. She was dazed, struggling to understand what was happening to her body, to her life. Everything she had wanted was within her reach but the overwhelming emotion she was feeling was fear. If she let herself believe in the vision that she would have painted for herself if she was allowed then that would break the rules and she would lose, even though she didn't agree with those rules.

Ashley had asked her to call Ji. To try and talk to her mother and tell them about the baby if she got a chance. She dialled the number.

Ji answered, his voice tired. His tone changed when he realised who it was.

"Kiran, I told you not to call."

"Dad, I have to talk to Amma. I did not do anything wrong. You can't punish me for something I didn't do. Otherwise I'm going to get on a plane and get there and you won't be able to stop me seeing my mother. Surely she must be wondering why I haven't called?"

Kiran waited.

Ji was silent for a few minutes. She could hear his breathing; could feel the turmoil in his mind.

"You can't talk to her. She can't come to the phone. But I will tell her you called. And anything else you want me to tell her."

Kiran sighed in relief. "Tell her I love her. Tell her she will be fine. Tell her she has to be fine." She paused. "Dad, tell her this exactly. Tell her I can't afford the childcare here and she promised."

The silence stretched between them again. Ji's voice when it came was hushed and thick. "You got your sense of humour from Elizabeth. Though you are my crazy daughter too, I hope your child gets that from both of you. Kiran, some day you will understand why I can't tell them everything here. They never understood Elizabeth. They will certainly never understand you."

"Dad, they know I paint. You said they allowed it because I was in Ireland not there. Why can I not say anything?"

He didn't answer. She said, "Dad?"

"I never told them you had the gift." He was whispering.

"What do you mean? I thought you asked permission from Dinesh's father to train me and that you told them I was working in Ireland?"

"Yes, yes. But I lied to them." His voice was so low she pushed her mobile tighter against her ear. "When you were young you showed the gift. I told them that. I was trying to help. But it didn't work. So I told them later that it was just a talent for painting that you had. That nothing materialised. Kiran, please, you need to take something seriously in your life. Please understand that I am trying to protect you, I have always tried to protect you."

"From what, Dad? How can I understand if you don't tell me?"

She heard a male voice speak in Malayalam in the background and Ji said in his normal voice. "Amma will be fine. I will tell her you called and that your work will not allow you to travel so soon after the last time. Don't worry."

The phone went dead in her hand. There was a sound in the hallway. It was low but she jumped and dropped the mobile phone which bounced off the bed and clattered to the floor spilling its battery. Kiran opened the door and the light spilled from her room into the dimness of the hallway.

Vijay looked uncomfortable. He was dressed in pyjamas but still managed to look quite formal. The hallway table was askew; a vase was lying on the carpeted floor, a dark stain spreading from its mouth. Vijay was trying to wipe water off the books that had fallen onto the floor.

He said, "I am so sorry. I was on my way to the bathroom and did not want to put on the light and disturb you." He placed the books back on the table and rubbed his thigh which was next to the sharp edge of the table.

Kiran walked back into her room and picked up her phone. She inserted the battery back into it.

Vijay said from the doorway, "Are you alright? You look troubled."

She smiled. "Troubled would be one word for it."

The battery was in and she switched her phone on. She gestured him in.

"I need your help with something." Kiran had decided she had no choice.

Vijay moved a few feet into the room.

Kiran retrieved the copy of the documents that she had taken from Ji's safe and handed it to him. The Malayalam script was beyond her. She hoped Vijay could read it.

Vijay unrolled the wad of papers. His eyebrows rose as he examined the first page.

"How did you get this?"

Kiran tried not to look guilty. "From my father."

His eyebrows remained raised as he flicked through the sheets with his thumb.

"Can you read the script?" She asked, her voice remaining casual, not betraying the desperation she was feeling.

He nodded. "I did not think we would be allowed to read this kind of material though." He narrowed his eyes as he examined her face.

"Could you please translate it for me? It is very important. I won't tell my father you read it." Kiran sat heavily on the bed. She was suddenly exhausted.

Vijay stared at her and at the papers in his hand and as he moved towards the door, he said, "Give me a little time. I'll start after work tomorrow."

He closed the door behind him with a soft click and Kiran fell back against the bed. She wanted desperately to sleep but she reached for the rest of her father's papers.

CHAPTER SEVENTEEN

Kerala, 1964

The old house looked cool and dark inside, a welcome refuge from his own. Ji slipped past and through the fronds of the banana trees and climbed through the window of the shack at the end of the garden.

Ji had cleared out the shack over the past few months and he escaped here to sit and think, to be an ordinary young man. He never saw the occupants of the house but there seemed to have been more movement behind the windows in the last month.

Ji landed on the dirt floor and felt a tug on his chest and realised his shirt was caught in the latch of the window. He turned to detach the sleeve and there was a thunderous roar in his head as something hard but brittle shattered off the back of it. Fragments of dirt and what felt like metal showered around his head and down his collar.

He matched the roar in his head with a yell as his free hand flew to see whether his head was still on his shoulders. A warm stickiness greeted it. Ji tugged at his trapped hand as he twisted to see in the gloom.

She was holding the remains of a frying pan like it was a rounder's bat and she had it raised to strike again. The flat base had disintegrated around his head, but the handle had a jagged edge and was long enough to reach him. Her face was determined, her eyes wide and blue-green and clear despite the dim light. Ji felt something inside him trip and fall into those eyes even as he tried to find his voice.

He held up his bloody hand and stammered in English, "No. I won't hurt you. I just come here to sit." He pointed behind her at the space he had made into a comfortable retreat.

She didn't take her eyes off his face.

He pointed again.

She backed away a few feet and glanced over her shoulder. There was a stack of books leaning against the wall beside a threadbare cushion. She looked back at him. Her eyes were still suspicious but the weapon had come down to waist height.

Ji kept his face turned to her as he yanked at the sleeve. He heard a soft rip as his arm came free.

She lifted the handle again.

Ji raised both his hands and said, "My name is Ji. I live in the village." He gestured in the direction of the window. "Down the road, the house at the bend of the road. The big house."

The handle moved down.

"So, you're one of those vision painting people." Her voice was like a breath of wind over his heart, soft, surprisingly strong for a girl.

He nodded. He couldn't seem to find his voice again.

"So you're one of the crowd of men who get to sit and paint all day and don't think that women can do what you do."

He jerked his head back in shock. She must not be Indian, though her skin was a creamy brown and her hair long and black. Anglo? No Indian girl would ever talk to a vision painter like that.

She laughed at his expression and he didn't know if it was anger that spread through his chest at the sound. Whatever it was, it was painful.

"I am a Vision Painter." He drew himself up to his full six feet and tried to convey the weight of that announcement through his eyes. "We are revered in India. As we should be. You are obviously not from here otherwise you would never speak to me like that, or speak about the profession with such disrespect."

She snapped him a salute. "Yes, Sir. Sorry, Sir." Her face was serious but her eyes were turquoise pools of laughter.

"What is your name? Who are you?" His eyes had become accustomed to the dimness and he took in that she was wearing trousers and a blouse.

"Can you not find all that out through a vision?" She put the handle of the frying pan down on the ground. Her feet were bare and a silver anklet peeked out below the hem of her trousers.

He frowned. "It does not work like that. We talk to people and ask questions about their dreams, their hopes for their lives. We listen and learn and then we can use our inherited gift to paint these visions into reality."

"And people believe this?"

"Yes, of course they believe this! They have seen it happen. What is your name?"

"Why? Are you going to report me to the Guardians of the Faith?" She tilted her head and gazed at him. "What will the punishment be?"

He stared at her. He was surprised to hear himself stammering again as he said, "There is no such group. There is only a Council. And it does not punish ordinary people, just vision painters who break the rules."

"You seem like a person who would like to break the rules if given half a chance. As I see from your breaking into my grandparents' house."

Ji's head was beginning to throb furiously. He tried to steady his voice. He was a vision painter, a future leader, and most of all, a man. No young woman, however beautiful, was going to get the better of him.

"I am not breaking into the house of your grandparents. I just come here to this shack sometimes when I want to read or think in peace and quiet. I am sure they would not mind." He put up his hand. "Though, it would be better if you did not tell them."

There was a call from the house. "Elizabeth!"

She ran her finger across her lips and his eyes were drawn to their perfect shape. She smiled and opened the door and slipped out silently.

∞ ∞ ∞

"What happened to you?" Dinesh reached up and prodded Ji's head. Ji jerked back as the sting from the cut bloomed into pain again.

Dinesh lifted up the dangling flap of shirt sleeve and waggled it in time to the movement of his head. "Did you meet a tiger in the jungle?"

Ji shook his head and then regretted the movement. He realised Dinesh was still staring at him with naked curiosity in his eyes. He tried to think of a reason for his appearance that did not involve a fiery raven-haired beautiful Anglo girl. But all he could think about were her eyes, the laughter in those pools of blue green.

He ignored Dinesh and walked over to the shelf covered with silver tins of paint. He picked up the blue and the green and put them on the table and wedged them open.

"You are going to paint now? You need to clean yourself up. Father will be back soon with the girl." Dinesh snorted as he laughed. "She will find it hard to be with you like that if you are covered in blood and your shirt is torn. You look like a madman not a vision painter ready to meet his woman."

Ji was barely listening. He dipped one finger into the blue and another into the green and ran the colours together onto the wooden surface of the table. He felt his heart leap as the mix swirled into the exact shade of her eyes.

"Ji, you cannot just stand around painting on a table looking like a madman. He will be here soon. You cannot just paint. You know the rules. What are you doing?"

Ji stopped his fingers as he realised they were molding the colours into the shape of eyes on the wood. He grabbed a rag and wiped down the surface. He pulled off the remnants of his shirt and the rust and dirt fell off his shoulders and onto the floor.

Dinesh shook his head. "You do not know how fortunate you are. You resist when you should be grateful. At least clean yourself up out of respect for Father."

Ji frowned. "I am grateful. I am respectful. I have done everything that has ever been asked of me. I do not even argue against the fate that took my father away, and turned my path into that of a follower rather than a leader."

"Well, you do not show your gratitude. You question him. I hear the two of you discussing everything. You are always questioning him."

Ji turned to Dinesh and smiled down at the earnest face of his friend and brother. "That is how I show my gratitude and respect. I question him so that I can learn from him."

Dinesh was still looking at him without understanding. Ji took him by the arm and led him out of the room that had been set up as a training studio. What he would not say out loud to Dinesh was that he listened and learnt from Manoj not only out of love and respect but also because he knew that one day he, Ji, would be leader, not Dinesh.

∞　∞　∞

Ji walked into the front room of the house. Manoj had summoned him for noon and it was now after 2 pm. Manoj was sitting bowlegged on the wicker couch. He looked up from his task of removing the dried pigment wedged under his fingernails, and his eyes showed irritation.

Ji stood beside a chair. "I am sorry, Sir. The painting took longer than I expected. The man was not clear about his vision."

Manoj looked back at his fingernail and scooped out a speck of yellow with a piece of smooth metal. He examined his fingers one by one, turning them over in the light from the window. Ji waited.

Manoj gestured to the chair. "Did you explain to him that it would be better to come to a vision painter with a clear idea of what he wanted?"

Ji sat down. "Yes, Sir. I told him that the clearer the description of the vision, the better the chance of a manifestation. That is why it took so long. We worked on a very clear vision. I think the manifestation will be excellent."

Manoj frowned at him. "Ji, you did not encourage him, did you? You did not put words into the man's mouth I hope."

Ji tried to control the stammer in his voice. "No, Sir. I do not think so."

Manoj's voice was stern. "What have we worked on with you? Patience. As well as acceptance. You cannot dream their dreams for them, Ji. No matter what your person requests, you must paint that."

The stammer was suppressed in the fervour. "He was asking me to paint rupees. A large amount of rupees. I simply asked him to consider what might make him happy."

Manoj sighed. "My son, I know you are very idealistic but we are not here to paint *our* ideals, we are here to help people achieve *their* ideals." He held up his hand. "Enough. I called you here to discuss other matters. We will return to that in our training tomorrow, for the hundredth time."

He looked at Ji in frustration. "Why is Dinesh able to paint whatever they ask him to paint? But you must question everything." He help up his hand again as Ji tried to speak. "Enough, I said." He sat back and put his feet on the ground. "Now, we must discuss your future."

Ji sat straighter in his chair. He was 23. Would they start talking seriously about the leadership at this early stage?

Manoj tapped his fingers on the wicker arm of the couch. His voice was hesitant. "We have chosen the girl."

Ji slumped back in the chair as he was blinded by a blue-green image of Elizabeth. She had rarely been out of his mind since he had seen her first a month ago. He had gone to the shack and waited but she'd obviously left again, and he did not want to ask her grandparents.

Manoj said sharply, "It is not all about the techniques or type of pigment or the philosophy that underpins our profession. We must also carefully consider the future. The decision has been made. I am just informing you of that. You can go." He waved a hand towards the door.

Ji got up slowly. He wanted to say something but the look on Manoj's set face froze the words on his tongue. There was no point anyway. Elizabeth could never be his.

CHAPTER EIGHTEEN

The traffic was bad as usual on the Bridge and Kiran rested her head on the steering wheel as the line of cars stood still. She felt herself dozing off and jerked awake to the sound of a horn behind her.

Half an hour later, she pulled into the driveway of Ron's house. Kiran felt slightly guilty that she was relieved that Ron's car wasn't there. Ashley was moving back to the house as her job was in Galway. They were going to tell Ron about the baby later, when Ashley got in from Connemara. Until then, Kiran just wanted to lie down under the covers and sleep. The sky was heavy with rainclouds and even on a spring evening, she was craving an evening lying by an open fire, snuggled into Ashley.

The house was quiet. Kiran dragged herself up the stairs and into her room where she flopped across the bed. She shook off her shoes and pulled a pillow under her head. The sound of the toilet flushing startled her. She groaned and pulled the pillow over her head.

She sat up suddenly. Ron wasn't home. Vijay was not due back until later. They had arranged to meet about the documents.

She heard the water rushing from the bathroom sink. She got up and opened her bedroom door and peered down the hall. Rishi came out of the bathroom and stopped when he saw her. He smiled.

"You're back. Excellent. I hope you don't mind me using this bathroom. Ron let me in earlier and it is so formal downstairs, isn't it? I did not want to disturb anything."

He was dressed casually, though his clothes seemed to have been chosen to try and increase his height. His receding hairline was not disguised by a comb-over but by expert styling of his hair.

Kiran sighed inwardly. Her eyelids felt like they were ready to give up.

"Where did Ron go?"

"Something to do with a Board function. He said he'd be back as soon as he could."

He walked down the hall and examined her. "You look very ruffled."

"Just exhausted. How can you look so fresh? I take ages to recover after a trip to India."

Her jaws trembled as she tried to suppress a yawn. Her sense of smell seemed heightened, she could get his aftershave and the slight smell of sweat, but there was also a scent of alcohol, very faint as it swirled gently under the others. She moved back slightly and felt the jamb of the door prod her in the back. She smiled.

"Do you want me to wait downstairs with you? Vijay should be back very soon."

"Vijay might be delayed." He leaned against the other door jamb. His eyes were level with hers. A shine of brown and black. He was close enough that she could see the tiny cracks in his lips until his tongue flicked, drowning and filling them. "It was you I was hoping to spend some time with anyway."

Kiran could hear that his voice had thickened even through the alarm bells clanging in her ears. "Actually, Rishi, I'm really exhausted. I might just go to bed." She slid sideways, but realised that her room would not be the best place in which to end up. She stopped mid-slide and started to reverse direction, her back rubbing against the edge of the doorjamb.

His arm snaked out and landed beside her head and he adjusted his weight forward. He was still smiling. He didn't seem to have noticed her subtle but desperate manoeuvring.

His voice on her cheek was a whisper of bad breath and alcohol. "Kiran, my little kitten. You have grown up into a beautiful tiger." She felt and heard what seemed like a giggle. "I have to say I was nervous, I knew you used to be a pretty little thing, but one can never tell after so many years."

She moved her head away from his face but it came to rest against his forearm. A feeling of nausea rose up in her chest. His eyes widened at the contact. She could see that his pupils were dilated, the black taking over most of the brown. He moved his face towards her, his lips aimed for hers.

She ducked and slipped out under his arm. She said, her voice shaky, "Rishi, I think you should wait downstairs. Please. Our fathers are friends. They are making plans but I have nothing to do with that, and I don't want to. No offense to you."

His eyes narrowed as he took in her words. "You are saying 'No' to the proposal?" The level of disbelief in his voice made her wonder what had been discussed, whether any promises had been made.

She nodded. "Yes. I am not available to marry you." The sudden anger at her father and Dinesh and him made her add, "And even if I were available, I would not be marrying you just to join our families and produce a great vision painter."

Kiran didn't see his hand as it flew towards her; she just felt the heat and the pain on her bare arm as he gripped it. She was surprised at the strength in his grip, he was her height and build, but she was now in no doubt who was stronger. That doubt never seemed to have crossed his mind if his swagger now was to be believed. He dragged her towards him and as she struggled against his chest, he ground his mouth into hers. She tried to turn her face and he pushed her into her room. She tripped and caught herself on the bed frame.

He strode into the room and closed the door. His hand felt for a key, his eyes fixed on her, but there was no key in the door. He walked towards her.

"Rishi, you don't want to do this." She backed around the bed and towards the window. Her room looked out over the manicured garden at the back of the house. The solar lamps glowed like evenly spaced sentinels trying in vain to push through the falling darkness.

He didn't acknowledge that she had spoken. He reached the window in three steps and she hit him in his solar plexus with as much force as she could muster. Rishi bent over, holding his stomach, his face contorted in shock and pain.

Kiran moved around him and rushed to the door. She swung it open and ran into the hall. She could hear footsteps and Vijay appeared at the top of the stairs. He took in the panic in her wide eyes, and automatically held out his arms to stop her pushing past him and falling down the stairs.

She pulled away and backed up against the wall. Vijay looked past her at the open door to her bedroom. He walked towards the door and stared in. His eyes were looking down so Kiran assumed Rishi was still on the floor. Vijay didn't say a word; he just stepped through into the room and closed the door behind him.

∞ ∞ ∞

Kiran heard the stumbling of footsteps down the stairs in the main house. She stayed where she was, on Ron's side of the house, the patio door open. One foot was inside the house, the other was on the paved stones outside. The front door opened and she heard the sound of a car door slamming. The click of the front door closing was followed a few moments later by a gentle tap on Ron's door.

She made a noise and the door opened. Vijay came in only when she gestured him into the room. She still hadn't moved from her position.

"I put him in a taxi. You won't have to see him again." His eyes were hard as he looked at the glass door beside her.

She nodded.

"Do you want me to stay or to leave you on your own?" He still couldn't meet her eyes. His voice was gentle.

She brought her foot into the room and turned towards him. Her hands were trembling and she realised her fingers were throbbing. "I heard him yelling at you. What did he say?"

Vijay shook his head. "It was nothing. He was angry. He will forget about it."

"Vijay, what did he say?"

Vijay shifted his weight on his feet. "He said he would be speaking to his father and that he would tell him I got between you and him. And that I disrespected him and the family." Vijay cleared his throat. He looked very uncomfortable and seemed to be searching for words. "He said he would tell his father that you tried to have relations with him and that I got jealous because I wanted you myself."

Kiran grimaced as she guessed at the actual words that must have spewed from Rishi's mouth. Her legs were still trembling. She sat on one of the stools.

"Can I make you a cup of tea? Or perhaps you might like an alcoholic drink to steady your nerves?" Vijay was looking at the kitchen counter and she got the feeling he would struggle to make a cup of tea.

"Here, you sit. I'll make us tea. He seems to have got to you too." Kiran put the kettle on and busied her hands getting out the teabags and the mugs. Vijay sat at the counter. He seemed quite shaken. She noticed the scrape and the swelling on his knuckles.

"I don't know if your religion allows you to use the steak that's in there so this will have to do." She handed him a bag of frozen peas from the freezer.

He smiled and accepted the balm, wincing as he positioned it.

She made them tea and sat down beside him.

"I guess you're in trouble now, aren't you? With Dinesh and therefore the vision painters, I mean."

He shrugged.

She said, "Thank you for doing what you did."

"I did no more than what any decent person would do."

"Aren't you a vision painter? Won't this mean problems for you?"

Vijay shook his head. "No, not a vision painter. But Dinesh has been very good to me. He missed having his son there. I think Rishi is used to having everybody do what he wants. To get what he wants, when he wants it. His father is so happy to have his son back that he does not control him."

"So that does mean problems for you with Dinesh."

"I think there will be problems for both of us. Your father will get the same version of the events that happened."

"My father won't believe I tried to 'have relations' with Rishi. In fact, he would probably be over the moon if he thought I had tried." She took a gulp of tea and added as she saw his face. "Over the moon...it means extremely happy."

"Ah. I see." But he still looked confused. "Why would he want that?"

Kiran took a deep breath. Ashley was moving back home. The stories that would get back to her father and Dinesh were out there. It might as well be out in the open. "Because I am gay. And I wouldn't accept the proposal from them."

She could see him processing the information. She could see the discomfort in his deep brown eyes. "Ashley?" He asked after a few moments.

She nodded.

"So, you're the right person for his daughter that Ron was talking about."

"Yes."

He smiled suddenly. "You're the first gay person I have acquainted."

Kiran laughed. "Well. I'm sure I won't be the last. In fact, Ashley will be here soon. That is two." She stopped laughing as she remembered why they were sitting there. Why her insides were still shaking.

What if Rishi had hit her in the abdomen?

Her hand went over her belly.

Vijay said, "You are pregnant, aren't you?"

She couldn't speak. She nodded.

He said, "This is very unusual for me to take in."

Kiran mumbled, "Tell me about it."

Vijay glanced at her and said, "I am not used to the idea."

"Sorry, yes, I got that. It is an expression."

He said, "Is there not a concern? Will the child not need a father around?" His hands were gripping the mug. He seemed quite disturbed by the idea.

Kiran shook her head. "The child will get enough love from the two of us. Ron is a lovely man. He will be a good role model."

Vijay had bowed his head. He looked up. "My father was a terrible role model." His eyes were haunted. The sudden change in his mood took Kiran by surprise. She waited for him to continue.

He said, "We lived all over the world. He worked for an oil company. He was a violent man. I am afraid I took some anger out on Rishi. Your fear brought back things I do not wish to remember."

"Your mother?" she asked gently.

He nodded. "And me." He smiled. "When you get frustrated at your father, remember how lucky you are."

She patted the bag of peas. There was a pool of water around his hand.

She said, "Don't tell him, but I know."

CHAPTER NINETEEN

Kerala, 1966

Elizabeth wandered down to the shack at the end of the garden. Warm raindrops dripped onto her hair as she brushed by the fronds of the banana trees. The door was open and she pushed it against the accumulation of dead leaves and mud.

The interior of the shack seemed to be the same as she had left it two years previously on an afternoon when she had smacked a young man on the head with an old frying pan. And the day when that same man had charged his way into her heart and mind without her permission. She had not seen him since despite her casual visits to the shack for the rest of the last few days of her month-long stay with her grandparents.

Her first visit to her grandparents had been traumatic enough without the unwelcome intrusion of the handsome vision painter. She closed her eyes and turned her face towards the window on which he had hung helpless. She could see his brown almost black eyes, the sparkle even through the dazed look that crept over them. The set of his shoulders, the confidence of his stance, even when it was startled by her laughter.

The books were still there, perched in a zigzag stack in the corner of the room. The cushion was damp and mouldy. Elizabeth picked up the topmost book. It was in Malayalam, the script packed in dense paragraphs of circles and curves.

There were two books in English, a tome on philosophy and religion in ancient cultures and a textbook on business methods. The pages were speckled with black and clumped together in parts. Elizabeth put the books back as she'd found them. Then she smiled and re-arranged them. She left the shack, pulling the door shut behind her.

Her grandfather had come out of the house and was watching her as she wound her way back through the wet trees. She stopped to pick two bananas from a bunch and handed one to him before sitting down on the stone steps and peeling the other one.

"Do you not like bananas?" Elizabeth asked, biting into the sweet white flesh.

Her grandfather shook his head, his eyes coming back to focus on her. He nodded. "I do, thank you, Elizabeth." He was in his fifties but his face was lined, his eyes heavy-lidded.

He sat on the rough surface of the low stone wall that lined the steps down to the garden. His face reflected the discomfort that he must have felt through the thin cotton *mundu*. He wasn't wearing a shirt and the grey hairs curled across his thin chest.

He turned the plump yellow fruit around in his hand. "One of these was responsible for you coming here."

"A banana?" Elizabeth laughed. "Now you have to explain that."

He smiled but there was a raw pain in his eyes as he looked at her. "Your laugh is exactly like your mother's."

She said, the sadness falling into the echoes of her laugh, "That's what my father used to say, on his rare visits."

Her grandfather's eyes narrowed. "I can keep saying we are sorry, but I hope you understand why we did what we did."

Elizabeth looked away and he continued with a hint of desperation, "We did not know what would happen. We were trying to deal with the shock of what happened to our daughter, the scandal. You have to see, it was so shocking to us. We did not want anyone to find out who the man was."

She looked down at the pattern of brown swirling through the grey of the step. Her grandfather got up from the wall and sat on the step beside her.

"Your mother died giving birth to you. She was only 15. We did not even know she was carrying a baby. That night when you were found," he paused and his voice had thickened when he continued, "that night was the worst of our lives. Because she could only say a few words before she died. She could only tell us who the father was. And there could be no way for you to be kept in the village. Everyone would know who the father was."

Elizabeth asked, "What would have happened to him? Why couldn't he just stand up and accept that it happened?"

Her grandfather placed his hand on her knee. "He was a priest, Elizabeth. A priest who was young and frightened. He had made a 15 year old girl pregnant. He told me he loved her. His church would have moved him. That is all they would have done. But his career as a priest would be over before it really started. My daughter was dead." His eyes filled with tears. "I wanted to kill him. Instead, I ignored my wife. I ignored her screaming and her pain. I took you to your father and I told him to take care of his daughter like I would have taken care of mine if I had a chance."

He sighed, a deep heavy sound that enveloped the two of them. "I did not know he would leave you in an orphanage in Ireland. I thought he had left you with his parents and I did not want to think about anything. Otherwise I would have known there was no way he would have let it be known to his family. He came back and worked in this place, right beside us. And I never asked. I never talked to him again."

She said in a small voice, "So, why did you ask for me? What made you look for me?"

"Your father left without a word to anyone in 1958. And a young man said you were in pain. Something he said woke me out of the monsoon of pain over your mother. It took a few more years to find you. At least you were with your father." He handed her the banana. "The young man couldn't take payment, but I hope he will be able to feel even a little of the happiness you have brought back to this house not just when you visit but in the time in between when we know you are happy now. I cannot paint but I hope my thoughts for him will be enough."

She looked puzzled and he smiled. "Never mind the ramblings of an old man. Come. I think your grandmother has employed the services of every woman in the village to prepare for your birthday party. They are making every type of food you like."

Elizabeth laughed. "I will be too fat to get back on the aeroplane. My Irish grandparents will be jealous."

He took her hand and patted it. "I am so happy you forgave us. You are a beautiful sun that has come into our lives and brightened every corner." He looked embarrassed but continued, "Your grandmother can tell you more than I can. I do not talk well like she does, but I wanted you to know it is not only her who is so happy you are part of our lives."

Elizabeth grinned as she squeezed his fingers, "You're ok. You're my favourite grandparent at the moment. Even though she does make me *dosas* every morning."

He smiled as he got to his feet. "My cheeky granddaughter. Some poor man is going to have a difficult time in the future." He looked at the house and frowned at the sounds of preparation. "I hope a long time in the future. You are only twenty."

∞ ∞ ∞

Her grandmother's fingers were deft as they pleated the sari and tucked the top of the pleats into the long skirt. She stood back and examined Elizabeth with a critical eye. She adjusted the fall of the folds and the fit of the blouse and stood back again. Her face broke out into a smile that lifted her earlobes out of their droop. Her grey hair was pulled back into a severe bun but her face was gentle with lines that had settled over the years into sadness and were now trying to figure out why they were more often pulled up into unaccustomed positions.

She only ever wore a white sari, without any of the embroidery that adorned the turquoise gauze that was draped around Elizabeth. The only colour on her grandmother was the sparkly red and gold of the earrings that Elizabeth had given her. Elizabeth leaned down and kissed the top of the grey head. Her grandmother clucked and turned her around and moved her towards the door but there was a smile crinkling her lips.

She said in Malayalam to the back of her granddaughter as she guided her out of the room, "No mischief, Elizabeth. You will drive those young men mad. Especially those young vision painters. They cannot be married. Remember that."

Elizabeth's heart had jumped at the mention of vision painters. "Are all the vision painters coming to my party? I did not think they would socialise with us mere mortals."

She felt her grandmother's fingers grip her waist and stop her. The grey head poked around her and whispered, "They are invited to everything that happens in the village. They cannot accept payment for their services but they are welcomed into the homes of everyone here."

"Do you believe they can do what they say?"

Her grandmother nodded. "Why would I not believe? They have lived amongst us for generations. They have proved they have nothing to prove. We believe and they paint. Did you know we have the two great families of vision painters in our small village?"

Elizabeth shook her head. "No. I don't know anything about them. I'm not sure I want to. All men. All getting whatever they want in return for putting some paint on a canvas. I do not have any time for religion. Too much pain is caused by the few who control it."

They were still standing outside her grandmother's bedroom and Elizabeth could hear and smell the bustle of preparation below. The scrape of table legs as the furniture was moved around, the spicy air rising in the stairwell. The front door of the house was open and she heard male voices on the veranda.

Her grandmother nudged her towards the stairs. "This is not religion. They are just a part of our lives. Just remember, keep away from them as much as possible, especially with that mouth of yours."

Elizabeth turned to protest but her grandmother's fingers were firm. They went down the stairs and as she stepped off the last step, she came face to face with Ji who had just walked in through the front door.

Elizabeth tried to stop the blush of red that spread on her cheeks, but she was sure it was obvious to everyone. Ji had filled out into his tall frame. His hair was combed back but a lock of black fell across his eyes. Eyes that were as deep and dark as she remembered, and bore the same dazed look as they had after she'd hit him with a frying pan.

Ji collected himself and smiled at her grandmother who had emerged from behind Elizabeth and was beaming at him.

"Ammachi, thank you for inviting us." He bowed his head and her grandmother giggled. Elizabeth glanced at her in surprise at the sound.

Her grandmother said, "Elizabeth, this is Ji. He is one of the vision painters. His family are one of the families I mentioned." She turned to Ji and said, "But even more than that, he is responsible for our happiness."

Ji shook his head. "I did nothing, Ammachi."

"Nonsense. Come. Let me get you some food." She took his hand and led him into the living room. Her other hand was holding Elizabeth's hand and Elizabeth followed with a grin as she took in Ji's discomfort beside her.

The living room was crowded with people. Tables had been moved into the room and lay covered with dishes of food. Elizabeth entered the room, pulled in by her grandmother and in line with Ji. Everyone turned to look at them and there was friendliness in their smiles along with the curiosity.

A man detached himself from a group of younger men and came over to them. He seemed to be around the same age as her grandparents, in his fifties. He was mostly bald, the remaining grey hairs tufting over his ears. He nodded at Ji and smiled warmly at Elizabeth and her grandmother.

"It is so good to see this home as it used to be, Mariamma."

Elizabeth's grandmother nodded. She nudged Elizabeth forward and said, "This is the reason, Manoj. This is Elizabeth, my granddaughter."

"Happy Birthday, Elizabeth. Welcome to our little village." His eyes were kind but Elizabeth could feel herself being assessed by someone who she sensed was experienced in such examinations.

"Thank you. I'm very happy to be here." She glanced at Ji as she spoke. She caught him staring at her and he looked away quickly.

Manoj said to Ji in Malayalam, "The rest are mostly all here. Why don't you join them? Dinesh is late as usual." He gestured with his head towards the group of young men with whom he had been standing. His eyes and voice were stern.

Ji straightened up to his full height and nodded to the two women before moving hastily to join the others.

Manoj turned back to them and smiled again. "It is sometimes hard to keep control of young men but we must do it, for their own good. Is that not right, Mariamma? They are at the age now and things have been set in motion that cannot be halted." He looked back at the group and said quietly, "Not without severe consequences."

Her grandmother followed his gaze at the group of young men, the tallest standing out from them, his eyes escaping from them to steal a look at Elizabeth. She nodded slowly as she looked back at Elizabeth who had not heard Manoj. Her grip tightened on Elizabeth's hand and she said, as she pulled Elizabeth towards the table of food, "Manoj, enjoy the party. Remember to bring Dinesh over when he arrives."

Elizabeth could feel their eyes on her as she filled her plate with an assortment of freshly cooked cutlets and *wadas*. Her tongue was adjusting to the new spices after the blandness of the Irish diet on which she'd grown up. But then, the colour and heat of this place was a continued shock to her system.

She felt a strange mixture of feeling at home combined with a restlessness in her blood. Must be the half of her that was Indian. Nothing whatsoever to do with the handsome Indian vision painter into whose eyes she could have stared all day.

CHAPTER TWENTY

Kiran spent the hour drive to Connemara trying to forget what had happened with Rishi. She'd left the house before Ron got back. She couldn't face him or anyone other than Ashley at the moment. She wanted to spend the night at the house in Connemara, in her own bed, in her own room, with Ashley.

She knew if Ashley had already left for Galway, they'd meet up on the narrow road. She was glad they hadn't by the time she pulled up to the front of her house. Ashley's car was parked outside, the back seat full of boxes. The passenger door was open and Kiran went to close it as she passed. They could go to Ron's house early in the morning. She noticed a rectangular object that seemed to have fallen into the footwell and lay resting against the passenger seat. Kiran reached in to retrieve it.

It was a canvas. She got a rough impression of shapes and swirl, of cream and auburn waves, before her heart contracted painfully. The woman in the painting was beautiful except that she was screaming in pain. Her body was covered in a sheet but the face was Ashley's, instantly recognisable to Kiran even in its agony.

Kiran dropped the painting back onto the seat and ran. She couldn't control her breath which was coming out in short gasps and muffled sobs and cries. As she approached the open front door, she heard other cries. She held her breath and still heard them. The study. They were coming from the study. The door was open and she ran through tripping and falling over the legs that lay across her path.

Kiran landed on her side, beside Ashley. The sweat mixed in with the tears on Ashley's face which was a reddish-brown mixture of heat and auburn hair. Her mouth was open and the high-pitched cry that escaped from it tunnelled through Kiran's chest wall and dug into her heart.

Kiran grabbed Ashley and held her close as she searched for her phone. The cries became whimpers against her shoulder. There was no point waiting, the ambulance would take as long to get here as Kiran would to get Ashley to Galway. She knew there were no obvious wounds. The only thing she could think of was to get Ashley out of pain.

Ashley helped as much as she could but her body was limp between the attacks of pain. Kiran half-dragged, half-carried her to the car. She lowered the back of the passenger seat down and put Ashley lying down on it.

The drive back to Galway was a twisting hour of hellish thoughts and sounds. The car kept on the road by sheer strength of will and luck. Kiran phoned Ron as she drove, explaining as best as she could, telling him to call the hospital, to meet them there.

He was waiting, anxiously pacing in front of Casualty. He rushed over to her car as it slammed into the kerbing and came to a jolting stop. They didn't say anything as they carried Ashley between them past the casualty reception towards the closed swing doors.

Ron had obviously warned the staff and the doors to the treatment area opened immediately much to the surprise of the crowd in the waiting area. A porter pulled up a trolley and they lifted Ashley onto it. She was shivering and a keening sound was coming from her mouth. Her face was still twisted in pain. Kiran grabbed a blanket from the ledge below the trolley and threw it over Ashley. A young intern hurried up and gestured at the porter and he wheeled the trolley towards the examining area.

A few minutes later, a grey-haired man in a suit came through the doors and nodded at Ron before following the trolley out of view. Kiran slumped against the wall and slid down to the floor. She buried her head in her knees, her hands pressed tight over her ears, but the sounds were inside her head and they deafened her. She felt someone sit beside her on the floor and an arm around her shoulder. She heard someone else ask if they wanted chairs. She shook her head.

Kiran and Ron sat in that position on the floor of the corridor in the emergency unit until the consultant came out and looked for them. His knees clicked as he crouched to get to their level. He tried to smile but his blue eyes were serious. He addressed the two of them though it was obvious he knew Ron.

"We have given Ashley morphine. The examination shows nothing. We're going to arrange for a lot more tests but I'm afraid we're going to have to induce a coma as we can't keep her comfortable."

Kiran couldn't stop the sob that escaped from her. Ron's arm tightened around her shoulders and she could feel his body shaking.

"Can we see her? Before you do..." Ron's voice was shaking too.

The consultant nodded. He winced as he got up and held a hand out for each of them as they scrambled to their feet. They followed him down the corridor, their steps silent on the speckled linoleum. The treatment area was busy, most of the curtains pulled across, doctors and nurses going about their business as if nothing titanic had happened. The consultant approached a curtained area at the far end of the room and pulled the flowered fabric aside.

Ashley was awake. Her forehead was sweaty, the strands of hair still stuck to it in red hugs. Her eyes were like ash clouds but they widened at the sight of Kiran.

Kiran took Ashley's face gently between both hands and kissed her cheeks, her eyes, her nose. A tiny smile attempted to play on Ashley's lips and she said, the words stringing out on the thread of her voice, "If childbirth is a quarter of this, you might regret you chose to do the carrying."

Kiran shook her head and touched the curve of those lips. "I just wish it was me instead of you in this too." Her voice strengthened. "I'm going to fix this, Ashley. Whatever it takes. I promise you. I'll fix this. Whatever it takes."

"Don't do anything dangerous, Kiran. You need to think of the baby."

Ron had taken Ashley's hand on the other side of the trolley and he gasped. Ashley said to him. "Meant to tell you tonight." Her face scrunched up and she sucked in a breath. Her skin was noticeably paler within seconds, the only colour a flush of red in her cheeks. The consultant moved up and put his hand on Ashley's leg. He nodded at Kiran and Ron.

Kiran said, "You'll be asleep for a little while. I'm going to go and fix this." She looked at Ron. He nodded, and Kiran continued, "Your dad will be here with you." Ashley moved her chin down in an attempt at a nod. Kiran kissed her and whispered, "I love you more than you will ever know. Whatever it takes, I'll do."

The porter had come over at a wave from the consultant. He waited for Kiran to straighten up and pulled the trolley away from Kiran and Ron and out of the room. They followed the trolley out of the treatment area and down the corridor until it turned out of the double doors into the Waiting Area and towards the main hospital. A few curious eyes turned to look at her from the rows of people waiting.

Most kept staring at the TV hung from the corner of the room droning its message into their fixed and tired stares.

"Kiran! Ron!" They both turned at Delilah's voice.

Kiran felt herself surrounded by warmth as Delilah grabbed her in a hug. "Where is she? How is she doing?"

Ron gestured down the corridor. "I'm going to go and sit with her."

They looked in the direction and Kiran could see the trolley moving towards the corner. Jennifer appeared from the direction of the main hospital. She skidded to a stop at the trolley and took Ashley's hand. The trolley turned left and disappeared from view.

Kiran could feel Delilah squeeze her waist. "Why are you two still here? Come, let's go and sit with her."

Kiran shook her head. "I have to go and sort this. I have to go and find out what is going on." She moved towards the exit then turned back. Her voice was strained and tight. "Will ye tell her she's loved. Even when she's asleep. That she has nothing to feel bad about."

Ron nodded. He seemed unable to move without help. Delilah took his hand and they walked away down the corridor. Kiran turned and moved in a daze out of the hospital. The night had fallen and in the yellow glow of the emergency unit sign, she could see the purple shape of her car still tilted up, one wheel teetering on the kerb.

The security guard was hovering at the door of an ambulance chatting with the driver, sucking smoke in to his lungs. She could see him thinking thoughts about women drivers, Asian women drivers at that, but he just nodded at her and flicked his cigarette ash onto the ground.

Kiran eased her car off the kerb and concentrated on driving back to Connemara. She had to forget Ashley's screams. To forget that she was responsible for bringing such pain to the woman she loved with all her heart.

Otherwise she wouldn't be able to stop this nightmare. She needed to examine the painting, to check her studio, her paints, her canvases. She had to get back to Ron's and talk to Vijay to find out what was in that script. If there was anything at all she could find that would save Ashley.

CHAPTER TWENTY-ONE

Kerala, 1966

Elizabeth heard what sounded like a chuckle as she approached the shack. She smiled through the thudding of her heart. The party was dying down in the house behind her. The music from the sitar slid through the air and pushed her forward. She nudged the door a little further open.

Ji had bent down to the books she'd re-arranged into a circle around the handle of the frying pan. He straightened up and frowned as he turned to her. He rubbed his fingers on the spot where the frying pan had hit him before disintegrating.

"This is your joke about hitting me with that thing. You created a bald area there. My ancestors had very thick hair. No baldness. And now, I will bear the scar. And my son as well."

Elizabeth put her hand to her mouth. She mumbled, "I am so sorry. I didn't mean..."

She took in the smile that was trying to escape from the corner of his mouth.

She smiled very suddenly. A smile that reached from her lips and eyes and dragged an answering smile from his lips. He seemed to be frozen in place, his fingers motionless and stuck to his hair.

She walked forward slowly and reached up for his hand and moved it out of the way so she could examine his scalp. He was taller than her and she had to pull his head down to see. His hair was thick and a lustrous black with no hint of a bald patch. She could almost hear the lack of breathing in the shack as the wind cackled through the leaves in the doorway. Her fingers smoothed his ruffled hair back into place, her eyes and skin taking in every strand.

His eyes closed. The skin around them bunched. Her fingers moved to his eyelids. She watched her hand as if from a great distance. His breath came out in a long exhalation and his eyes opened. He grabbed her wrist and stilled her fingers. She could see the fog over the earth plains of his eyes.

Ji stammered as he spoke. "I am a vision painter. I am not allowed this." His grip on her wrist was tight but she did not feel any pain, just the heat of his fingers on her arm.

The notes from the sitar stirred in the restless air. Their tone matched the haunted look in Ji's eyes as he stared at her face.

Elizabeth whispered, "What are you not allowed?"

His eyes were intense. "To feel what I do. To remember you the way that I do. Every moment for two years. I saw your face, your eyes, your smile. I heard your laugh in the leaves when I came here to wait for you."

Elizabeth felt her recognition of his words, his waiting. She said, trying to keep her voice steady though it felt like her pulse was shaking each word, "Why are you not allowed?"

His hand fell away from her wrist and the chill raced through the hairs on her arm. He turned to stare at the books on the ground. "I am a vision painter. Our path is set. We do not marry." He paused and looked embarrassed. "I mean, if we wanted to marry someone."

She smiled at his discomfort, stopped, suddenly aware that she wanted to marry him. She groaned at herself. Her father was right. She was headstrong and impulsive and a little crazy. Well, a lot crazy, according to him.

Ji kept his head turned away from her. She could see his silhouette etched against the wooden sides of the shack. He said, "Will you be here tomorrow? At the same time?"

She wanted to tease him but it seemed too important so she nodded and whispered, "Yes"

∞ ∞ ∞

They lay against the cushions she had sneaked out from the house. Her head was nestled against his shoulder and she could feel the steady beat of his heart against her ear. The thought hung heavy between them. Elizabeth was leaving in two days.

They had spent the month walking through the coconut groves, alongside the paddy fields, laughing as they hid from passers-by. Evenings in the shack were spent sitting and talking, holding hands. Lying with her head on his shoulder, talking, not thinking. Trying not to plan a future he couldn't give her.

They had said more in this month than she had ever shared with anyone and she knew it was the same for him too. The desperate avoidance of their reality took an effort that drained her. He spoke every day of his path, his training, the burden of history. And she felt it like a long shadow reaching from the past to cast its darkness over their love.

She knew she loved him. Not in the flighty flirty way she had remembered him from her first visit. That had served to keep him in her mind. This feeling was from her heart and her mind, from deep in her soul. But how could compare with almost 200 years of history? With the respect and love he felt for his calling and with duty and honour.

His hand came up to her face and she realised her tears had dampened his shirt. Ji lifted her chin and tightened his other arm around her.

"When will you be coming back?" His voice was a whisper of sharp edges.

Elizabeth closed her eyes. "I can't come back, Ji. How can I come back? I cannot separate from you again. I can't watch you from a distance. We have been stealing time together and now we have to give it back."

He was silent.

Elizabeth sat up and wiped her eyes on her sleeve. She took his hand. She turned and kissed him once on the cheek and got to her feet. His hand was still in hers. She hoped he would hold her back, ask her to stay, but he covered his eyes with the palm of his other hand and she gripped her fingers around his for a moment before pulling away and hurrying out of the shack.

The banana fronds added their tears to those on her face as she ran towards the house. She burst through the kitchen door and sat at the table, her legs giving way as she fell onto the stool. Her grandmother was sitting in front of the large mortar, the heavy curved base of the pestle squeezing and grinding the rice and urad dal into the dosa batter. She looked at Elizabeth's face and her hands stopped their circular motion. She wiped the white batter off the pestle and lay it down on the gray stone of the mortar.

"You know he is not allowed, Elizabeth. You knew that when you met him." Mariamma eased herself upright and slowly walked over to the table. She used her plain cotton sari to wipe Elizabeth's face and sat on the stool beside her.

Elizabeth said, "I knew that, Ammachi. But I thought..."

Her grandmother patted Elizabeth's hand that was resting on the table between them. "You thought he would leave everything for you. His family, his profession, his gift, his very life."

Elizabeth shook her head. "I know he cannot. I didn't mean to feel this way. I knew after I met him first that I wanted to see him again. But when I did, when we talked, spent all that time together. I love him. I feel like I have known him forever. And I know he feels the same. It hurts so much, Ammachi. I have to leave and I don't know if I can come back." The tears started again as she realised she would not see her grandparents either.

Mariamma pulled the sari off her shoulder and wiped Elizabeth's face again, before rubbing at her own. "Maybe in some years you will be able to come back without this pain, Elizabeth. But you are right that you cannot come back for a few years. We cannot take the risk."

"Why are the vision painters so restricted? Why can they not be allowed to marry?"

Mariamma's voice was firm. "They believe that the man must remain without distraction. That all his focus and his love must be channelled into the visions that are requested of him. The attention of the vision painter must not be taken away by the love of a woman. The only family is the son they will train and the other vision painters."

Elizabeth said, "Surely they can love someone but still paint for others?"

Mariamma shook her head slowly. "They are not allowed to paint for themselves or their loved ones. They sacrifice their personal happiness to help others experience happiness. It is a gift that bears punishments for the giver, but I think the giving brings them peace too. The satisfaction of giving without seeking anything in return."

She stroked Elizabeth's forehead and used the sari to wipe off the streak of batter. Her voice was tender. "My dear little granddaughter, if you could paint people's visions into reality, if you knew what happiness that could bring to people, would you jeopardise that gift?"

Elizabeth struggled with the words, her heart screaming that she would give up anything to be with Ji, her head bowed under the weight of the knowledge that she couldn't ask that of him.

She shook her head. "No, I wouldn't ask him to jeopardise that gift." The last word was muffled as she lowered her face into her arms as they rested on the table. She felt her grandmother rubbing her back.

CHAPTER TWENTY-TWO

Kiran was finding it difficult to take in a deep breath. Her chest was tight and the panic curdled around her solar plexus. She parked her car beside Ashley's car, its passenger door groaning as the wind nudged it on its hinges. Her house was dipped in darkness, her path lit only by the sprinkles of a cloud-covered moon on the sleeping leaves and stones.

She got out and approached the other car, her reluctance to see the painting weighing down each footstep. It was still lying where she'd dropped it. Kiran switched on the light in the car and ignored the painting. She saw what she hadn't noticed before. A brown package, ripped, fallen between the two front seats onto the footrest at the back.

There were postage stamps plastered all over the surface, but they were from many different countries and were partially obscured by the black ringed stamps of post office clerks. The package was addressed to Ashley, care of Kiran.

Kiran threw the paper down and picked up the canvas. She could not look at the painted surface. She slammed the car door shut and hurried into the house. Her combined office and studio smelled faintly musty after months of neglect. She dragged out the easel and propped the painting on it. Kiran took as deep a breath as she could, and looked at the painting.

She noticed the details in the rest of the painting now as her eyes stubbornly refused to settle on the face of the screaming woman. The bed was plain, a hospital bed. There

167

was a window in the room but a black night was all that was visible through it. The sheet was white and covered the woman's body like a shroud, loose and hiding any definition, just the hint of curves.

But the curves of the face, the hair, the rugged terrain of those irises, were all Ashley. Her mouth was stretched in a scream that echoed through Kiran in its silence, in the cold of the room. The chill sneaked its fingers around her heart and squeezed as her mind took in the familiar use of colour, the brushstrokes, the style that made her fingers tingle in recognition.

Kiran shook her head and her hands trembled as she raised them to the canvas, as she tried to stroke away the pain. Her eyes could not bear to see anymore and she looked out of the bay windows, at the trees, at the spot where she had sat with Ashley, at the place where she imagined Marge and Sarah walking away, hand in hand, Ashley's little sister clinging on to her mother.

Kiran thought they had worked through the guilt Ashley felt over Sarah's death, that Marge had used so effectively on her. Or did Ashley have a different guilt she had not shared?

Kiran took a cloth from the bookshelf and draped it over the canvas. She counted out her canvases, touched the tips of her paintbrushes, tried in vain to take stock of her paint supplies. There didn't seem to be much change that she could make out from the last time she had painted. Again, her spirit dipped as she remembered what one of her paintings had been. She put off the light in the studio and paused. She switched it on again and went to her desk. The top drawer held the completed Vision Painting Application Form she had placed there, out of her sight. She touched the writing, Ashley's scribbled request for love with Jennifer, the detailed list of words that had speared through Kiran as she read it. The list she had never been able to excise fully from her mind.

She folded the paper carefully and put it in her pocket. A slip of paper that felt heavy as she walked out of her house, as she drove the road to Galway and contemplated the night ahead.

∞ ∞ ∞

It was after midnight but the light was on in the main living room of Ron's house. Vijay was sitting in one of the formal armchairs with the papers spread out on the coffee table in front of him. His shirt was open at the collar, his tie hanging tired and blue. Kiran sat on the marble hearth of the fireplace. She suppressed the shivers that were rippling through her muscles.

Vijay said, "What are you looking for in these papers? There is a large amount of material. The history since the first Guru, his notes, the proceedings of Council meetings. And there is the codebook as well to read." He shook his head. "I am not sure I am the right person for this. It is a struggle to read and understand for me. The old papers. They are written in a variable of Malayalam script."

"But you can get the general idea, can't you?" Kiran tried not to let the fear in her voice spill out into panic.

Vijay nodded. "Yes, yes. Do not worry. I will keep trying. What do you want me to focus on?"

Kiran tried to think. "I need to know if there are any mentions of vision painters doing negative paintings. Where would they mention that? Would they even write about it? I don't know." She buried her head in her hands. "I need to think."

Vijay's voice was gentle. "If they have inducted the coma, then your Ashley will not be feeling anything. You must concentrate now on searching for answers."

Kiran raised her head from her hands. He was watching her with pity in his eyes.

She murmured, "You mean 'induced'," then took a deep breath and said, "You're right. I'm wasting time." She got up. She was getting used to the feeling of exhaustion trickling through her body. "It is going to be a long night. I'm going to make us a cup of tea and then you can tell me what you've found out so far."

She came back in a few minutes with two cups of tea and pulled the other armchair up to the coffee table. Vijay took a gulp of tea and placed the cup on the floor. He picked up a notepad and she saw he had made detailed notes.

He read them out. "Guru discovered his gift in 1841. He was 25 at the time. He writes about the process of discovery. He writes about his early attempts and how he trained his son. He felt it was a gift that was bestowed on very few men and that by discovering those men as boys, he could breed a generation of vision painters."

Kiran interrupted him. "Why is it only bestowed on men? Why did he think that?"

Vijay shook his head. "I do not know. But he went and searched out a particular type of man. It was a very detailed search. He looked for men who were considered the people that everyone went to with their difficulties. Men who provided advice. Who were respected as healers."

"Surely, there would be more women like that?"

"You must remember that in those days, women were not treated equally. I remember reading about some strange behaviours in Kerala. Did you know there was a breast tax on women in the 1800s?"

Kiran shook her head. "What, they had to pay tax to have breasts?"

"No, women of some low castes in India had to pay a tax called *mulakkaram* if they wanted to cover their chests when they went outside because this type of modesty was considered a privilege of upper caste women."

Kiran was looking at him in disbelief.

"It happened. The tax rate was high. It depended on the size and attractiveness of the breasts. It only stopped in 1840 when it was repealed after a woman in Cherthala in Kerala refused to pay the tax. She cut off her breasts in protest and presented them to the tax collectors."

"You're joking!" Kiran realised she had her arms across her chest and she lowered them.

"No, the woman died of blood loss later that night, but the tax was repealed the next day."

Kiran took a few moments for the story to sink in. Vijay looked back at his notes.

"Should I continue?"

Kiran nodded. Her chest hurt.

"Guru found those men over the years and he explained to them the great honour involved and he asked them to let him train their sons. Most of them agreed. And he developed the sons into vision painters in many cases."

Kiran was still distracted by the image of a woman bleeding to death from her sliced chest. She tried to focus on Vijay's words again.

"Guru was in charge till the age of 75, when he died in 1891. His son was 50 at the time and took over. Guru's son continued and formalised the rules into a codebook. He developed further rules as the need arose. Sometimes to quell disputes. But everything was done to fit in with the society around them. And to make them the elite in that society."

Kiran glanced at his face but Vijay did not seem to be making a judgement. He just continued in a formal tone.

"The son, the second Guru was in charge from age 50 to 75. He passed over the leadership to his own son at age 75 and died at age 80. His own son, the third Guru, was 50 when he took over. He was an excellent vision painter but not good at leading people. Two of the young boys who were picked and who developed the gift and became vision painters were yours and Rishi's ancestors, your fathers' great grandfathers. It was in the time of the third Guru that the Council was formed. The third Guru was weaker and the other vision painters wanted representation. When the second Guru died, his son was not able to stop other strong personalities from taking over. They formed a Council after five years, in 1921 and Ji's great-grandfather became Leader of this first Council of Vision Painters. Dinesh's great grandfather was on the council. They completely formalised the rules into a codebook and developed the punishments."

Kiran asked, "So before that, there were just rules but no punishments for breaking the rules?"

Vijay looked up and nodded. "It would seem that way. The Gurus had a faith that their words and rules would be enough to keep the vision painters on the correct path. The Council must not have shared that faith."

He looked back at his notes.

"Ji's great grandfather led the Council until he was 75 at which point he passed tried to pass leadership on to his son, Ji's Grandfather, in 1941. However, Dinesh's grandfather was also on the Council and wanted the role but after a bitter leadership battle, it was Ji's grandfather who became leader of the Council and held that post for many years. He wanted to pass it on to his son, Ji's father, but Ji's father died suddenly in 1958 at the age of 42. Ji's grandfather never recovered from that and left the council that year at the age of 67."

Kiran said, "So that is when Dinesh's father took my father into his family and took over the leadership."

"Yes, that was in 1958. Manoj was the man who stepped into the crisis and took charge. He trained Ji and Dinesh and he led the Council until 1991 when Dinesh took over. There are not so many notes from the time of Manoj. I need to look through the codebook and match it with the notes and see why the rules were developed as they were."

Kiran shook her head. "That would be very useful. So far, that's a lot of dates to take in. The leadership of the Council has been in my father's line for most of the time. It passed to this Manoj and then Dinesh and now it is back with my father."

Vijay nodded. "And it will go to an open election when your father decides to retire."

Kiran sat back with a sigh and closed her eyes. "What is so important about the leadership? Why do they have to add all the trappings to everything? I didn't want to examine my gift too seriously. I hate the way they took something so wonderful and slapped on rules and regulations and punishments. They can't see the beauty in the idea that we can take people's visions for their lives and help them to achieve it. I can't even seem to paint anymore, since I started worrying about it." She rubbed her temple to try and stop the thudding pain. "It was so much easier when it was just a mystery. A part of me that I didn't have to question. When I just knew that the visions were positive and their manifestations would have no severe consequences for anybody."

She stopped when she realised what she'd said. She opened her eyes. Vijay was staring at her. She smiled and said as calmly as she could, "Ignore me. I just dabble. I like to think it has good effects but as everyone knows, women can't be vision painters. Some of us can just paint."

His eyes showed doubt and a little confusion.

Kiran got up and stretched. "It has been a long horrible day. I'm very grateful for your help. We'll continue tomorrow?"

Vijay nodded.

Kiran picked up the cups. "Okay, I'm going to bed. I'm going to read through more of my dad's journal and notes."

Vijay stood up as she passed him. She heard the rustle of papers as he gathered up the sheets.

Great. Hopefully he wouldn't say anything to Dinesh or Rishi. He probably wouldn't. They were not on the best of terms at the moment. But she certainly didn't need for them to know.

CHAPTER TWENTY-THREE

Kerala 1966

Elizabeth packed the saris her grandmother had given her into the suitcase. She was trying not to cry, but was close to breaking at the sight of Mariamma's face as she sat on the bed

Her grandfather had said his goodbyes, his voice gruff with his unspoken thoughts, before collecting his fishing rods and disappearing down the track to the paddy fields and the river that flowed beyond.

Mariamma asked, "How long will you stay away?" Her fingers were absentmindedly playing with the sparkly earring that hung from her earlobe.

"I think it will be a long time, Ammachi. I cannot come back when I still feel like this for him. And I don't know how long that will be or if that will go away."

Elizabeth closed the lid and locked the suitcase. She pulled it off the bed and placed it on the floor. She sat down and put her arm around the plump shoulders of her grandmother. They sat in the silence of the bedroom and listened to the sounds of the church bells competing with the wind through the palm trees. The air that moved through the room was hot and scented with jasmine and coconut.

Elizabeth breathed in the scented air mixed with the spices that piggybacked up the stairs on the bustle of sounds from the kitchen. She wanted to store every scent and sound and sight with the memories of the home she had found here, the joyous sparkle of red and gold against her grandmother's lined face, the laughter in her grandfather's hands as he demonstrated how he had fished from a little boat in the main street of the village when the floods came, and Ji who had reached into her heart and painted the colours of every vision she had ever felt for her life.

A horn sounded from the street and Elizabeth tightened her grip around her grandmother. She could feel Mariamma's shoulders tense then droop.

Mariamma said, her voice subdued, "I will stay here. The car will take you to the station." She clasped her hand around Elizabeth's knee and pushed herself off the bed. She walked to the door, the shuffle of her feet on the floor slower than her age.

Elizabeth remained sitting on the bed until another blast of the horn poked through the window. She got up slowly and took a last look around the room before picking up the suitcase and walking out.

There was no sign of her grandmother as Elizabeth said her goodbyes to the women sitting downstairs who had been a noisy presence during her stay. They had talked and laughed through the cooking and cleaning, sometimes staring in fascination at Elizabeth's fair skin and blue-green eyes, other times combing her long black hair and clucking over her inability to eat as gracefully with her fingers as they did. They did not speak English as her grandparents did, and Elizabeth struggled with Malayalam, so the communication had been loud but mostly through gestures.

Elizabeth felt the pangs of loneliness as she walked away from the noise and liveliness of her Indian grandparents' home. Her Irish grandparents tried to make her feel at home and she loved them but the house there was quiet, the oppressive frowns of the saints dulling her natural enthusiasm.

She could feel the shutters in her eyes snapping the images that she would carry with her as they drove away from the house where she felt most at home, past the church where her father had worked, the curve around the vision painters' houses where her love lived. There was no one waving goodbye. She leaned back and let her eyes close as the village faded out of view behind the glass.

∞ ∞ ∞

Elizabeth felt the sweat drip from her temple and into her eye. She raised her head and wiped at her face. The road looked narrower than the normal route from the village. Rubber trees leaned in unison, spirals of white sliced through their barks, sap dripping into the coconut shells fixed to their trunks.

She leaned forward and tapped the top of the seat in front of her. The driver glanced back and waggled his head. He said something in Malayalam and pointed down the road. Elizabeth could see the road stretch ahead cutting through the plantation of rubber. It did not look familiar. There were no people, no animals, and no movement.

Elizabeth tried to suppress the fear that curled through her stomach. She knew the driver had worked for her grandparents for the last few years. The thought occurred to her that she had said her goodbyes and they might not expect her to contact them again for a while. If she disappeared, would they assume she didn't want any further contact with any of them?

She assumed she could jump out of the car if necessary, but then what? She looked around the back seat. There were no objects that could serve as weapons. The car slowed and she looked up quickly. The wheels went over ridged earth as they turned off the road onto a dirt track.

Elizabeth kept her voice calm. "Where are we going?"

The driver smiled and waggled his head again. He said some words in Malayalam that she wouldn't have understood even without the fear that was dulling her comprehension. She didn't think the way could get narrower but the branches of the trees scratched against the sides of the car as the track started to ascend and wind its way up.

The driver obviously sensed her distress now and continued to smile and gesture up the hill. She ignored him and stared through the window at the diminishing rubber plantation below. The car turned around a bend and she saw a house that looked like it was just big enough to have one room. There was a clearing in front and it fell away into the hill. A coconut tree towered over the house, the coconuts hanging high over the tin roof.

The driver stopped the car and pointed to the house and then to his chest. His smile was even wider than before, the black of his moustache lifting, showing his teeth stained with the red of betel leaves. He got out of the car and opened her door.

Elizabeth shook her head. His smile changed to a frown and he looked up at the house. She followed his gaze and saw the figure of a man standing in the darkness of the doorway of the house. Her heart jolted with fear before she realised as he moved out of the shadow that it was Ji.

Elizabeth climbed out of the car, her heart thudding with the remnants of fear and the start of hope. Ji's brow was furrowed but the rest of his face seemed helpless to stop the smile that took over his features as he saw her.

She was conscious of the driver standing there so she walked over to Ji but did not make any physical contact with him. He turned and led her to a wooden table to one side of the house and pulled out a chair for her before sitting down himself.

Ji said something to the driver who went into the house and came out a few minutes later with a cutlass. Elizabeth watched as he slung a rope around his ankles and clambered up the coconut tree, drawing his feet up the trunk in snatches of fluid motion. He cut off two coconuts and threw them down before reversing down the trunk after them. He retrieved the coconuts and chopped off the tops and presented one to Elizabeth first, the other to Ji. She smiled at Ji. He'd remembered that she loved drinking the milk straight out of the coconut. Her eyes drank in the sight of him.

The wind moved through the leaf shards of the coconut tree and raised a puff of dust that sank back down into the red earth. The driver was sitting in the shade with his back against the trunk of the tree and he shook his feet to flap the dust out of his sandals.

Ji said, "I will miss that in your country. They do not grow coconuts there, do they?"

Elizabeth laughed and shook her head. Her face stilled and reflected her hope and her fear at the suddenness of change.

Ji took a deep breath. His eyes held hers in their depths of earth-brown. He said, "I will miss many things, Elizabeth, but I do not want to miss you." She could feel the pain in his heart as he spoke but his voice was firm and sure as he continued, "I have thought very deeply about this. There are many sacrifices that will need to be made. Sometimes those we meet are a test of our strength, of our abilities to remain on a path that we have been taught is the correct one for us." His hand moved forward a few inches on the table, towards hers, but he stopped before he could touch her. "I believe with all my heart that this is not one of those times. This is not a test for me to see whether I will remain on the path. It is a new road, and it is the right road for me. You are my signpost, my destination, and most of all, my travelling companion."

She felt the words settle into her skin, like they were hers. She felt his certainty but she needed to ask, to be sure.

"I feel it too, that you are my path, Ji. But I have no ties to another destiny like you do. Will you have to give up everything, all that you are? How can I ask you to do that? Your gift is strong, stronger than the others. There are many people whose visions you would paint, whose happiness I will have stolen. Why would you give anything up for me? I am a nobody." Elizabeth felt her hope fade as she spoke.

He took her hand. "You have never been and never will be nobody. When I saw you first, I felt a physical pain in my chest as my heart and mind and soul recognised you. I tried to deny this. But when I saw you again, when we talked and spent time together, it grew even more. It grew from recognition to knowledge. I feel your goodness, your care, your very nature. And even though you have suffered, I hear your laughter and it blesses me and shows me that even in the depths of the pain there is the possibility of light if one knows where to look for it. And you have the gift of knowing where to find the smallest ray of light in the darkest of shadows. You are and always will be more valuable to me than anything else. You are my gift."

He touched the teardrop before it could release itself from her eyelash. "I may be able to persuade Manoj to let me continue. He has mentored me and he has always said my gift should be treasured. There is a chance he would rather change the rules than lose me." His palm was warm against hers as he squeezed her hand gently. His eyes were steady as they looked into hers.

"Elizabeth, even if he refuses, I will not change my mind. Your happiness is as important to me as any other human being's, even if mine is not. If you say that I can bring you even a small amount of the happiness you bring me, I will not waver. Your road is my road from now on. We will move forward on it to the same destination, in this world and after. That is my promise to you."

He whispered, "There will be difficult times ahead but we will face them together. I cannot paint for myself or now for you but our love will be strong enough to create the future we envision together."

She held his hand and felt the teardrop soak into their skin.

CHAPTER TWENTY-FOUR

The corridors of the hospital were cluttered with trolleys and Kiran walked through avoiding the gaze of the people lying on them. Ashley was in a private room at the end of the corridor, next to the ICU. Kiran could hear voices in the room as she pushed the door open.

Delilah was speaking, her voice a loud whisper in the otherwise still room. "So, I told him that writing about gay men in that way would just not cut it unless he went off and got some experience himself." She was grinning as she looked up at Kiran. "Hi, Kiran. I was just telling Ron about the latest group of baby writers we've acquired. Their teacher is not impressed with my efforts to broaden their horizons."

Ron had a trace of a smile on his lips. They were in chairs, sitting across the bed from each other. They both looked exhausted, faint shades of blue were smudged under Ron's eyes and Delilah's wrinkles were protesting against the grin on her face.

Delilah said, still in the same forced whisper, "You look terrible. Did you find out anything?"

Kiran shook her head and walked over to the bed. Ashley's face looked peaceful despite the tape that pulled at her skin as it criss-crossed the breathing tube. Kiran found herself holding her breath and consciously let out an exhalation which swirled and was lost in the pressured hiss of the ventilator that measured out Ashley's breaths.

Her finger shook as she smoothed the skin on Ashley's brow. She leant down and kissed Ashley, leaving her face resting on the pale cheek for a few moments. She heard the chairs scrape gently on the floor and felt Ron's hand on her shoulder, squeezing. The door opened and closed behind them.

Kiran's legs gave way and she collapsed into the chair Ron had vacated, her hands reaching for and holding Ashley's. She sat slumped against the bed, listening to the silence between the forced breaths. The seconds turned into minutes and she found herself counting the mechanical clicks that heralded the start of another hiss.

"I don't know what to do, Ashley." The whisper hung in the air between them before wandering off to join the other lost sounds in the room. "You said for a negative vision painting to work, there must be a negative energy that the painter can capture. And you must be right. It was obvious; I was just too panicked about my mother to see it." Kiran sighed. "And I could not believe there was anything negative in my mother." Her hands gripped tighter. "Or in you."

She continued, the whisper strengthening, "But we all have negative in us. Of course we do. We're all a mix of positive and negative. And it is not fair that I put this pressure on you and on my mother." She smiled at Ashley. "It must be cold and lonely up there on the pedestal I put you on. I should either have you nice and warm with us mortals or I should join you up there and expect to be completely blameless and perfect as well."

There was no change in the pace of the machine.

Kiran felt the desperation creep into her voice. "Whatever it is, Ashley, it doesn't matter. You have nothing to be guilty for. Everybody makes mistakes. You have to move on and accept that each mistake makes you less likely to make the same one again. You can't take on other people's pain, even if you caused it especially as you never meant to cause the hurt. Your mother should never have done that to you. I know she was the strongest influence on you. I see it in all the ways you try not to be like her. And you are not. You are nothing like her. You didn't give up. You didn't stop being able to love. You care too much some times. Even when that eats you up inside."

There could be no response from the still figure on the bed. Kiran knew that but she couldn't seem to stop herself trying to reach through the veil and shake Ashley awake. She looked down and willed herself to stop her hand as it pushed and pulled at Ashley's arm.

"Ashley, I wish I had said this when you were awake and able to tell me what an idiot I have been. I always felt less than others here. I felt like I was an outsider here. No matter that I'm almost fully Irish, I never seemed to fit in. And of course I don't fit in India either. And I have this gift that seems like the most natural thing in the world to me, and it would be in India, but it must be so weird to the Irish. When I met you, I remember feeling like I had just fallen into another time and place. Somewhere I belonged. My heart and soul felt this, but my mind wouldn't let me forget that I have never belonged anywhere. And you and Jennifer, you're the right match for each other, aren't you? She's everything I am not. She's perfect for you and I won't blame you for still being in love with her. I won't blame you if something happened with her. I know you feel guilty for leaving her after promising to be with her for the second time. I don't know how that would feel but if it is anything like the fear and pain I feel at the thought of losing you, then I would never want to have been in Jennifer's shoes when you told her."

Kiran got up and moved to the window. The glass was warm as she laid her forehead against it, but the sun had obviously given up and crept behind the gray clouds. She watched people drive up and park and go about their business. She spoke into the glass, watching her breath make patterns in time to the hiss of the ventilator.

"I would never have wanted to be in Jennifer's shoes, but if you love her then they would be the best place on earth to be standing. I will never be her, Ashley. I'll never be perfect for you like she is. I'll never be good enough for you."

She took the Vision Painting Application form out of her pocket and unfolded it. "You wrote this for Jennifer and I painted it for you. You asked for a gentle, loving, funny person. Impulsive but who would never let you down. Someone who cares about everyone else as well as looking for what she wants. Someone who sees you and loves you for who you are, not the image of you that they want to see. I painted Jennifer into your life and you went to her but you left your vision of your happiness and came back to me. Did we mess with the way things should have been? Do you regret that?"

Kiran placed the creased page down on the sheet beside Ashley. She heard Delilah's voice in the corridor outside the door and shoved the paper under the cloth and smoothed the sheet back over it.

The door opened and it was Jennifer who walked in first. Delilah and Ron followed with cups of coffee in their hands and looks of unease on their faces. Jennifer was wearing casual clothes and her blonde hair was damp and subdued.

Kiran smiled at Jennifer. It felt like pushing a mountain with her lips but the worry and exhaustion in Jennifer's eyes were a mirror of her own. Ashley had loved this woman. Might even still love her. There was no room for jealousy, only for discovering what would get Ashley well again.

Jennifer smiled back, the relief apparent in her eyes. Her eyes moved to Ashley and she asked, "We can come back later? I just needed to clean up a little before the next watch."

Kiran shook her head and walked towards the door. "No, I'm just leaving now." She controlled the shake in her voice and said to Ron as he sat down, "I have to call my father as well. Vijay and I have been looking through old material and I need to continue to find out as much as I can."

He nodded as he took Ashley's hand. "I will be back to the house shortly. We can search together. Delilah and Jennifer will be here with Ashley."

Delilah gave her a hug and took her seat and Kiran left the room trying to erase the image of Jennifer standing beside the bed, leaning forward to take Ashley's other hand.

CHAPTER TWENTY-FIVE

Kerala, 1966

Ji heard the sound of children's voices coming up the track. He squeezed Elizabeth's hand and got up from the table. The driver stirred but stayed sleeping with his back against the trunk of the coconut tree.

The little boy and girl coming up the track were accompanied by a woman carrying a bundle of wood. She acknowledged Ji with a bow of her head and smiled with curiosity at Elizabeth before dropping the bundle at the side of the house. The children stopped talking and stood by the table staring at Elizabeth. She lifted the girl onto her lap and smiled at the large brown eyes as they gazed in fascination at the blue-green of Elizabeth's eyes.

Ji felt a spark of what felt like recognition as he watched Elizabeth hold Shalini, and a thrum of fear. The driver got up and spoke in Malayalam, ushering Babu and Shalini into the house, the little girl reluctantly climbing off Elizabeth's lap. The smell of smoke and food being prepared filled the clearing.

Ji sat back down. "I will come to your country but first I need to talk to Manoj and make the necessary arrangements."

Elizabeth asked, her voice quiet, "If they let you stay, if they let you continue as a vision painter..?"

Ji felt the desperate hope rise within him. Would Manoj ever allow that?

He asked, "Will you come and stay with me here?"

Elizabeth's smile was shy. "Yes, Ji, I want to be with you wherever you are."

Ji said, "I will come for you, Elizabeth. Whatever happens here, I will come. I want to be married to you." She smiled wider as his cheeks darkened.

He felt his heart move again as he watched her smile. He knew his decision would devastate Manoj who had championed Ji over his own son but he also knew he could not live without Elizabeth. He would never be able to paint again anyway if she was not a part of his future. He had to let her go for now. He had to make an attempt to allow both sides of his nature to be expressed.

The family carried out food and proudly laid the simple fare on the table. Ji and Elizabeth ate the tasty food with difficulty both knowing they had to separate after the meal and not knowing when they would see each other again.

∞ ∞ ∞

Ji stood at the front door to the house, his former family home, now his new family home. It had torn him to say goodbye to Elizabeth. He held on to the thought that he would see her again, a thought he had felt lost without over the few days when his old life begged him to make a different decision.

There was no noise from inside the house. Dinesh's new son, Rishi, would not be brought back to the house until he had left his mother's breast. Ji went through the door, his heart heavy with the anticipation of disappointing the man he looked up to almost as much as he had looked up to his own father. He was closer to Manoj than he had been to his father. The time in training and discussion bonding them together in a way he had never had a chance to with his father.

Manoj was in his studio examining miniature pyramids of colour that dotted the landscape of the table. He glanced at Ji, took a pinch of ochre pigment and rubbed it between his thumb and finger.

"No matter how many times I tell them that I need it smoother, they still deliver the same texture. See." He pointed at the pile with his paint-stained finger.

Ji wandered over to the table and stuck his fingers in the ochre powder. He nodded and sat down on the bench beside the table.

"What do you think?" Manoj picked up a rag and wiped his fingers.

Ji said, "Yes"

"That was not a question that could be answered by Yes or No, so Yes does not answer it." He threw the rag towards Ji and it landed on the floor beside Ji.

"What is wrong? Ji? You normally get angry when they do not do it the way we want. That is something we have always had to work on with you. Patience."

Ji looked up from the piles of pigment, the colours hurting his eyes. He could feel his chest get tight and his breaths felt shallow. He took a deep breath, trying to get the air to reach his centre.

"Sir, I have something to tell you. You will not be happy, but I hope you will not be too angry to think about what I have to say."

Manoj sat down. He rubbed at the shine on top of his scalp and his eyes narrowed. "You always tell me what you think. We argue about issues but I have always listened to you with an open heart, Ji. I do not even listen to Dinesh like that. So speak freely."

"This is not about issues of vision painting. This is about a matter that will change everything, a matter that I hope you will be open to and consider deeply."

Manoj patted the table. "I said speak freely, Ji. I meant that you should tell me what this is about, not that you should use more words than necessary."

Ji said, "It is difficult."

"When has that ever stopped you before, my son?" He used the term Ji had become used to hearing from Manoj since he was 17 and his world had collapsed. Manoj had rebuilt a boy into a man, into a leader. Ji felt the burden of responsibility, the knowledge that he was about to cause the collapse of this man's world, the loss of a father replaced by the loss of a son.

Ji spoke carefully. "Sir, we have spoken many times about our profession, about our dreams and hopes for its development. You know I hoped to lead the Council and to make our plans into reality."

Manoj stole a look at the doorway. He got up and closed the door. "Dinesh does not know that. I do not wish to disappoint him. He would expect the leadership as he is my blood line. And he has produced a son first. It is true that I wish you to take on the leadership. I just have to find a way to tell him. Though he does not seem to care about the substantial issues like we do." He placed a hand on Ji's shoulder and sat down again. "So, tell me what is this matter that has you so troubled."

Ji bowed his head and sighed. He said quietly, "I am going to marry Elizabeth."

There was silence. Ji looked up. Manoj was staring at him as if he had just announced that the earth was flat. Ji waited. He could see the realisation dawn in Manoj's eyes.

Manoj said, "No. I told you not to go near that girl. I told you it was against the rules. You are a vision painter," he stood up and his chair fell over with a clatter, "the best vision painter we have seen. You are our future leader. I chose you over my blood son. You cannot do this. You will not throw everything away for a woman."

Manoj's knuckles were pale as he gripped the edge of the table. The gray hairs bunched and shook around his ears. His eyes were full of anger.

Ji said, "I love her. I cannot deny that anymore. Surely you will not deny my gift, my place here."

The shock in Manoj's voice was a knife into Ji's chest. "The son of my blood has just produced a son. And you are taking one away. This is not the way I saw. You are my chosen one." Manoj steadied himself against the table.

Ji held out his hand. He said, "It can still be the way you saw. Please do not do this."

Manoj pointed to the door. "Get out of my sight."

"Will you not listen to me?" Ji felt the panic rise through him.

"I cannot look at you. I cannot listen to you. Did *you* listen to me? All the years I worked with you, trained you, treated you better than my son. Did you talk to me before you decided to throw everything away? Before you threw us all away?"

Ji stood up. "Why must that be the only way? You are the leader of the Council. You could change the rules. The rules were made by men who lived a long time ago. They did not always choose the right way. We have spoken of this many times. You agree with me on this matter."

Manoj straightened up to his full height and Ji suddenly felt shorter though he had always been taller than his mentor.

Manoj pointed again to the door and turned away. He said, "Go."

Ji walked towards the door. He thought he heard words follow him out and they sounded like "my son" but the sound was muffled and he closed the door to the sight of his mentor burying his face in his hands.

CHAPTER TWENTY-SIX

The paint fell onto the canvas in brown and cream, plump folds of skin, tiny fingers and toes. A body enclosed in maternal love and care. The painter's strokes were hesitant and even the canvas rebelled against the picture being painted, the paint sliding over its bumps and sticking in protest on hairs that separated from the brush.

The painter slipped in a slick of paint on the floor, the involuntary movement of the brush creating a line cutting down across the brow of the mother looking on in fear. The painter's hand was stiff and the rag jerked over the vertical line, smoothing it out, leaving only the horizontal lines of worry. The rag was soaked in colours, absorbing the mistakes that marred this painting like no other before.

The painter laid the brush down and took a deep breath, stood in front of the canvas with closed eyes and dragged up memories. Painful, searing memories, until tears squeezed through eyelids and hands clenched in rage and fear and pain. Until those hands gripped the paintbrush like a weapon and the tiny body surfaced in the oily pools of paint on canvas, its silent weight dragging out a mother's flowing tears.

When the canvas was finally subdued by its unwelcome subject, the painter flung the brush onto the floor. The turpentine and paint followed, and the colours ran into the crevices in shadowed swirls of pigmented spirit.

CHAPTER TWENTY-SEVEN

"So the canvas is restricted in size as a way to contain the visions?" Ron asked.

They were sitting on the couches in Ron's living room. Vijay looked up from his notes, his eyes bloodshot and his jaws a deeper shade of black than Kiran was used to seeing on him. Kiran was reaching the edges of the cliff of exhaustion herself. She had stayed up the whole night reading her father's notes and journal, Vijay sitting beside her reading through the script while she continued her search. Ron had come back to the house in the morning and had slept but not for long.

Vijay looked worse than the two of them, his normally neat appearance crumpled. His voice was tired. "Yes. That was the purpose. To restrict the size of the painting and allow some structure and limit to the visions."

Kiran didn't say it in front of Vijay, but she had been grateful for that rule and others that restricted the materials. The rules meant she didn't have to think about the physical things around her. She could just focus on the words of the client's vision that needed to be expressed onto the canvas.

She asked, "I know vision painters are not allowed to influence the client with words or images or deeds, and I can understand why. Why would they only have one session for each visualisation?"

"That is a container as well. It restricts the spread of the vision. It focuses it by forcing the client to spend whatever time is needed to think deeply about what they want in that particular area. And when the painting is done, they must not come back with changes and new desires for that area as it will make the colours dirty." Vijay seemed to be struggling to find words to fit in with the translation.

Kiran said, "And they used the threat of the visualisation failing to stop the vision painter or the client breaking any of the rules."

Vijay snapped a look at her. "They believed that the visualisation could fail for many reasons and they tried to avoid those circumstances."

Kiran said, "The harshest rule, the one that leads to the immediate loss of the gift, is if a vision painter paints for another. I guess that makes sense. Though even therapists are allowed to have therapy themselves." She smiled. "I find it hard to believe that someone along the way did not see how to make money out of this. That rule about not accepting payment seems to have survived even in these greedy times."

Ron frowned. "I didn't think you were so cynical, Kiran. You always seem to think well of people."

Kiran sighed. "I do believe that thinking good things about people and expecting good from them brings the best out of them. I've just always had a hard time with the idea of the Council, with the organisation behind vision painting, with the rule of a bunch of old men."

Vijay said. "They do lead very comfortable lives, especially if they are powerful vision painters. They are highly respected and people are very grateful. What started as a way for the first Guru to avoid placing a burden on poor people has developed into a good system of remuneration for the vision painters."

Ron sat forward. "Are you saying that they are now getting paid despite the rules?"

Vijay wiggled his head and held up his hand. "No, no. I did not mean that. I mean that Guru knew that the people could not afford to pay him so he passed them off by saying they should paint their gratitude to him. What he actually said, according to the records and the closest translation, was 'Paint me into whatever you would like me to have.' I think he did not expect any payment and probably did not get any. But as time went on, the custom developed into the clients painting for the vision painter if they felt gratitude."

Kiran sat back and closed her eyes. She said slowly, "So, ordinary people have the ability to paint for vision painters." She opened her eyes and Vijay was nodding.

∞ ∞ ∞

"Why can't vision painters paint for their loved ones?" Kiran threw the question out in frustration. The clatter of her fork on the floor sounded loud in the kitchen.

It was getting dark outside and they had decided to try and eat before Kiran went to the hospital for the night. Vijay and Ron looked up from the plates on which they were pushing around their food.

Vijay put his cutlery down on the counter with what seemed like relief. He said, "From what I understand, the vision painter would be influenced to a great extent by their love or closeness to the subject."

Ron got up and collected the plates. He scraped the uneaten food into the bin. His movements were slow, his shoulders bowed in exhaustion. He said, "So they thought the painting would be more of what the painter wanted than the client?"

Vijay nodded. "Yes. When we love someone, when we know them well, we cannot help but want what we think is best for them. I assume the rules are there to stop the vision painter from controlling those they love."

Ron put the kettle on and Kiran could see him resting his weight on the counter as he stood by the kitchen sink. The late evening light through the window was weak but it showed the lines on Ron's face.

Kiran said, "I understand that they could influence the manifestation. But surely that could be incorporated into the training?"

Vijay said, "Remember that their families consisted of their son and the other vision painters. So, it makes sense that they were not allowed to paint for each other."

Ron said, "Could you imagine if they could? It would be chaos."

Kiran's voice grew stubborn. "It wouldn't be the same in this case. I know I love Ashley and she is my family but there could be no doubt that she should not be suffering in pain. Surely I should be able to take it for granted that she would want to be painted better?"

She looked at the two men who had gone quiet. "What?"

Vijay and Ron exchanged a look. Ron brought the cups of tea over and put them down on the counter. He said in a gentle voice, "Kiran, have you thought about what you said before? About how a vision painter could only have painted negatives that existed in the subject." He was picking his words with care but Kiran felt like blocking her ears. She nodded.

He continued, "So we do not know what Ashley would want -"

Kiran cut in, "She wouldn't want this! No matter what she did."

Ron was rubbing his silver hair. "I know that Ashley said she felt guilty about what she did to Jennifer. I know Jennifer has been more in her life since they started discussing Ashley working in Galway. I have been talking about Sarah a lot in the last while. I have been trying to understand what that experience could have done to Ashley. When you mentioned about the baby, I found myself examining so many things." He sat down on a stool. "I know now that Marge did so much damage to her and I was oblivious. I was in shock as well. I thought a mother would take care of her daughter. I did not know that she would blame Ashley. Or that even if she did in her own head, she wouldn't make it obvious to a nine year old child."

He put his face in his hands. "We went from a loving family unit to a group of damaged strangers. I let Marge send Ashley to boarding school." He looked up at Kiran and his face was tortured. "She must have felt like she was being punished. At the time when she needed me the most, when she needed our love and support, she was pushed away. What kind of a father does that?"

Kiran could not answer him. She was in the child, feeling the terror of abandonment, the fear, the guilt. She was in the lonely nights crying herself to sleep for the missing sister, the lost parents. She could feel the emotions creeping through her cells, the pain sizzling at her nerve endings. The darkness was falling outside and she felt it encroach, running cold hands over her skin. The kitchen was fading away into the darkness and she gripped the edge of the counter, her fingers reaching for solidity in the river in which she was drowning.

Kiran heard Vijay say to Ron, "You have been a great father. Ashley was loved and cared for by you. It is obvious to anyone to see that you love your child. There are many people that would consider Ashley to be so blessed."

She could hear the voices continue but could not make out what they were saying. Her body was immersed in the pain while her mind reeled as it was battered by the emotions that could be used against Ashley.

"Kiran!" She felt Ron's hands on her shoulders as she surfaced. The pain eased as oxygen returned to her cells, ejecting acid.

Ron turned her around and held her, standing beside her as she leaned off the stool. She could feel him trembling. His voice was shaky. "You went there, didn't you? Like you went into my pain before. You went into Ashley's visions." His voice caught in a sob. "And it was bad."

Kiran stayed silent. She could not add to the cycle of pain and guilt. She hugged Ron's thin frame and shook her head. She said, her voice muffled against his jacket, "Everything will be okay. She will be fine, Ron. I promised her and I will promise you. I will find a way." Her voice was weak and she sank back down on the stool as she said, "Sometimes we have to let go of someone to help them."

She could feel Ron's stillness for a few moments. He squeezed her gently before releasing her. He avoided her eyes but wiped at his as he went into his study.

Vijay got up and said, "I am going to continue reading. Thank you for the food." He left the room, closing the door behind him.

Kiran tried to stand. Her limbs felt heavy, like she had run a marathon at the pace of a sprint. She leaned against the hard edge of the counter and rested her hand on her belly. She had been feeling the growth of a life within her. Along with the nausea and a bone-aching tiredness that she could not seem to shake.

She was going to be a mother. Kiran wondered if she was strong enough, whether she had the courage to make the necessary sacrifices.

CHAPTER TWENTY-EIGHT

Kerala, 1969

The Ambassador made its way slowly through the throng of schoolchildren and pulled up in front of Ji's old house. Ji gripped Elizabeth's hand tighter. The plastic seating felt hot and sticky underneath their hands, and he could feel his palm stick to hers, the gold bands rubbing together. Ji had not thought two years in Ireland would make him find it so hard to cope with the heat and humidity of Kerala. He took out a white handkerchief from his pocket and wiped at his forehead.

"Nerves or humidity?" Elizabeth smiled as she asked but he could see the waves of tension in the blue-green sea of her eyes.

"I am not nervous. Everything has been settled with Manoj. His letter was clear. He wants me to return." Ji cleared his throat.

She squeezed his hand. "Go on in. I will be waiting with my grandparents. They are so happy that we could come back. They are eager to see me. I don't think Manoj wants to see me anyway."

Ji nodded. "That will change. It will be fine. He will get used to the idea and once he sees that being married will not affect my care for our profession, then he will return me to my rightful place." He had said the words many times in his head since receiving the reply from Manoj. A reply that had taken months but gave him permission to return. There were no specific details of what that return would mean. Ji had filled in the blanks.

Ji rested his hand on her shoulder before opening the door. He got out of the car and loosened the sticky clothes, the Western trousers and shirt, off his back and thighs. Should he change? The children stared at Elizabeth with wide eyes as they moved aside again for the car. They watched it around the curve to the house of Elizabeth's grandparents and turned to stare at Ji. He recognised most of the older ones and nodded at them. They smiled shyly and he could see them glancing back over their shoulders as they continued on their way home.

Ji looked at his old family home and tried to work out whether that was their new home. To work out whether he was supposed to move his wife into a house of vision painters, something that had never been an issue before, when the door opened.

"Brother? Ji, you are back?" Dinesh stood on the threshold. His round face was shocked and a little fearful.

Ji smiled. "Brother! Yes, I am, Dinesh." He held out his hand and Dinesh looked over his shoulder and pulled the door closed before taking the outstretched hand.

"Our father asked me to return." Ji pulled him in closer and ruffled the hairs that were already starting to recede off Dinesh's forehead. Ji smiled again at Dinesh's grimace. "It has only been two years. If you keep losing your hair, you will not have any left soon. You are not even thirty years old yet."

"Did father really tell you to come back?"

Ji released him. "Yes. I should go and see him. Where is he?"

Dinesh waggled his head towards the studio room and Ji looked in the direction to see Manoj turning away from the window. Ji smoothed down his shirt. He took a deep breath and walked to the front door. He had been invited back, he reminded himself, as he entered the coolness of his old home and felt the smell of paint and turpentine greet him.

∞ ∞ ∞

Manoj looked older. It had only been two years, but he looked tired and older than his 53 years. The remnants of his hair still clung to the sides of his scalp but they didn't overhang his ears anymore. But it was in his eyes that Ji saw the deepest changes. There was a sense of defeat, of having given up something precious.

As he faced his mentor and adopted father, Ji felt guilt drift and settle onto the layers of emotions floating through his body. He bowed his head and took the seat Manoj had left askew for him.

"Where is your wife?" Manoj sat in a chair by the window. He looked out onto the street in the direction of the church.

"Sir, she has gone to her grandparents' house." Ji tried not to stammer. He was a 28 year-old man with a gift and a wife. He just wanted to keep both.

Manoj smiled but it was a sad expression. "Mariamma will forgive me now maybe. She understood why it had to be the way it was, but I know that it broke her spirit again."

"Elizabeth found it difficult too. She feels at home here. They are the closest people to her parents." Ji cleared his throat. "As I found it difficult. I had to leave everything I knew and loved. And I could not express my gift."

Manoj said, "But that did not stop you."

Ji leaned forward in his chair. "Sir, I know I let you down. But have you ever felt so much love for someone that you cannot be who you are meant to be unless they are by your side?"

Manoj stared out of the window, his eyes focused on nothing. He shook his head and Ji did not know if it was a no or if it was a clearing of thoughts. Whichever it was, Manoj's voice was stronger as he turned back to the room.

"We have a situation, Ji. I asked you to come back because I am prepared to consider your return to our profession. This has never happened before so no one knows how to be with it. We vision painters deal with our lives by setting rules and living by them. We set punishments for breaking the rules. The biggest punishment is losing the gift, the entry to our profession. We punish our own for being capable of feeling, of loving, because for some reason we believe that this self-sacrifice is necessary to purify us, to allow us to be the channel for love in this world. So, if we do not allow love to dirty us, we might be cleaner channels for the love of other people. You and I know my views on this. I have always wondered how empty channels can be better for the world than channels filled with love that would flow out to other people." Manoj sighed and turned back to the window. "But I am just one man. I am not even a strong man like your father. We lost your father before he could change us, and I needed his strength, like I needed yours."

"I am here now. We can still do all the things we planned. I can still try and find the ancient scripts." Ji stood up.

Manoj shook his head. "We will do nothing, Ji. There are those in the Council who hate you. I have only been able to persuade them to have you return if you stay to yourself. You can paint and you can live with Elizabeth at her house, but you must not talk. You must not shake things up. You must be an ordinary man with an extraordinary gift. I can only support your return, I cannot support your future. When I retire, my son will take over the leadership. He believes in the past, in our history, in our rules. He has provided a son who will receive his gift. The cycle will continue as it has. I am sorry you are on the outside, but I have done the best I can and I am now almost on the outside too."

"But we could find out what is happening. We could stop the..."

Manoj's voice was sharp. "Ji, I have said all that I am going to say on this matter. You should think of yourself as supremely blessed that you can even return and paint. If you know what that required from me, you would remain silent and thank me with all your heart."

Ji stood silent. This was not what he had expected, but he knew it was more than he could have hoped for. He nodded.

Manoj turned back to the window. "Go to your in-laws. Mariamma was happier than I have ever seen her even just at the thought of Elizabeth coming back. I believe that she will be unable to hold in her joy now."

"They are good people. Elizabeth is a good person, Sir. She can only make me a better person and maybe a better vision painter."

"That may be, my...Ji. That may be. Maybe you will paint better visions for the people who come to you. But what about our hidden history that we wished to know? What about the good you and I could have done? The changes we could have brought in?" Manoj shook his head and his shoulders slumped. "No. I will not remain in the lost hopes. There may be more souls who will regret this but I must proceed under the direction of the Council. And I am a lesser man for that. Go on, leave now."

"You will never be a lesser man to me, Sir. Though I can see you do not consider me your son anymore, you will always be the best father a young man could have had." Ji's voice choked and he turned away and walked out of the room.

CHAPTER TWENTY-NINE

The hissing of the pump as it descended was a hypnotic backdrop to Kiran's thoughts. She sat in the chair beside Ashley's bed, her finger gently stroking the pale hand in hers. Her eyes were doing the same to Ashley's face. The features that were so familiar that Kiran didn't need to have her eyes open to see, but she kept her eyes open as she stored as much as she could. The hospital room was lit by a strip bulb; its sole window was a black eye to the outside world that slept through the pain.

Kiran gathered Ashley's hair until it lay red and tame across the pillow. She ran her finger down the line of Ashley's profile until its smooth path was disrupted by the bump of the tube coming out of her mouth.

Kiran thought of the people she had visited in hospital. Her mother lying peaceful in a paint induced sleep, Ashley in a pain induced coma. Tony and his tears glittering in the dim light of ICU. She felt the familiar guilt over Tony. She still had negative emotions washing through her after the events of the previous year.

But a vision painter could not paint for or against another vision painter. If they could not paint her positive emotions then they could not use her negative emotions against her.

So were the women she loved being targeted because of her? Kiran could not paint them better because they were family. She closed her eyes tight against the tears. She could not paint her mother better but she could do something about Ashley.

Her voice was low as she leaned over Ashley but it sounded loud and harsh in the hush of the room. "Ashley, there is something I need to tell you. I don't love you. In fact I'm not even gay. Not really. I am going to marry Rishi."

Kiran sat down heavily. She muttered, "This is stupid. She'll never believe that. No one would believe that."

"Damn right! That was the stupidest thing I've heard." Delilah's voice came from the doorway and Kiran looked up in fright.

Delilah walked in and closed the door behind her with a sharp push. She looked fresh for someone who had spent the last two nights in a hospital. She had a bag in her hand and she dropped it beside the bed. She was still glaring at Kiran.

"Well, I was just trying to find a way to tell her that I'm leaving." Kiran kept her voice low as she stared back at Delilah.

"You're not leaving. You love her. I haven't seen anyone more completely and utterly besotted over a woman than you are over Ashley. Don't forget, Kiran, I know you. You try and pretend that you are not that involved. You think if the world doesn't know how much you care for something, it can't take it away from you."

Kiran frowned. "That's not me. I care about people and they know I do."

"I watched you for years. You're a beautiful woman." Delilah pointed a finger at Kiran. "You have those features, that skin. Your eyes are a stunning surprise." Kiran looked down embarrassed. "And you have a sweet, funny personality. So why the hell weren't you with someone serious for so long?"

Kiran watched the shadow of the pump shorten and lengthen on the floor by her feet.

"I'll tell you why. You wouldn't give anyone a chance. Yeah, I know you went with women but did you actually give any of them a chance?" Delilah continued without letting Kiran answer. "No. You didn't. Because somewhere in there you can't seem to let yourself go. And now that you have. Now that you've found the woman you were waiting for, the woman who, by the way, even I can see fits you like a glove. And you've opened yourself up, what do you do? You shut it down again."

Kiran shook her head slowly, her eyes still fixed on the ground. "It is gone. I don't know what happened. Since I went to India to see my mother." She looked up, straight into Delilah's eyes. "And I'm not the one she loves anyway. She won't even notice I'm gone. Jennifer has been here the whole time, hasn't she?"

Delilah looked uncomfortable for a moment. "Jennifer is still in love with her. That does not mean anything, Kiran."

"Then isn't it better that I am not here? Ashley will be able to work through her guilt over Jennifer. She'll be able to sort out her feelings for Jennifer." Delilah looked uncertain. "Delilah, they were together for a long time. They were getting married. I know that Ashley was confused when she broke it off with Jennifer. She met me during a really tough time, her dead mother was back and pushing her. I mean how many people do you know that had to face that situation?"

Delilah snorted. "I don't know many people who had to face a person like a live Marge not to mention a dead one."

"So you agree?" Kiran slumped back on her chair.

Delilah sat on the edge of the bed, her short legs dangling. Kiran watched the swinging sandals seeing them blur through her tiredness and the tears in her eyes.

Delilah said, "I don't know what is going on here, Kiran. I can only go on what I have seen between the two of you and more recently, what I have seen of Jennifer."

Kiran shot her a look. "Not just in the last two days?"

Delilah shook her head. "No." She looked at Ashley. "They were at the castle with me for a coffee."

Kiran felt a jolt through her body. "When I was away in India?"

Delilah nodded. "They were just talking. About a job, I think."

Kiran looked down. "Ashley told me about the job. But she didn't tell me they'd met up or anything." She sighed. "It doesn't matter anyway, does it?"

Delilah said, "Yes it does! Why are you doing this, Kiran? I know you love her. I may be a bitter old woman but I recognise love when I see it. You know, the kind of love that feels so right. Not the twisted kind I had from Sam. Or the destructive love from Marge. You said it when you met Ashley, she feels like your complementary colour. I teased you about putting it like that but I envied that so much. You were so sure." Delilah's face was strained with the effort of keeping her voice low.

Kiran got up. She felt the blood draining downwards, its pull taking her energy with it. Her voice was steady. "I was wrong, wasn't I? It happens. Even vision painters get it wrong when it comes to themselves. And if I got it wrong about her being the one, I need to stop messing up Ashley's life."

Kiran didn't look at Ashley. She kept her eyes focused on Delilah. "I need you to tell her. When they wake her up. Ask them to try in a few days. When she wakes up without pain, tell her I had to go to India." Kiran looked away from Delilah and stared at the door. "Tell her the pregnancy wasn't real. It was a false positive. I did the test again and it was negative." She heard Delilah's gasp but ignored it. She needed to get out of the room. She spoke fast. "Tell her I am sorry that I had to leave without talking to her myself but that she will be better off without me. She's free to explore what she feels about Jennifer and she definitely needs to feel no guilt doing that."

Delilah stayed silent and Kiran said, "Will you remember all of that?"

Delilah nodded.

Kiran placed her hand on Delilah's shoulder. "Thank you. I'm not sure when I'll be back. Could you check in on my house for me?"

Delilah nodded and Kiran could see the glint of wetness on her face. Kiran walked to the door and opened it. There was a nurse passing with an IV tray in her hands. Kiran forced a smile at the startled nurse who hurried past. Kiran turned back with the smile still laid over her mouth. "I know two people whose colours flow together. They let their past and their fears keep them from each other. Even Marge wouldn't want them to be apart now." She turned quickly and walked out of the room before Delilah could answer.

∞ ∞ ∞

Kiran called Vijay as she drove out to Connemara. The sound of his voice echoed through her car as she drove through the boggy darkness.

"Did you find out anything more?" She had let the tears fall freely after she'd left the hospital but her throat was still tight from the effort of holding them in there.

Vijay said, "I took a break from the script. I had a pain in my eyes and my head and I could not see anything anymore. But I read your father's Malayalam notes, his journal."

"And? What did you find out?" Kiran controlled her impatience. She could hear the reluctance in his voice.

"There are events and practices that take place, took place, that you would not understand, Kiran. There are customs that have been passed down through the generations. It keeps the entire structure in place."

"What are you on about?" Kiran swerved to avoid the first of the sleeping sheep on the road. She slowed down.

"I am confused. I am not on anything."

"Vijay, please just tell me. I'm on my way to do something that I really wish with all my heart that I didn't have to do. Tell me something that will help me find this...this...I don't know, this crazy vision painting lunatic bastard, who can take such a beautiful gift and use it to cause such pain and suffering to two wonderful women. Tell me something please." Kiran slowed to a crawl. She was conscious of the car veering across the narrow road.

There was a long pause before Vijay answered. "Ji mentioned in his journal that he had been entered into the process that all vision painters follow."

There was silence and Kiran felt like beating her head against the sheep that stared at her car lights with frustrated eyes. "What process? The training?"

"No." More silence. She stopped the car and rested her head against the steering wheel, rocking it gently against the plastic.

"Vijay...?"

"The process of finding a suitable woman."

Kiran stopped rocking. She sat up straight.

"And did they find a suitable woman?"

"I think so. I think they chose one just before Ji met your mother. Ji wrote that Manoj, that is Dinesh's father, had chosen a girl from a neighbouring village."

Kiran sat in silence as she tried to get her mind round the coldness of the process.

Vijay said, "Ji was feeling very guilty because Manoj had announced to the girl's family and village that she had been selected. But Ji had met Elizabeth, your mother, and he left the village."

"So what happened to the girl? Did my father know? What would her family have done?"

Vijay paused again and Kiran could feel the tension in his voice when he spoke. "Ji wrote that she was sent to England. He thinks the family was furious. It is a great honour to be chosen, for the girl and for her family. It would have been so shameful to them when he ran off with another woman and married her. No one had ever done that in the history of the vision painters."

Kiran thought aloud. "So is it me or my father that is being targeted?"

Vijay answered, "Have you angered a vision painter here in Ireland?"

Kiran shook her head and then realised he couldn't see her.

She said, "No, there are no vision painters here." She had stopped herself from saying automatically 'I'm the only vision painter in Ireland'. *And no one in Kerala actually knows that.*

Kiran continued slowly, "So it must be my father, and that means it could be anyone there. He could have annoyed anyone. He can do that without even meaning to. Maybe something to do with that family? What did they use to select the girls? Would there have been any vision painters in their family line or something?"

Vijay sounded tired. "I do not know. I will read more tomorrow. Maybe the selection process or criteria will be present in the script."

Kiran nodded. "Get some sleep. I'll be there tomorrow evening. I have something to do at my house, and then I'm going to India."

She clicked off the connection as he mumbled a goodnight. She was exhausted but she had a job to do, a job she had earlier qualified herself to perform.

∞ ∞ ∞

The paintbrush fell to the floor and Kiran reached down and grabbed it with an angry motion. She straightened up and rubbed at her back and sighed as she realised that her white top now had a smudge of red across the back. She was shaking and nervous and this was not going to work if she did not calm down. She put the paintbrush down on the table and picked up the rag.

The hallway was dark and she didn't bother putting on the light. She went out to the porch and sat on the steps. In the darkness she heard the trees welcoming her back with excited rustling of their leaves. The stars packed the dense sky, their clustered whiteness overpowering the deep indigo canvas on which they lay.

She felt the cold on her face. It trickled with the sweat down her back. She did not know if this would work but she had to do it. She knew the hurt she was causing Ashley with her words, she knew she didn't believe her own words but she had to make them true to her. She sent a silent thanks wrapped in regret to whatever had sent Ashley into her life.

Kiran felt the cold curl its fingers around her heart and she let it in until her breath hung in her lungs refusing to swirl in foggy puffs around her mouth. The vision of her life without Ashley demanded entry into the vision Kiran was trying to create. A vision of Ashley happy and healthy with no pain. Kiran could not bear to include Jennifer in the vision. She had done that once before and it had stained her thoughts and her happiness since then. She shook her head and refocused on the picture of Ashley.

She could feel her heart thumping harder at the images. Ashley sitting at her desk writing, her glasses lost in the wilds of her soft hair. Ashley waking up in the morning, the shy look in her eyes. Ashley speaking in her gentle voice, words of love. Ashley smiling, her eyes shining with love. Kiran stopped the images abruptly. These visions wouldn't work. The love in Ashley's eyes was for Kiran. She needed a vision of Ashley happy, but without Kiran.

Kiran focused on Ashley standing in the house she would be living in with Ron. Smiling at something he had just said. Ashley walking down the wards talking to her patients in that gentle voice, the empathy that shone from her and surrounded the person with her. The strength in the gentleness that held her upright against the battering. The strength that would get her through.

Kiran let the visions play through her mind and her heart. When she was confident that the next image would not include her in it, when she felt she had excised herself from Ashley's future happiness at least in her own mind she opened her eyes. The dawn light felt harsh.

She got up stiffly and walked back into her studio. The paintbrush still lay on the table and her movements were slow as she soaked it in turpentine and wiped the hairs with the rag. The canvas was waiting. The paint felt like sludge as Kiran translated the vision into pigments on canvas. She kept the thought alive in her subconscious. A vision painter cannot paint for their family. But they can paint for everyone else.

The stranger on the canvas smiled in the dark as Kiran slumped onto the armchair. She let her heartbreak sink into the cushions as her heart switched off the lights and her mind slipped into a dreamless abyss.

CHAPTER THIRTY

Kerala, 1975

The baby's cry swept through the opening doors of the delivery room and was cut off as they swung back into place. The doctor's eyes were bloodshot and his white coat hung to one side, the pocket weighted down by his stethoscope. He hurried down the corridor to where Ji was standing. Ji's eyes were fixed in hope, his palms sweaty, his heart beating in slow waves of panic.

The doctor smiled, mistaking Ji's worry for that of any new father's concern. "Mr. Ji, Sir, you have a healthy baby."

And you don't know who I am. Ji asked, "Is he a boy or a girl?"

The doctor's smile faltered at Ji's impatience. "A beautiful baby girl." The smile fell away completely at the expression on Ji's face. "She is healthy and perfect."

Ji took in a deep breath and tried to calm the flames of panic. He had been so sure—too sure. He should have prepared for this, had a plan. But instead, his world was falling down around him, and he had no answer. He controlled his expression into a calmness he did not feel.

"How is my wife? How is Elizabeth?"

Ji could see the look of curiosity that the young doctor gave him before saying, "Your wife is fine. There were no complications. You can see them now." He started to turn away and paused. "You must be grateful. You are so blessed." He wandered off down the corridor and Ji could hear him mutter, "These people."

Ji felt like yelling after him that he had no problem with baby girls. He was an advanced thinker, unlike the people who surrounded him. He shook his head at the image of the Council, the twelve men lined up to judge his latest mistake. No, not Manoj, so eleven men. What would they say? Ji felt his heart start to race again. More importantly, what would they do? He walked towards the doors to the delivery room, his footsteps slowed by fear.

∞ ∞ ∞

The house was quiet and Ji rocked back and forth in the chair on the porch trying to keep the baby quiet too. He had her in the crook of his arm and she felt like a bag of rice. The warmth of her tiny body spreading further than the space she occupied.

He whispered in a singsong voice, "Kiran. My little kitten. Sleep for your father."

The moon was low in the sky and it sparkled in her eyes as she turned her face towards him. He smiled in awe. She had cat's eyes, the blue green darker than Elizabeth's shade of turquoise but just as beautiful.

He said, "If you sleep for me, I can get some sleep and I will not be tired for my painting tomorrow. Can you do that?"

The baby stared past his face. Her mouth opened.

"Ssh...ssh...I should not have brought you outside like this. Your mother is tired, your grandparents are tired. I think you have tired out the servants too."

Baby eyes moved back to his face. Nothing emerged from her open mouth which he knew was capable of a sound that would wake the whole household.

"You have spirit, my little kitten. Maybe we should call you little tiger." He moved his elbow up and down gently so that it seemed she was agreeing.

Ji smiled again and looked out at the street, the vague outline of houses, the church looming beside them, its stained glass windows throwing dark patterns in the weak moonlight.

"Did you get your spirit from your Irish side or from me? Your great-father and your grandfather were great leaders. On my side, of course. Your grandfather would have been a great leader too." He sighed. "Was that the end of our line? When your grandfather died, it all changed so much. Everything was in place for us before that."

He looked at the baby. She yawned. He put his finger against her plump cheek.

"Have some respect, little tiger. It is a great honour to be Leader of the Council. A great honour, indeed. When you lead men who have such a wondrous gift, then you can change the world for the better. But what am I now? I cannot change anything. The Council looks at me with scorn. They all do, because of you."

Ji picked up the little hand that was curled into a fist against his chest. He pried back the fingers. "They are mad, little tiger. How can they not see the beauty and wonder in these little fingers, and these little toes, and in the heart beating in your chest, and in your beautiful eyes. You are going to be trouble for me. I can see it. Just like your mother."

"And there I was thinking I was a wonderful addition to your life and that you loved me." Ji jumped in his chair and the baby screwed up her face and let out a scream. Elizabeth's voice was tired but there was a teasing note in it that turned into dismay at the noise.

"I was just calming her down and it worked. Now look at this." Ji clambered out of the chair and handed Kiran back to her mother.

Elizabeth held the crying baby close and swayed from side to side. She said, "What were you saying about the Council? Are they fine with us having a baby? You told me they were, Ji. Are they?"

Ji looked out at the road. "Everything is fine, Elizabeth. I was just telling Kiran about her great family line."

Ji put his arm around his wife's shoulder. He stared at the baby who was now snuggled and fast asleep against Elizabeth's chest. "That was fast. She sleeps immediately now while I was trying for half an hour."

"Maybe if you didn't talk so much about your Council?" Elizabeth smiled. "Actually, I'm surprised she didn't fall asleep for that." She laughed and Ji experienced the feeling he was finding familiar now, a surge of love tinged with fear.

He looked around at the leaning coconut trees and the slumbering village and tightened his arm around Elizabeth and his baby daughter. "Come inside, let us try and sleep while there is peace."

They walked into the house and Ji locked the door behind them.

∞ ∞ ∞

"How is he still here?" The voice buzzed through the meeting room and Manoj shook his head. Ji shifted uncomfortably in his seat at the back of the room.

Manoj said, "Ji is still a vision painter. And he is a very good one." He stared at the man who had spoken. "Better than you, do you not agree, Devdar?"

Devdar frowned and shook his head. His hair was a frizzy grey and his fingers on the table were shrivelled from the years of turpentine. There was a snicker from the man beside him and Devdar turned to glare at the other council member who stopped immediately and rubbed at a paint stain on the wooden table.

Devdar looked back at Manoj. "You have always treated Ji like he is the best. You treated him better than your own son." He smirked. "Until Ji disgraced himself and you." His grin got wider and even from the other side of the room Ji could see the yellow stains on the few remaining teeth in Devdar's mouth. "And not just once by marrying that, that Anglo, but now he has produced a *girl* child."

The disgust in Devdar's voice and the nodding heads around the table filled Ji with a mixture of fear and anger.

Manoj smacked his hand down on the table and the nodding stopped. "We agreed that Ji would come back and practise as an ordinary member of our profession. I promised in return that we would not consider the changes I requested, that I have spent many years trying to persuade the Council are necessary. But can we at least behave with some degree of civilization?"

The old men around the table looked like guilty children and none of them would meet Manoj's eye. Only Devdar was looking up. He was staring at Ji and his eyes were full of anger and hatred.

He turned to Manoj and said, "We do not want to hear any more of your proposals, Manoj. You are still the leader of the Council and you will be there after we have passed. We are happy that your son will take over then. Dinesh understands our history. He is a diplomatic young man. He will make a great Council Leader." Devdar's grin was back and he glanced around the table before leaning forward and saying in a loud whisper, "Don't you agree, Manoj? That your real son will be worthy of the role?"

Manoj looked straight ahead, his eyes fixed on the shelves of equipment that lined the room in his house that they were using as a meeting place.

"Dinesh will be a worthy leader. Now, can we please get back to the reason we are here." He turned to nod at Ji. "We have to agree as to whether Ji can continue as a vision painter now that he has failed to produce a male child."

Devdar leaned forward again. "Do you not mean, now that he has produced a girl child?"

Manoj shook his head. "No. We have had to face some unpleasant duties in our time. Times have changed, we must move with the times. We are painting the visions of people who live in these times and so we must at least try to understand them. That is one of the secrets of our skill."

Ji looked around at the eyes of the men sitting around the table, all older than him and older than Manoj. The anger was obvious in the eyes of a few of the men and Manoj continued quickly, "Would you lose a man with such a gift? He has brought happiness to so many people with his painting. Would you want to deprive your people of that? The child is not important. Like her mother, she will exist in the village and be a part of the community. She will not encroach on our profession or our lives in any way." He looked across the room and Ji felt the warning in Manoj's eyes.

Ji had a sinking feeling as he thought of the stubborn yell of his new daughter, but he nodded vigorously at Manoj and the rest of the Council who had all turned to stare at him.

Devdar snorted. "How many more rules will you try and break for him? You know what should have been done when he first broke the rules. But you persuaded the others. Against my counsel, you allowed him to set foot in the village again. Even to paint. Now he has shown us all what he is. An ordinary man. Not a vision painter. Why would you have us break the rules again? What does this..." Devdar's lips were drawn back in a snarl, "this 'man' have to do before you will agree to banish him like he should have been."

Devdar looked across the room and Ji could feel the waves of hatred flow towards him. He wondered how such a man could paint the positive visions of his clients without that negative energy in him seeping onto the canvas.

Devdar said, still staring at Ji, "Send him out of the room please. Let us talk amongst ourselves. His presence is making my skin itch." He scratched at his arms to emphasise the point.

There was a general murmur of assent around the table. Manoj sat back and sighed heavily. He did not look in Ji's direction but gestured at Ji and pointed at the door. Ji felt the fear weaken his legs as he stood up.

As he opened the door, he heard Devdar's sly voice. "He even had the woman we picked for him. Was that not enough? Our pure Indian girls were not good enough for the great vision painter after he tried one, he had to go with an impure mongrel."

Ji clenched his fist on the handle of the door as he felt a wave of fury sweep through him. He felt the handle cut into his palm and he struggled not to turn around. He was not sure if he would be able to kill Devdar with his bare hands for saying that about Elizabeth but if he let go of the handle they might all know the answer.

Manoj's voice was sharp. "Devdar, do not speak of anyone like that! Ji, leave now."

Ji rested his head against the door. He took in a deep breath and straightened up before opening the door and walking out. He closed the door to the sound of Manoj's voice. He had to leave his future in the hands of these old men. He knew what they were capable of doing. All he could do was hope that Manoj's power as Council Leader, despite being weakened by Ji's first mistake, would prevail. As he left the building his rage at Devdar's words was followed by guilt. The debris of his past was never far behind him.

CHAPTER THIRTY-ONE

Kiran threw the paper down on the coffee table and jumped up from the armchair. Vijay's hand jerked in surprise and he muttered under his breath as his coffee swirled in the cup but did not overflow onto the copies of the script he was studying.

"What have you read?" His voice was sharp.

"My father...my father wrote in there that Devdar said he was with that woman." Kiran pointed at the paper she had been reading. She grabbed the offending sheet and it wavered in her hand.

"What woman? What are you talking about?"

Kiran waved the paper in front of his eyes. "The woman that was picked for him. Before he met my mother, he must have been with this woman."

Vijay reached for her hand and stilled its waving. He took the sheet and read the handwritten words. He frowned. "I knew they had picked a girl but I did not realise that the process had gone so far. It is no shock then that she fled to England, if she did."

Kiran was looking at him with wide eyes. She could feel the adrenaline coursing through her and jolting at her heart. Her voice shook. "Do you know what this means?"

"Well, I do not know if it means anything. Perhaps it means something."

"What?" Kiran steadied herself against the low table.

Vijay shifted uncomfortable in the chair. "I mean, yes, they seem to have had relations, your father and this girl, but that does not mean anything resulted from that. But on the other hand, it is a possibility."

Kiran stared at him, opened her mouth and closed it.

After a few moments she said, "Let us consider the facts. There is a lunatic vision painter with a gift strong enough to paint my mother and my Ashley into sickness. We worked out that it is unlikely that I am being targeted as I am not really in much contact with vision painters, and besides that, why did the lunatic not paint me?" She quirked her head at Vijay but didn't wait for an answer. "So, it has to be someone targeting my father who for some reason thinks that getting to me through Ashley will affect my father in some way." She paused as her theory started to unravel. "Well, the lunatic is attacking my father through me as well as through my mother. And then we discover that my father might have produced a child with some girl who either ran from the village or was smuggled away to England. And you think there is not a strong possibility that all of this could be related. And that the lunatic is my father's son."

Vijay looked at her with an expression that conveyed an uncertainty regarding her sanity. He said, "You have a vivid imagination. And you jump to conclusions based on that imagination rather than on facts."

"You already admitted you thought it was possible my father might have had a child."

"Yes. It is possible. But from that you extrapolate to this? You don't even know if it was a boy?"

Kiran said, "Well, if he can do vision painting, it must be a boy, right?"

Vijay nodded. "Yes, according to the script, only males can be vision painters."

"You didn't find anything in there that mentioned why they think that?"

Vijay shook his head.

"Right, so what if my father had a male child and the boy had a gift that was as strong or stronger even than my father's very strong gift? This boy might be very angry with my father. He would have every reason to hate him."

Vijay said slowly, "Have you considered that the vision painter might be angry with you as well? And that is why he went after your Ashley?"

"But I haven't done anything to anyone." Kiran sat down and put her head in her hands. "Not that I can think of anyway." *Except reject Rishi and get him beaten up.* She looked up suddenly and said, "The girl moved to England, didn't she?"

"Yes. London, I think. But that was a long time ago. She could have moved anywhere."

"So how do we find out more about her? About where she went?"

Vijay sat back in the armchair and covered his eyes with his hands. He rubbed at them and when he opened them again the redness was more pronounced in the whites of his eyes.

"Do you know anyone in Kerala who might know? Could you call someone?" Kiran jumped up from her chair and the papers slid off the table in the gust of movement.

Vijay sighed and leaned forward to gather the stray papers off the ground. He put them carefully back on the table.

"I might be able to ask around." He sat back again and closed his eyes.

Kiran felt like shaking him but she could see the exhaustion in his body. Neither of them had been able to get much sleep over the past few days.

Vijay opened his eyes again and seeing her still staring at him with a question in her eyes, he said, "Now?"

"Yes. Please. Now." Kiran said as she picked up her father's journal. "I need to go to India as soon as I can. If I have to stop off in England and find this woman, I will." She had no idea what she would do if she found the woman but she didn't wait for that question from Vijay.

Vijay said, "It was a long time ago. Some of her family might still be in the next village. But a lot of people from the villages moved to the Middle East or the U.S. This is going to be very hard, Kiran. I am not from the area and my knowledge is just from what Dinesh has spoken about."

"Is there any hint in the papers about where the girl was from? You said the neighbouring village."

Vijay nodded. "We have the name of the village and the family name."

"Do you know anyone who knows the family?" Kiran continued when Vijay shook his head, "Do you know anyone in Dad's village who is not a vision painter?"

Vijay said, "No." He screwed up his eyes. "Well. Maybe. I know the teacher at the primary school there. I met him when all the schoolteachers went on strike a few months ago."

"Can you call him? See if he or anyone he knows can tell you anything about that family."

Kiran got up as Vijay nodded. She said, "I need to go and pack and I want to read more."

She hurried upstairs with her father's papers.

CHAPTER THIRTY-TWO

Kerala, 1980

Ji examined the area of the canvas where the client's head overlapped the hospital building. He focused on the line of hair making sure the oil blend did not have concrete buildings seeping into human hair.

His eyes felt tired and he sighed, feeling sorry for himself. Other vision painters had the support of their colleagues. Other vision painters did not have to stay up all night with an inquisitive five year old girl. Other vision painters could sleep well the night before a painting and could spend the morning absorbing the vision into themselves. Other vision painters could—

Ji felt a tug on his *mundu* and looked down along the slope of the canvas into the wide blue-green river of expression that was his daughter's eyes. He sighed again. He could not even complain to himself about his complaints.

"Yes, little tiger? I know I told you to always come to me about anything but you know your father is not to be disturbed when he is working."

The river turned even more fluid and he shook his head. It was no use, why fight it?

He put his brush down on the easel and reached down to pick Kiran up. She smiled as her face reached his shoulder. He squeezed her to him, feeling the little body wriggle as she got ready to question him from her new height. He sneezed as the talcum powder Elizabeth had patted onto the child after her shower entered his nostrils.

"Why is the man wearing white?" She pointed a finger at the canvas.

"It is a white coat, Kiran. His vision is to be the best doctor in Kerala."

"What is that behind the man?"

"The best hospital in Kerala. If he is going to be the best doctor in Kerala, surely I must put him in the best hospital in Kerala?" He tilted his head to look at her and his beard grazed her cheek.

Her fingers rubbed at her cheek and she nodded with all the seriousness she could muster. "Good plan, Appa."

He hid his smile behind her hair.

"Why did you use the Burnt Umber for his skin? He looks sick? Is he going in the hospital too?"

Ji smile faded away as he stared at the painting.

"The Burnt Sienna is better for him. The man who was here yesterday with you."

Ji's eyes fixed on the client's face and now he could see nothing but the subtle shading. He lowered Kiran to the floor and she wandered towards the shelf on which the tubes of paint were placed. Ji glanced at the open door as Kiran pulled up his chair and climbed on it to be able to see the paint. She touched the tubes, running her palm across each one.

Ji closed and locked the door to his studio. He walked over to the window and pulled down the bamboo blinds.

Kiran chose the colour she wanted and clambered off the chair. She was wearing a simple cotton dress and Ji groaned as he saw she had already got a smear of blue on its cream blankness. He glanced guiltily at the door again. The paint stain would probably be the least of Elizabeth's accusations if she found Kiran in the studio painting with her father.

Ji checked the chair and found the offending drop of paint and wiped it off with a rag. He moved the chair, its back facing the front of the canvas and to one side, and lifted Kiran onto it. He took the tube from her and squeezed the Burnt Sienna onto the canvas. He mixed it and worked the new colour carefully over the features of the client. Even as he blended the oily pigment into the forehead he could see she was right.

Kiran nodded.

"Why do you paint people?" Her elbows rested on the back of the chair and she had her chin in her hands as she watched his every move.

He didn't look away from the canvas. "Because I want to bring them happiness."

"How do you bring them happiness?"

"I have a gift, my little kitten, which enables me to paint happiness for people. If they ask me in the right way."

"What is the right way?"

"They have one visit with me in which they tell me what will make them happy. They should think about it before they come here otherwise they waste their time and mine."

"How do they know what to ask for?"

Ji turned away from the stretched skin around the mouth of his client. He looked at his daughter, at the shine in her eyes, the contentment in her face.

He pursed his lips. "Sometimes people forget what it is that will make them happy. They listen to everyone around them, to the multitude of voices that carry in the wind and blow worry into their souls. They do not listen to the voice that is in them, that rises from the earth in through their feet and rises through their heart and will emerge from their mouths if they only let it out. If they can be quiet, if they can shut out every other voice and listen to this true voice, then they will know what to ask me to paint. Then I take their words and I do the same but I connect with my feet in the earth and my eyes to the stars above as well and I let my heart become the meeting place from which my hands draw their vision." He placed his hand on his chest.

Kiran's eyes had become dark pools of serious thought. "What if their feet are in the air? Like when I lie on my back on the tree and put my feet in the air? Can the voice rise from the earth into me?"

Ji smiled. "Yes. When you need to hear it, you will not be lying in trees with your feet in the air. You are full of happiness now, are you not?" Kiran nodded vigorously. "So do you need to fill up from the earth? Are you not able at any time to walk with your feet on the ground when you want?"

Kiran nodded again, her hair hitting off her shoulders in black waves. Ji tucked a lock of hair behind Kiran's ear and grimaced as he realised she now had a smear of paint on her hair and ear. At least it was skin coloured, though darker than her creamy skin tone.

He wiped the paint away gently. "People when they grow older, they forget how to be filled with happiness. And they listen to everyone else tell them how to fill up again. Until they are filled up with things that will make everyone else happy. And that can never make them filled with the same pure happiness that they had, like you have." He smiled at Kiran's worried face. "When they come to me, I am a way to make them stop and put their feet back on the ground because they know I don't like my time to be wasted. They know they have to think and listen to that true voice and when they hear it, they tell me and I use my gift to paint their vision. If they have listened to the true voice their vision will be pure and true for them and their lives will follow that true path. Do you understand?"

Kiran nodded but he could see another question forming. He checked the grandfather clock and realised with a start that the afternoon had slipped past and he would be in serious trouble with her mother.

He pinched her cheeks and kissed her forehead. He unlocked the door and opened it a little, peering through the narrow opening to scan the hallway. There was no one in sight though he could hear the bustle from the kitchen. He turned back to his daughter. "Go, little tiger. Before your mother finds you here. I will find it hard to find my happiness if she catches you here." He held his fingers to his lips. "So do not tell her."

Kiran climbed off the chair and put her finger to her lips too. "I will tell her I was climbing trees of happiness with you."

Ji smiled. "Yes, we were."

Ji felt his heart fill with happiness as he watched her wander towards the kitchen. He sighed a moment later as he noticed the stain on her dress and remembered the streaks on her face. Maybe Elizabeth would believe that the trees of happiness they were climbing had trunks of blue and dark-brown.

∞ ∞ ∞

Elizabeth looked up and smiled as her daughter wandered into the kitchen. The little girl looked so pretty in the dress that Elizabeth had made for her, trying out her newly acquired skills.

Shalini was fussing over the basket of dirty clothes. She looked at Kiran and let out a little scream followed by a string of words in Malayalam. Elizabeth shook her head at the highly-strung girl. She could not understand the outburst but it was obviously about the dress which Shalini was now tutting over.

"Shalini! What is it?" Elizabeth asked in Malayalam. She knew it sounded strange in an Irish accent but she was getting a lot better after five years in Kerala.

Kiran looked guilty, an expression Elizabeth was becoming as used to as the sweet smile she preferred seeing.

Shalini pointed to the smear off blue that marred the cream of the dress.

Kiran said, "I climbed a tree." She swallowed back some words and Elizabeth eyed her suspiciously.

"A blue tree?"

Kiran nodded.

Elizabeth got up from the table and marched Kiran over to the window. The sunlight showed up the stain in even clearer detail. As well as a dark patch of brown on Kiran's face that had remained after an obvious attempt to wipe it away. Elizabeth wiped at it and rubbed the trace of oil between her fingers. She gestured at Shalini to get some clean clothes for Kiran.

When Shalini had left the room, Elizabeth asked, "Were you in your father's studio?"

Kiran nodded. She looked down at her feet.

Elizabeth sighed. She went through the motions anyway.

"Kiran, you are not allowed in there. Your father is working and he is not to be disturbed. He will get into trouble if he lets you stay there with him. Do you understand?"

"But I was helping him."

"Are you listening to me at all? Your father cannot say no to you. But there will be trouble if anyone finds out you were there."

Kiran looked up at her mother. "I want to be a painter when I grow up. I want to paint the happiness for people."

Elizabeth knelt down and put her finger on Kiran's mouth. "Hush, now. You cannot be saying things like that to anyone. Promise me. You won't say that to anyone in the village."

Elizabeth cursed inside at the Council as she saw confusion and hurt cloud her daughter's eyes. She took her finger away from Kiran's mouth and ruffled the black mop of hair. "Kiran, you can be anything you want to be. I promise you. Do you believe your mother?"

Kiran nodded and Elizabeth smiled at the look of hope that came over her daughter's face.

"So will you promise me not to say anything to anyone or in front of anyone about wanting to paint? Or about being in the studio with your father?"

Kiran said, "I promise." She looked around at the hallway behind her and back at her mother and leaned in to whisper into her ear, "Can I say it to you?"

Elizabeth hugged her. "Of course, my little kitten." She turned her around and starting unbuttoning the long line of buttons that ran down the back of the dress. "I guess I should be grateful you managed to wear this for even one morning."

∞ ∞ ∞

Elizabeth placed the bowl in front of her husband with a firmer clink than usual and the cloudy liquid spilt over the edge and onto the table. Ji looked up quickly at her face, but she turned and walked back to the stove without meeting his eyes. She ladled *kanyi* into another bowl and walked back to the table careful not to let the hot rice water spill as she placed it in front of Dinesh. He was grinning at Ji.

Elizabeth snapped at him, "I don't know what you are smiling at. When I get my hands on your Rishi, I will have a few questions for him."

Dinesh stopped grinning. He lowered his eyes to the *kanyi* and slid a look towards the window of the dining room.

Elizabeth filled her bowl and sat down at the table. The clink of spoons was the only conversation as they ate.

Dinesh said, "I think that Rishi was not the one who made the construction."

"How do you know that? Kiran is only five years old. She couldn't have managed to build that 'thing' by herself." Elizabeth's face screwed up as she said the words.

Ji said, "She just likes to build things, Amma. You know that."

"Like father, like daughter. You always stick up for her. Do you know what a fright it gave me? You saw it, what did it look like to you?"

Ji played with his spoon. "It is just unfortunate that the cardboard box had that shape. Our daughter did not intend to build a moving coffin." He couldn't help a proud smile. "But it really was good, was it not? To take the roller skates and fix them to the box like that. The kids will be able to play for hours with it on the street."

Elizabeth got up and cleared his bowl before he had finished. He waved his spoon feebly at her but she ignored him. "If you think our daughter or any of the children in this village are going to ride down the streets of the village in a moving coffin then you are crazier than your daughter." She turned to Dinesh. "And you can stop laughing as well. I am going now to find that boy of yours and give him a talk."

She stormed out of the kitchen and they heard the loud exclamation and a clatter before her voice filtered back into the kitchen. "Ji, I thought I told you to burn this 'thing'". They heard the sound of dragging and muttering and the back door opening and slamming.

"She has learnt most of our customs well, Ji." Dinesh spooned some kanyi into his mouth.

Ji nodded. He was still hungry and was about to get up and help himself from the pot on the stove when he noticed the look of discomfort in Dinesh's eyes.

"What is it, Dinesh?"

Dinesh cleared his throat. "Ji, you know I love Elizabeth and Kiran like my own family."

Ji nodded. "Like I care for Rishi. We are all family."

Dinesh waggled his head. "Yes, but Rishi is a boy. And I am still a proper vision painter. And one day I will take over from my father as Leader of the Council."

Ji suppressed the urge to argue. He had made the choices that led to this. He had to live with the consequences, as galling as they were.

Dinesh continued, "There has been talk on the Council."

Ji said, "Devdar?"

Dinesh nodded. "He is saying things, Ji."

"What kind of things?" Ji jumped up. "That man should not even be a vision painter yet he is on the Council. He has not got the right spirit for our profession."

Dinesh waggled his head again. "You are always saying things like that yet you are the one who continues to break our rules."

Ji sat back down. "What is that man grumbling about now?"

Dinesh frowned. "I don't know. I just know that there has been a lot of murmuring and he starts it every time."

"And it is about Kiran?"

Dinesh nodded miserably.

Ji jumped up again. He walked over to the window and looked out on the street. A bullock passed, its muscles rolling as it pulled the cart of bananas, the layers of yellow wormlike bodies crowding on to the simple platform.

He heard Dinesh put down the spoon and get up from the table. "Ji, there is only so much my father can do and that I will be able to do when I am leader. I do not share your views, you know that."

Ji smiled bitterly at the glass. "*Your* father would have been able to do something if I had not married Elizabeth. He would have changed things with my support." He turned around to face Dinesh. "What if it was Rishi? Would you do it for him?"

Dinesh shook his head. "But it is not Rishi. Kiran is not one of us. Elizabeth is not one of us. You have made your choices, Ji."

"Kiran could be a great vision painter." The words burst out from Ji's mouth before he had time to consider them. They bounced off the shock on Dinesh's face and fell on the ground between the two men.

"Brother...Ji! You must not mention her name in such a way. What are you trying to do?" Dinesh hurried over to the door and closed it. The sunlight through the window glistened on his forehead.

Ji drew himself up to his full height but his heart was jolting as he spoke. "She is my daughter. She could have my gift, maybe even—"

Dinesh held up his hand. The dust in the air between the two men shifted and Ji realised this was the first time in their lives that Dinesh had stopped him speaking.

Dinesh's voice was firm. "Enough. There is only so much I can do. If you insist on speaking in this way, I will not even be able to do that."

Dinesh opened the door and walked out before Ji could find his voice.

CHAPTER THIRTY-THREE

She'd heard Vijay on the phone to India, phone call after phone call. He'd spoken quietly but urgently to what seemed like an army of people, writing down little pieces of information, mostly names. Ron and Kiran paced. She'd packed her suitcase. Ron seemed sad but resigned as though he understood.

When Vijay had finally given up, she'd said nothing, just leaned across and given him a hug. His body had stiffened in surprise, in awkwardness, but he had smiled back when she smiled at him.

She had booked the tickets for the next day to leave from Shannon on Monday afternoon and be in Cochin on Tuesday afternoon. With almost seven hours in Heathrow in between. She needed to use them.

She called her father from her car on the drive down to Shannon. The phone was picked up after the third ring but the silence reverberated through the car.

"Dad?"

"Yes."

"How's Amma?"

"She is the same, Kiran."

She came to a traffic light and stopped.

"Dad, I'm on my way. Can you send Babu to the airport for me tomorrow?" She reached for the ticket printout on the seat beside her and gave him the arrival time at Cochin.

"I will send him."

"Dad, it will be ok." The words sounded as hollow as the silence after.

Kiran waited but he didn't say anything. The traffic moved off again. She took in a deep breath. She didn't know what Rishi had said to Dinesh or her father.

"Dad, do you know Rishi's address in London?"

"Of course I know it. Is Dinesh not my brother? Would I not know where his son lives? Rishi has invited me many times but I am a busy man here."

"By any chance then do you know where Rishi's mother lives?"

He didn't reply.

"Dad?"

"I'm thinking. Why do you want to know anyway? We don't need her permission for anything. If you are interested in Rishi, I will take care of everything with Dinesh. Why do you want that woman's address?"

So Rishi had not gone ahead with his threat to tell her father his version of events.

"I just want to get to know more about him. Please, Dad, can you find it. I'm on the road, on my way to the airport. I have a few hours in Heathrow. Ashley has been sick. Someone did a painting of her too. I left her so that I could paint her better. Please don't be happy about that." Her voice caught in a sob.

There was a long pause on the line before his voice softened as he said, "I will never be happy about your unhappiness, my little tiger. But of course I would be happier if you were not with..." his voice dropped to a whisper, "a woman." His voice rose to a normal level again. "What did you say? Did you say someone did a painting of her?"

He listened without interrupting as she explained what had happened.

His voice was quiet and defeated. "This is all wrong. This is all wrong. This gift cannot be used in this way. This painter cannot do this. I do not understand any of this. And we cannot retaliate or manipulate our gift. We cannot defend ourselves."

Kiran said, "I can't sit back and do nothing. Somebody is doing this to our families. You may be tied down by your rules and Council, but I can't stand by and let this happen. Surely you can see that? We need to at least try and protect them." She realised the car had speeded up over the motorway speed limit and she slowed down.

"Kiran, be careful. When you come here, don't say anything to anyone. We will talk."

She nodded in the empty car. "Do you have the address?"

"I will get it and ring you back in a few minutes."

∞ ∞ ∞

This was her second time in Heathrow within a few weeks but this time she was going into the city. Kiran tugged the suitcase off the conveyor and dragged it and herself towards the exit. She had an address and a name. That was all she had.

The taxi driver barely looked at her when she read out the address to him and she was content to sit in silence for the journey into London. Though she'd never thought she would miss the rambling questions of an Irish taxi driver. There was too much silence for thoughts, for doubt and fears to come whispering their words into her tired mind.

Her eyes took in the motorway, the buildings, the traffic, but her mind was in the hospital room where Ashley would be waking up. Those beautiful eyes opening and searching for Kiran. There would be pain to follow when Delilah repeated what Kiran had asked her to say and showed Ashley the painting Kiran had left with Ron. But there might be no physical pain for Ashley. And the chance of that was enough for Kiran. She closed her eyes and the movement of the taxi lulled her to sleep.

When she opened her eyes again the taxi was turning into a street lined by houses. The taxi pulled up in front of a detached house and the driver gestured to it before checking the meter. Kiran paid with the Sterling notes she had thought to bring.

The house looked expensive. All the houses on the street looked well cared for, lawns tended, patios and conservatories neat, driveways covered with decent cars. Kiran walked towards the front door, her suitcase wheels bumping noisily across the paving stones. She had no idea what she was going to say but she rang the doorbell and waited.

The door opened after a few minutes. The Indian-looking woman was wearing slacks and a blouse and an expression of enquiry on her face that got more pronounced when she noticed the suitcase.

Kiran said, "I'm sorry to trouble you and just land here unannounced but I'm looking for Rishi." She tried not to fidget with the handle of her suitcase as the woman frowned.

"Rishi? Are you a friend of his?" Her accent was strongly Malayalee.

"Yes. I'm on my way to India and had some time to spend in London so I thought I would look him up." She could see the woman start to relax. "I live in Ireland. He visited us there. I lost his address but he had given me yours."

"Ireland, you say?" The woman looked vaguely uninterested.

"Yes, have you been there?"

The woman shook her head.

"If you visit, you must come to Connemara. I live there. We Malayalees should stick together, as my father always says." Kiran knew she didn't look in the slightest bit dangerous but she was a total stranger. She shifted her weight onto the suitcase and tried out the most innocent look she could muster.

The woman smiled for the first time. "Thank you. Would you like to come in? I don't know if Rishi is back from his trip to India yet. How long before your flight?"

"I have a few hours. Thank you so much." Kiran picked up the suitcase and moved towards the door before the woman could change her mind.

∞ ∞ ∞

The woman's name was Seeta. She made them each a cup of tea and sat Kiran in the formal living room with floral couches and an ornate brass mirror above the mantelpiece. There were no photos in the room, just framed posters of the English countryside. The house had an air of loneliness despite its comfort.

Seeta sat on the edge of the armchair and sipped at her tea, the brown skin of her hands wrinkling as she wrapped it around the china cup. She was not what Kiran had expected. She did not look like she had challenged anyone in her life.

Kiran said, looking around, "You have a lovely house. Did Rishi grow up here? He said you moved here in 1980, the same year my family moved to Ireland."

There was a slight frown on Seeta's forehead. "Yes, we moved to London that year. What was your father's name?" She put the cup down on the glass topped coffee table and winced at the click it made.

"Ji." Kiran watched Seeta's eyes and she saw the recognition as she said the name, and something else—fear.

Seeta's voice sounded like she was deliberately keeping it steady. "Ji, the vision painter? And Elizabeth."

Kiran said, "You knew my parents? Maybe we had met too." She kept her voice light.

Seeta shook her head. "I never met them."

"But you knew of them? My father was probably well known in the area, and my mother was half-Irish." Kiran smiled, trying to keep the desperation from her voice and eyes.

She must have succeeded because Seeta relaxed slightly as she nodded. "Yes, your father was well-known. He went against the vision painters and married the woman he loved, even though she was Anglo." There was a strain of envy in her voice.

"My mother, Elizabeth, she is sick at the moment. That is why I am going to Kerala now." The worry spilled from her and she closed her eyes trying to get back into control. When she opened them again, Seeta was looking at her with concern.

"Is it serious?"

Kiran nodded. Her throat was tight and she couldn't find the words she needed, the questions to ask. She decided to trust her instincts.

"I am trying to help my mother get better. But I need help to do that. I need some information." The desperation was now obvious and she could see the fear come back into Seeta's eyes.

Seeta started to get up and Kiran said quickly, "Please, I have to help her. She has done nothing wrong. I'm just asking you to talk to me. You don't have to do anything. Just talk to me about the past. If she dies, could you live with that?"

Seeta sat back down. She stared at Kiran for a few minutes, her eyes assessing. "Are you even a friend of Rishi's?"

Kiran said, "I used to be. A long time ago. We played together. Time has changed many things. We are not who we were."

Seeta smiled sadly. "Yes, that is true. We wake up one day and wonder how we got to where we are. I wonder that now. If things had not happened the way they did. Rishi woke up one day too. And he came looking for me. He was a boy of fourteen and I had not seen him since he left my milk behind." Her arms hugged her chest.

"He was taken away to be a vision painter when he was a baby?"

Seeta nodded. "That was the way. It was an honour for me. I was to go on with my life and I did. But he was so unhappy. And when he told me what was happening, I was frightened. I was not a young 18 year old girl anymore. I was a 32 year old woman. But sadly, I had not married; I had no family of my own."

Kiran frowned. Rishi had said his mother had been helped by her family in England.

"Rishi did not want to be a vision painter. And after what happened to your family and when he heard what I went through, he just wanted to leave. I went to see his father. I begged that the boy be able to leave. Dinesh agreed to let me take Rishi to England. He helped me set up here. We have had a good life here. It is more than I could have asked for." Seeta's eyes were sad.

"What happened with my family?" Kiran leaned forward, her voice strained.

Seeta shrank back. "You do not know?"

Kiran shook her head.

Seeta's hands were fluttering around her throat. "I cannot help you. I do not want to be involved. The past is the past. What happened there can stay there. They might still be in the present."

Kiran said, "Who? Who might still be in the present? Please, tell me. If it will help my mother..."

"I cannot tell you anything that will help your mother. I have been gone from there for a very long time. I only have my memories of then. I wish I did not. What makes you think I can tell you anything that will help your mother now?"

"I don't know. But the more I know the more chance I have of helping her." Kiran shook her head. "What did you say? When Rishi heard what you went through...? What did you mean?"

"What time is your flight?" Seeta looked at her watch. "We would not want you to miss your flight. Your mother will be waiting. I will call a taxi for you, if you want?"

"Please, will you not tell me what you told Rishi that made him want to leave there? Was it something that turned him against the vision painters?"

Kiran could see the smudge in the line of kohl under the brown panic in Seeta's eyes.

Seeta lifted herself out of the armchair and rested her hand on the mantelpiece. There was a note of finality embraced by the fear in Seeta's voice. "I am going to call the taxi for you."

Kiran let out her breath. She slumped back in the chair and nodded and Seeta went out into the hallway. Kiran heard her talk on the phone and go into the kitchen.

Kiran waited in the living room until she heard the beep from outside the house and Seeta's footsteps. Seeta had the front door open when Kiran went out into the hallway. Her suitcase stood propped up on its wheels on the polished tile floor. The handle felt cold and hard in Kiran's hand as she gripped it.

Seeta opened the front door. The smile on her face was polite but distant. The thank you and goodbye was brief and the trip to Cochin long.

CHAPTER THIRTY-FOUR

Galway, 1982

Something bounced on the paving a few inches in front of his shoes and Ji looked up from his thoughts. There were a group of teenage boys across the road, some seated on a wall, the others leaning against it. Ji looked back at the ground and into the grass verge beside the pavement. The rock lay gray in the green, staring back at him, as puzzled by its sudden flight and new position.

Ji looked back up at the young men. They stared at him, a sneering laughter in their eyes. He picked up the rock. Out of the corner of his eye he could see them straighten up. He smiled and kept the smile on his face as he stood back up and waved the rock at them.

"Thank you, young men, I was looking for one exactly this colour."

Ji tried not to laugh at the expressions on their faces as he slipped the rock into his jacket pocket. He strode past them and down the road through the housing estate with the smile still firmly fixed in place and by the time he reached home, it felt real.

The lights in the row of semi-detached houses were on and he felt again the strangeness to his blood of an Irish evening with its foggy greyness warmed by the glowing haze of yellow streetlamps. He unlocked the front door and braced himself for the onslaught of child but there was no sign of Kiran. He hung up his wool jacket and went into the kitchen.

Elizabeth was washing the dishes, staring out of the window behind the sink. She turned her face to smile at him and he felt the cold melt away. He put his arms around her from behind and she leaned back against him, her hands still immersed in the soapy water.

"Nice walk?"

He rested his head against her shoulder and said, "Yes. I even picked up a nice rock on the way."

"From the road?"

He nodded. "Yes. Where's the little tiger?"

Elizabeth finished scrubbing the last of the dishes and pulled the plug out. She sighed.

"Ji, I told her she could do anything she wanted to do in her life. I promised her. And I don't think she's doing any harm."

He felt a tingle of fear. "Kiran is painting?"

She nodded, the dishtowel rubbing furiously at the dry plate. "I don't want you to stop her. She's hurting nobody. Just don't tell your...your Council."

Ji stepped back. He felt his heart racing. "I know we shouldn't let them know."

She turned around and frowned as she faced him.

"Ji...?"

"I am not used to hiding anything from them. Manoj has been my mentor, my guide for so long. Dinesh, my friend, my brother. The Council members were always the men we looked up to, respected, talked to, received advice from. But they are now strangers. Strangers that I cannot tell the truth to about my child who might be a vision painter even though she is a girl." His hands were moving jerkily as he talked.

She gathered his hands in hers and he felt the calm radiate from her hands.

"Ji, it will be fine. You are not a vision painter now. You are a businessman with a wife and child. Your child is painting beautiful pictures. That is all that is happening." She gripped his hands tighter and he felt his heart slow to a more comfortable rate.

"What is she painting now? Did she ask you about painting something specific?"

Elizabeth smiled and said, "She is painting a picture of a beautiful cake. I was feeling lazy about doing her birthday cake. I'm hoping one will materialise soon." She giggled and then burst out laughing.

"Elizabeth! You cannot play with such things." Ji tried to keep a serious face but her laughter was too contagious. He sent a silent apology to all vision painters as they laughed helplessly together.

∞ ∞ ∞

"Ji, stop picking at your food. Even Kiran has eaten more than you."

Ji looked up from his plate. He was dreading telling Elizabeth the news. She would take it on and feel even guiltier than she did for their circumstances.

"Amma, when do you think the cake will appear? I forgot to put seven candles on it. It is very pretty, just like you wanted." Kiran was spearing the long beans with a fork, her brow furrowed in concentration.

Ji narrowed his eyes and Elizabeth smiled as she saw his expression. She said, "Soon, kitten, soon."

Kiran said, "I did not think we were supposed to paint things like that. Though it will make you happy, it will also make me happy. And I thought we could not paint for us." Kiran turned to her father with a worried frown.

Ji shot a look at Elizabeth, who grinned even wider. Ji sighed. He looked back at the intense face of his daughter.

"Kiran, you should not be painting." He continued hastily as Kiran's face fell. "But since you are, at least make sure to keep to the rules. Yes, you cannot paint for yourself. Even if your mother tells you to."

Ji realised he would need to spend more time with Kiran when he saw the look of horror on her face at that last instruction.

He said, "Tomorrow, I will tell you more of the rules. I will explain about the gift I have"

"That I have it too. Just like you. Right, Dad?" Her blue-green eyes were fixed on his.

He hesitated, wondering when he had gone from Appa to Dad and how he hadn't noticed, but her eyes did not waver. He nodded. "We'll see. You must learn how to paint properly first. You must be trained in the correct techniques not just using your instinct. I will explain our restrictions and how we do what we do. And later, much later, you will learn how to find out what a person wants and how to translate their vision onto the canvas. We shall see then whether you have the gift."

Her eyes lit up with such hope and pleasure that he felt his misgivings melt away.

And he was losing ties to his village anyway.

Elizabeth said, "Kiran, if you've finished eating, why don't you go up and get ready for school tomorrow."

Ji nodded. "Yes, go on Kiran." He patted her cheek.

When Kiran had left the room, Elizabeth said, "So, are you going to tell me?"

Ji pushed his half-eaten dinner aside. "Yes." He sighed. "Elizabeth, I am very happy with you. You know that. I would make the same choice a thousand times every day for the rest of my life if that was necessary."

Elizabeth nodded. She gave a gentle smile. "As I would too. What has happened? Don't worry about how I will feel about it, just tell me. I know I feel bad about the choices you have had to make, but I know we can deal with anything if we are together and Kiran is safe."

Ji said, "My father's house has had to be taken over. They had no choice. It was either they took it over or it would be lost." He knew his eyes showed his hurt and he closed them.

Elizabeth got up and came around the table. She leant down and hugged him. She whispered, "I am so sorry." She held him and he felt her warmth and the pain lessened.

He said, "It is just a house."

"It was your family home, Ji. You don't have to deny your loss." Elizabeth lifted his chin with her fingers. "You need to mourn now. But one day we will go back and you will have more than you had before."

He said, "I have everything I could want now. You and Kiran. What more could a man want?" He smiled. "But yes, one day, the Council, the members, the village, they will all know and respect me." He looked into her eyes. "One day, we will have more. But I will never need more than you and Kiran."

CHAPTER THIRTY-FIVE

"She's very hurt and very angry. What did you think she would feel?"

Delilah's voice down the line sounded harsh. Kiran held the handset a few inches away from her ear.

"What did you tell her?" Kiran asked, not wanting to hear the answer.

"The crap you told me to tell her."

"Delilah!"

"Well, it was. Why did you want me to lie to her, Kiran?"

"You didn't say they were lies, did you?"

"You want me to answer that?" Delilah's voice rose.

"No, sorry." Kiran moved the phone away and then closer to her mouth. She whispered, "How is she? Is she still in pain? What happened when they woke her up? What did Ashley say?"

"I thought you didn't care anymore. That you'd moved on. Lost that loving feeling and all that jazz."

"Delilah, please! Just tell me."

"She is still in pain, Kiran."

"No!" Kiran couldn't stop the word as it slammed against the mouthpiece.

Delilah said quickly, "Not as bad though. She is on strong painkillers and she refuses to let them induce the coma again. She says it is bearable."

Kiran felt a slight relief wash over her. She looked around in the hallway of her parents' home and saw a stool beside the telephone table. She sank down onto it.

"She asked for you, Kiran. The moment they brought her out of the coma. She asked for you." Her voice grew angry again. "Do you have any idea what it was like to look into those eyes and lie and tell her you had walked away? That you had lost the baby? That she had just lost her family? Do you know, Kiran?"

Kiran felt her breath catch in her throat, the sob strangled before it could escape. She could feel the muscles in her throat working to produce a voice. "But she is awake now, isn't she?" Her voice found its strength. "She will be able to talk through whatever negative emotion allowed someone to paint her into such pain. We have gotten her this far, she can now at least make the next few steps."

Delilah did not reply.

Kiran asked, "Did you show her the painting?"

"She looked like she was going to throw it at me. I love your little brown self, but I'm not too sure even I can handle a redhead in a temper."

Kiran had to smile. It lasted a few seconds before creeping away. "The painting is important. It is for her future happiness."

"Kiran, I don't think she was too curious about her future happiness. She was in pain, but managed to hiss at me."

"Ashley doesn't hiss."

"She does now. She asked me to take the painting out of her sight." Delilah sighed. "She won't even talk to Ron. And he's so upset too. He can't bear to see his Ashley in pain. He doesn't want you to be gone. The house is even quieter without Vijay, and to top it all off, I had to tell him you'd lost the baby. He's a pretty useless liar. I like that quality in him, really I do, but sometimes I could just smack him." She added quickly, "Not that I would. He's had enough of women pushing him around. Well, one woman. You know, I really did not like Marge, but I have to say she produced one hell of a daughter. The only thing they have in common is the red hair, though Ashley's is a much nicer shade. She's a wonderful woman. Kiran, what the hell are you doing?" Delilah took in a deep breath.

"I'm trying to save her, Delilah." Kiran's voice was sharp.

"Yeah, that's what Ron was trying to hint at. Do you know, I wonder how you two figure these things out?"

"It was the only thing I could think of. I just want Ashley to be happy. But I've done all I can. She needs to take the next step. I have to be here now. I need you to help Ashley if she needs it."

Delilah sighed again. "I've been talking to her."

"And...?"

"I told her what you said about Jennifer. About her needing to work out what she felt for Jennifer."

"And...? Delilah! Tell me."

"There's nothing to tell. She agreed to do that. Reluctantly, may I say. Do you know, I feel like knocking your heads together. Actually, no, I take that back. Only yours. But you're over there. So, we'll do what you asked...Kiran, if by some chance, Ashley still loves Jennifer, are you prepared for that?"

Kiran felt the stab of the words into her chest. *No, she wasn't.* "I will have to be, won't I?"

"And are you prepared to have and bring up a little one on your own?"

Kiran's hand automatically flew to her belly. She whispered, "He or she will be my little part of Ashley. Delilah, what can I do? She has to be happy. I can't see any other way."

"So how are you getting on there? How is your mother?"

"She's the same." Kiran answered automatically, bemused by the change of subject.

"Did you find out anything in London?"

"I met Rishi's mother."

"Oh, meeting the in-laws already?"

"Delilah! Her name is Seeta. She seemed frightened to talk about whatever happened here in the past. But I know that Rishi lied to us. He said they went to England and his mother got them through with the help of her family there. Turns out it was Dinesh who helped her out. Something happened here and Rishi wanted to leave the village. Something to do with my family and the vision painters and something that happened to Rishi's mother. She wouldn't say what."

Kiran looked around to make sure she was alone. The house was quiet. Babu and Shalini were at the market, her mother was asleep, and her father was in his study, the thrum of the air conditioner creeping under the closed door.

She lowered her voice anyway. "Delilah, I have to find out what happened. Why we left here. My parents would never talk about it."

"You have to get them to tell you."

"Easier said than done. My mother isn't communicating much and my father is in a complete state of shock." Kiran glanced across at the study door. "I'm going to talk to him now. I'll call you as soon as I can. Tell Ashley...tell Ashley...never mind...Don't tell her I called."

Kiran hung up without waiting for an answer.

∞ ∞ ∞

Her father was staring out of the window. Kiran tapped on the door to the study but he didn't move. She walked around to the front of his desk and pulled up a chair and sat in his line of sight. His eyes were focused on the coconut trees in the distance and he did not acknowledge her presence.

The young Ji and Elizabeth, dark heads bent towards each other, a light glowing in their eyes, stared out of the framed photo on the desk. A nine-month-old Kiran sat on her mother's lap.

Kiran took her eyes from the photo and her father was looking at her. Under the stray strands of white eyebrows, his eyes were sad. She noticed that his hair and beard were now completely white.

"How is Ashley?"

Kiran was glad that, for the first time, he had not called her 'that woman'.

"They took her out of the coma. She is awake but still in some pain. Not as much and it can be managed with painkillers." She tried not to let the image interfere with her voice but she could feel it cracking.

His voice was gentle. "You removed her from your family so that you could paint her."

Kiran nodded. "It wasn't enough though, was it?"

"You still love her. We can only fool ourselves for so long, Kiran. Our gift is not something that can be manipulated. Not for very long."

"I know. But it gives her a chance." Kiran shook her head. "She won't look at the painting I did of her happiness."

"You painted her without her vision. Just your vision. That can only provide temporary changes that spring from the energy you painted into it from your love." Ji's fingers were tapping the desk as he spoke. "It is your vision of what you want for her. Of what she needs to be happy. Even if she looks properly at it, she will need to create her own vision of her future."

Kiran said, "But I can't decide to go back to her, can I?" Her heart dipped as he shook his head. She looked down at her hands. "I knew at the time that I couldn't. I'm sorry I broke the rules last year with Marge. And I am sorry for all the times you had to make sacrifices for me."

She looked up again. His eyes were wet.

"We make sacrifices for the ones we love. You were brave to do it for your Ashley. I am a coward. I cannot do what you did for Ashley for your mother. I cannot leave her. But I could break the rules and paint her anyway. I could have done that when we found the negative painting. But I am restricted by my belief, by these rules. Why is it that when you want to do good, you have to follow the rules but somebody who creates bad visions can break the rules as if they do not even exist?"

His hands were bunched into fists on the table between them.

Kiran said, "Even if you or I could paint Amma, you said that would only be temporary." He nodded. "Then we have to find out what someone could use against her to make her sick. Amma will have to tell us."

Ji looked back out of the window. He said in Malayalam, "Sometimes I don't know if we have a gift or a curse. When men are given power to help people achieve happiness, they should do it without rules. They should be free to help those they love. They should not have to sacrifice their own happiness. If we have the responsibility to help strangers in a way that does not control them, then we should be able to help our own. We should be trusted with this gift, not treated like children."

Kiran stared at him. She had argued these things in her mind for so long, mentally debating her father and his profession.

His fingers started their tapping again. His voice lowered. "I am the Leader of the Council. For years I wanted to change the way things were done. But I made choices that took me away. And it took so long to get back to Kerala. By then, it was too late."

Kiran said in a low voice, "I took some of your papers. And a copy of that Malayalam script." She cringed at the shock in her father's eyes.

"I'm sorry. I saw them there when I was leaving and I was curious. Dad?" She realised that the expression in his eyes was more like fear.

He pushed back his chair and fumbled at the lock on the safe beside the desk. He took out two rolls of script and a sheaf of papers and put them on the desk. She could see his hands shaking before they disappeared back into the safe.

Her father crouched as he felt around in the safe and she said, "Dad, I took them the last time."

He straightened up slowly. Kiran looked away from the disbelief in his eyes.

"Where are they now?" His voice was hard but calm.

"Upstairs. In my suitcase. Dad, I'm sorry." She looked back at him.

"You cannot read Malayalam so you do not know what is in the papers." She looked down quickly and his voice was a low bark. "Kiran?"

"Who else has seen them? What have you done?" He gathered the papers up and shoved them back into the safe. The click as he closed the safe door was followed by the whirring of the lock.

"I needed someone to translate them. I was just trying to find out more. To help Amma. I asked Vijay to help me."

"Who?"

"You know, Vijay, the man at the training centre who was moving to Galway."

"Oh, yes." Ji seemed to be struggling to remember. "So, nobody outside of that?"

Kiran said, "No. He told me what some of it meant. And I read your journals and the notes for your autobiography."

"You are sure no one else saw them?"

Kiran shook her head.

Ji sank back into the chair. "I spent a long time trying to gather all those papers. It is our history, good and bad." He glanced up at her. "Did you get very far? The script is not easy to read and translate."

"It was very slow. We only found out the rules and the reasons for some of them." She paused before rushing on, "But I found out a lot from reading your writings."

He looked at her and she could almost see him reading through the papers in his mind.

"Dad, I know that you were in the process with a girl before you met Amma."

He jumped up from the chair. "That was not in my autobiography. You read my private notes."

She could see the white hairs in his beard trembling as he clenched his jaws and glared at her.

She kept her voice calm. "We need to talk about what could have happened."

"Like what?"

She got up and faced him across the desk. "Is it not obvious? You could have fathered a child."

He jerked back and Kiran looked at him in surprise. *How could it not even have entered his mind?*

His face had gone slack. "That is not possible. How is that possible? I would have been told. No matter where I was, I would have been told."

Kiran felt the doubt creep through her. *Had she jumped to that conclusion too soon?*

Her father looked pale under his brown skin. Kiran moved around the desk and helped him back into the chair. She could feel the muscles in his arms trembling.

"It is not possible. Do not speak about things that are not possible." He was muttering and she strained to hear him even though her head was near his.

"It is ok, Dad. I'm sorry I said it."

She walked over to the door and looked back. He was staring out of the window again.

CHAPTER THIRTY-SIX

Kerala, 1992

The faces around the living room were sombre, brown skin contrasting with the white mundus and shirts and saris worn for a funeral. The food sat waiting on a table. There was now only a murmur of voices from the kitchen which had been a hub of activity for the morning.

Ji sat on one of the chairs lining the room. He looked across at Manoj who he had helped onto a chair earlier and who was being supported by one of the young vision painters. Ji felt the weight of sorrow, not just at the loss of his beloved in-laws, but for the loss of the essence of the man who had been his father. The left side of Manoj's face was dropping towards the floor, pointing in bewilderment to the wasted arm and leg. A sliver of spittle drooped out of the left side of his mouth and Ji jerked his head at the young man beside Manoj. The man hurried to wipe Manoj's face.

Ji said, "Where is Dinesh? Is the new Leader still late for everything?"

Some of the other vision painters smiled. One of them nodded and then looked around at the others and stopped. Ji knew they had all been told about him. He needed to step carefully if he was going to fit back into the community. He had to curb his natural tendency to take charge.

Ji said, in a softer voice, "There must be something important keeping Dinesh. He is a busy man."

He got up and went to the table. He gestured at one of the girls standing at the door to the kitchen and she went in and came back out with serving spoons. Elizabeth followed with more plates. Her eyes were red and her face swollen.

Ji said, "Come, let us eat."

The men got up and filed along the table, helping themselves to the food. The women remained seated and Elizabeth joined them. They had been her grandmother's friends and Ji was glad she seemed to be taking comfort from the warmth of their pats on her knees and shoulders, the sorrowful nodding of their wrinkled faces.

Dinesh came into the room and walked straight over to Elizabeth and took her hand. "I am sorry I am late. My sincere condolences for your loss. Your grandparents will be highly missed in the village." Elizabeth smiled and nodded.

Dinesh looked around and saw Ji at the table. "I see you have started eating."

Ji took a plate from the stack on the table. He said, "What can I get you?"

Dinesh joined him and they served themselves and sat down. When all the men were seated with their plates of food, the women got up, one of them encouraging Elizabeth to the table and filling her plate.

Dinesh asked, "So, how is Kiran?"

Ji said, "She is good. She wanted to accompany us. I told her not to come. She is in the middle of her first year examinations."

Dinesh nodded. "What is she studying? Medicine?" He took a swipe at the curry with a piece of *appum*.

Ji said. "Engineering."

"Good, good." Dinesh waggled his head. Ji could see the shine of scalp through thinning grey hair.

Ji smoothed down his own hair, grateful it was still full and mostly jet black, apart from the grey at his temples which Elizabeth said made him look very distinguished. He looked for Elizabeth and he felt the comfort of her presence when he saw her sitting amongst the white saris, standing out from the women around her not just because of the creamy bronze of her skin and the turquoise of her eyes.

Dinesh's eyes followed Ji's gaze. He said, "It is good to have you both back in the village." He moved his head to look at the figure of Manoj. "Father has changed, has he not?"

Ji nodded. He couldn't speak.

Dinesh said, under his breath, "He will not be with us much longer. It is good you are back to be able say goodbye to him too."

Ji said, "I am going to build a retirement complex here. When we get older, we will need a place with good services, an excellent medical centre. The company of our friends." He turned to Dinesh. "What do you think?"

Dinesh looked at him. "That will cost a lot of money. I know they left the house to Elizabeth but I did not think her grandparents had that much money to leave."

Ji shook his head. "I was a successful businessman in Ireland, my friend. I have enough to build what I want here. I will use the land they left us beside the house. It will be the best complex of its kind in Kerala." He looked around at the wooden walls. "And I will modernise this house as well. Air conditioners in every room. When did it get so hot here?"

Dinesh smiled. "You have been too long in Ireland, Ji. It is as hot as it has always been. It never bothered you before." He got up. Ji stood up too.

Dinesh said, "It will be an interesting few years I think. Come and see me about rejoining the Association. I know you. You will want to start work on that too. Am I right?"

Ji said, "Yes. You are right. I would like to paint again."

Dinesh said, "It is probably better that Devdar is not with us anymore then."

Ji frowned. "That man should have been removed from the Council and the Association long before he died."

Dinesh glanced in the direction of the other vision painters. Some of the council members were present in the room. He whispered, "Ji, have you not learned yet to keep such thoughts to yourself?" He took Ji's arm and led him out of the room. He said in a firm voice, "You will need to convince the Council that you are ready."

Ji felt the anger rise through his body. He tried to keep it out of his voice. "Have you forgotten what happened? Why we had to leave?"

Dinesh shook his head. "I have not forgotten. But it was 12 years ago, Ji. The Council is made up of new members and I am now the Leader. Even though I was not officially Leader until last year, Father was not very involved since you left. I have been doing the job. If you are not comfortable with us, you should not come back."

Ji closed his eyes. The anger was still simmering and he needed to find his calm. "No one who was involved then is around now?" He was annoyed at the slight tremor in his voice. He opened his eyes.

Dinesh was looking up at him, his hand over his brow to shield his eyes from the light that hung above Ji's head. "Everything has changed now, has it not? Nothing is as we thought it would be when we were playing together as children. When we thought our sons would be following."

He put his hand on Ji's arm. "Come and present your case to the Council. What is the worst that can happen?"

Dinesh's smile didn't reach his eyes which betrayed a trace of worry. He squeezed Ji's arm and said, as he turned to leave, "Tell Elizabeth again that I am sorry for her loss."

Ji watched from the front door as Dinesh walked around the corner to their houses that were now joined.

CHAPTER THIRTY-SEVEN

Elizabeth opened her eyes and Kiran leaned forward to give her a kiss on the cheek. Her mother's cheek felt clammy and the bewilderment trapped in the depths of her eyes hurt Kiran in her gut.

"Thank you for coming, Kiran." Her mother's hand was warm on her chin.

"Where else would I be, Amma?"

"At home with your woman." Elizabeth's eyes turned curious.

Kiran shook her head. "There's only one woman in my life at the moment. We need to get you better. I'm going to lose my job if I keep gallivanting around the world like this."

"Kiran. What happened? Where is Ashley? And how is the baby?" Elizabeth struggled upright before leaning back against the pillows. Kiran wiped her mother's forehead. She could not admit she didn't know about Ashley. Two days had passed. Days filled with watching her mother, days filled with fear, and she had not had the courage to call Delilah.

"So Dad told you about the baby? I wasn't sure he would."

Elizabeth smiled. "Yes, he told me." She gripped Kiran's hand. "Your father can be a very difficult man. He is infuriating sometimes. But he loves you. And he is in a state of shock about the baby. He will not admit it, but he is secretly very pleased that he is going to be a grandfather. Don't tell him I told you. I wonder sometimes at how the two of you manage at all. You are so similar." She sighed deeply. "What are you two going to do if something happens to me?"

"Nothing is going to happen to you, Amma." Kiran took her mother's hand. "Amma, we need to try and find out some things." She paused, trying to find the right words. This was the first chance she had got to ask her mother, she didn't know if it would come again.

"What things?" Elizabeth's eyes were retreating behind shutters.

Kiran said, "There was a vision painting of you sick. Which means somebody targeted you and it worked. The same thing was done to Ashley."

Elizabeth's eyes widened. "Is she alright? What are you doing here if she is sick?"

"She is getting better. I did something." Kiran shook her head. "Amma, I need to know what somebody could have used against you. I need you to be completely honest with me."

Elizabeth looked at the door to the bedroom. It was shut and they could hear Shalini and Mala chattering in Malayalam on the other side.

"Amma, we can't lose you." Kiran tried to smile. "You don't want Dad to have to lead that Council on his own, do you? Think what a mess he could make. And he would have to face talking to his lesbian daughter on his own, without as interpreter. He'd miss out on his grandchild. You should see him. He can't figure out how to keep the house running. He has food stains on his shirt. Shalini is being driven crazy."

Elizabeth smiled. "Stop. I know he needs me." The smile vanished just as quickly.

Kiran said, "Please, Amma. Tell me. There is nothing you could do that would stop me loving you. I may be able to help."

Elizabeth closed her eyes and leaned back into the pillow. It clung to the sides of her face.

"When your father made the choice to be with me, I was so happy. I was scared and I was worried for him but I knew we were meant to be together. It was a feeling of coming home. My heart had found its home with him." She opened her eyes and looked at Kiran. "I think you know how that feels." Kiran nodded. Elizabeth looked at the window, through the slats of the blinds. "Well, there were many in the village and in the Council and amongst the vision painters who did not understand. They were horrified. He was a promising young vision painter on the way up, widely thought to be the eventual leader of the Council, from a family of leaders. I was a young 'Anglo' woman whose background in the village was already scandalous." She glanced back at Kiran. "You don't know that part, do you?"

Kiran said, "I know a little. I found Dad's journals and part of the autobiography he is doing for the two of you."

"So you can understand what kind of a reaction we got when we decided to get married." Elizabeth smiled. "I was in a daze though. I was so in love with him. We lived in Ireland for 2 years before Manoj replied to his letters and allowed him to come back. I knew he needed to be here. I wanted to be here with my grandparents. It was home."

"Do you feel guilty about it? About Dad having to leave?"

Elizabeth said, "I felt guilty then."

"Because he had to leave his profession?"

"That, and other things."

"Tell me, Amma." Kiran put her hand on her mother's arm.

Elizabeth looked away. Her voice was subdued. "When I met Ji, he had already been entered into the process."

Kiran said, "The process of finding a girl."

Elizabeth looked at her and glanced away. "Yes. They had found a girl for him. From a family that was one of the original families that let their son be trained as a vision painter. It is a long detailed search. There is no mixing of bloodlines but the families have connections through the years."

"That sounds awful, very mechanical."

Elizabeth shook her head. "Just because it is different to what we would be used to does not make it wrong. They want to keep the gift as pure as possible. These are the traditions that were passed down and they have not failed the profession. The vision painters are valued for the comfort they bring, for the happiness they can materialise for people. The lives of many people would be so much emptier without these men."

"But why are they all men? Am I not living proof that women could have the gift?"

"I don't know, Kiran. I know that your father questioned so much of what they stood for, but he was just one man and he angered some powerful men. After he came back, he had to learn to keep his thoughts to himself. But he never stopped thinking of these things. I did not want him to question. I just wanted both of you safe."

Elizabeth closed her eyes.

Kiran asked, "Did you know the girl that was chosen for him?"

Elizabeth shook her head.

"Was he with her?"

Elizabeth nodded. She opened her eyes. "But it was only once. She was chosen just after we first met but he was with her before I came back to Kerala two years later."

"What happened to her?"

"I don't know. Ji told me about the process and about the traditions while we were getting to know each other, but

I couldn't ask him about that. He was feeling guilty about it, but he could not have known we would meet again. I never heard about what happened to the woman after that."

"Did you wonder if she had become pregnant?"

"I felt guilty but I did not want to think about it. It felt very distant from what was happening with us. Almost as if it had happened to other people. We never heard anything about her after we left. It was a different time. There was no email or anything like that. Ji did not have communication with them here, just the letters he wrote to Manoj. After we came back I got the impression from Ji that everything had been sorted out and that the girl had gone to her family in England."

Elizabeth looked her daughter in the eyes and said, "I feel guilt that my happiness with your father caused people such difficulty. How could I not feel that? But I know it was the right thing for us."

Kiran put her hand on her mother's. Elizabeth smiled and took Kiran's hand in hers.

"I could cope with everything because he was so obviously happy with us. Yes, he grumbled about his profession, about leaving his family of vision painters, but deep down he was so calm, so sure. And so was I. And when we came back, he started painting again. I know it hurt him that he could not be involved with the leadership but he was happy."

"Then why did we leave? Was it because of me?"

Kiran could feel the tightening of Elizabeth's grip on her hand and the moisture.

"Amma, you have never told me why we left. I need to know. Was it because of me?"

Elizabeth whispered, "It was to save you, Kiran. It was not because of you. It was because of years of tradition, years of wrong." Her eyes were flitting between the closed bedroom door, the window, Kiran's face, Kiran's hand, refusing to settle.

Kiran leant forward. "Because I was painting?"

Elizabeth nodded. "Not just that. Ji had broken the rules. He was let back in and then you were born. A girl child. As if things could not be worse for him in their eyes. What credibility could he have? No vision painter produced a girl child. But Manoj spoke on his behalf and he was allowed to stay painting. You were not to be seen or heard. You and I were to be just a part of the ordinary community here. They could bear it then. No one questioning their powers, their traditions, their ways."

Kiran said, "But then I painted."

"Yes. And the wrong men found out about it. Ji could not hide his pride in his little tiger. He had been so hurt with the reaction to a girl child. He is a proud man, Kiran. He was shunned. He was laughed at. He was ostracised in a way. And now the 'weak girl child' was helping him paint beautiful paintings, sometimes even instructing him. He knew you had a more powerful gift than even he had." She smiled. "For a very competitive man, he didn't even grumble that your gift was stronger. He was just so proud."

"But when I started painting in Ireland, he talked about 'maybe' I might have the gift, 'maybe' I could learn how to paint."

Elizabeth smiled. "I said he didn't grumble, but he's still a man. He wanted to be able to teach you. And he was frightened of the consequences; of the Council finding out."

"How did the Council find out? He didn't say anything to them when we were here, did he?"

Elizabeth shook her head. "He struggled not to boast. But somehow the rumours started. And they got back to the wrong men."

"But surely they could just have asked that he should get me to stop?"

"It was not that simple, Kiran."

Kiran watched the years of conflict pass before her eyes. The battles with her father that had left them both injured.

She asked, her voice thick, "What happened, why did we have to leave?"

CHAPTER THIRTY-EIGHT

Kerala, 1980

Elizabeth shook out the pillowcase. There had been no creepy-crawlies the last hundred times she'd done this, but she wasn't taking any chances. The pointy spikes of an earwig may be harmless to humans but she didn't want them nesting in her ears. She was determined they had no squatting rights despite their name.

The heat of the morning sun wrung sweat out from her forehead. The village street was quiet and she could hear the rumble of thunder in the distance.

"That little girl. I do not know what I am going to do!" Shalini's usual complaint drifted out onto the porch and Elizabeth could not help the grin that crept onto her face.

"Kiran!" Elizabeth tried to keep the laughter out of her voice. Shalini was still a teenager at 19 and she was adjusting to being in their house. She was almost as fascinated with Elizabeth as she had been as a little girl staring with her brother at the Anglo visitor to their father's house on the hill.

Shalini's voice got more dramatic. "She has gone out the back. I will catch her now for you."

Elizabeth burst out laughing. She heard Shalini's footsteps slap out of the back door, her high-pitched voice triumphantly yelling Kiran's name.

"That little girl certainly creates a lot more trouble than her size would imply."

Elizabeth stopped laughing and jerked around at the sound of the male voice, a snigger hidden in its singsong tones.

She knew his name from Ji's description of the Council members. It was the difficult one, Devdar. She smoothed out the pillowcase in her hands.

"She is just a child. The normal playfulness of a little child, that is all." Elizabeth found her hands folding the cloth into a tiny square.

He smiled and shook his head. She noticed flakes drift down from his sparse grey hair onto his shoulders. Her eyes focused on the white flecks lying on brown skin, winking up at her. "That child would do well to keep herself quiet and learn that our customs are important. She is already such a, such a..." He paused, his hands gripping and seesawing the white cloth slung around his neck. "A 'difference' here."

"Difference is sometimes good." Elizabeth tried to keep her voice calm. She could not understand the fear curling in her stomach standing in the shade of the porch talking to this man. The occasional cart passed by and groups of women carrying baskets on their heads.

His toothless mouth grinned at her. "Do you think we are not good enough as we are? Perhaps a bit of foreign blood will improve us? You think maybe a little girl should be allowed to remain and try and be a vision painter?"

Elizabeth could feel her heart thudding against her chest wall. The sweat slid down her cheek and she turned her face slightly so he would not see it drip.

"My husband is the vision painter. We are just here to be part of the ordinary community like my family, my grandparents." She cursed him inside but bowed her head.

His voice got lower. "Yes. I see. That is right. I should be going. The Council meeting should not be delayed because I am talking to a woman on the street."

He turned, hitching up his mundu exposing bandy knees, and picked his way carefully over the stones in the driveway.

Elizabeth sighed. She sank down into a chair on the porch. The clatter of footsteps came and passed so fast that she could not react until it was too late. She watched in horror as Devdar's legs buckled as the weight of a small girl landed against the back of his knees. Kiran looked as shocked as he did. Her customary headlong flight off the porch steps was not usually halted by old men.

Elizabeth rushed down the steps and grabbed Kiran by the arm. A few women stood, swaying under the baskets. She could see them try to hide their smiles behind the cloth of their saris. Devdar's face was darkening to a deeper shade of brown, almost black. He glared at the women and they hurried on, whispering to each other.

Elizabeth said, "I'm so sorry. So is Kiran. It was an accident."

Kiran added, "Sorry, I was trying to see if I could fly if I went fast enough down the stairs. Shalini took the wings I made and…" Her voice trickled to a halt as Devdar got to his feet and she saw his face. Elizabeth could feel Kiran shrink behind her mother's legs. She put her hand on Kiran's shoulder and squeezed gently, pushing her a little further behind the curtain of her sari.

Devdar was staring at Kiran, his lips moving in a silent rage. His eyes narrowed and Elizabeth followed his gaze. She felt a jolt of pure panic when she saw what he was looking at; the smears of paint stood out in orange and green on Kiran's blue shorts.

She shoved Kiran behind her and said, "I am so sorry. Are you alright? Can I get you anything?"

His eyes flicked back up to her face. He did not say a word but in that moment Elizabeth knew with a mother's certainty that her child was in mortal danger. She straightened up and stared back at him. She gathered every bit of strength she could find and held his gaze until he dropped it.

His voice was low and hard, "This is what should have been done immediately. She will not see another day. If you are blessed, you may see a few, but they will be days of such pain for her loss, that you will wish for the end of your days too."

He spat at the ground and the glob of spittle landed beside Kiran's bare feet. Elizabeth felt the quivering against her leg as Kiran tried to push further in to her sari.

Elizabeth kept her gaze steady and watched as Devdar limped out of the driveway. She did not move or lower her eyes until he had disappeared around the corner. When she was sure he was gone, she bent down and scooped Kiran up into her arms and hugged the little girl's shaking body to her chest.

She murmured into Kiran's hair, trying to hold in the panic, "Why were you painting? I thought you knew not to take your father's paints."

Shalini appeared at the front door. "So, you have caught the little rascal." She brandished what looked like a pair of cardboard flaps. "I caught her just before she jumped out of a tree with these on her arms."

Elizabeth carried Kiran up the stairs. Kiran's head was buried in under the swath of sari that ran across Elizabeth's chest and over her shoulder. Kiran wouldn't take her head out so Elizabeth held her in place with one arm and held out her other hand for the two pieces of cardboard.

"Cheh, now I have paint all over me." Shalini wiped her hands on her plain white sari that already bore the stains of the day's cooking and cleaning. The bright orange and green now on Elizabeth's hand was mixed into a streak of orange-tinged green on Shalini's sari.

∞ ∞ ∞

Elizabeth thought her grandfather's face could not get any paler. She did not know if it was anger or fear. He stood by the window in the dining room, alternating between wringing his hands and twisting the cloth of his mundu. Ji was standing beside him, both men fixing their eyes on the road outside. The darkness outside was broken by pinpoints of lamps, the darkness inside by candles.

Elizabeth and her grandmother sat on a bench at the dining table. Their eyes were swollen from crying. Mariamma was holding Elizabeth's hand in hers.

Manoj stood by the door. He looked ill, his face stretched and sweaty. He said, "I cannot do any more. You have to leave. Get out of here tonight."

Ji said, "How can you let this happen? She is a child. I used to be like a son to you. Can you not see this is wrong?"

Manoj wiped his face with the cloth slung around his neck. "Ji, we both know I have never agreed with some teachings of our profession. But what would you have me do here? Devdar has convinced them the girl is an abomination. I could argue with them and change their minds again. That is not the problem." He lowered the cloth and his voice. "I cannot stop the few who would do much worse than talk. I can remove Devdar from the Council for what he said to Elizabeth. But he is a vindictive man. That will increase his hatred and his anger. He will do what he said. He will kill Kiran, even if it is just to save face now."

Elizabeth jumped up. "Ji, please. We cannot risk staying. He will be here soon. He said she would not see another day. It is almost midnight now."

Ji turned to face them. He looked at Manoj and his mentor looked down at the ground, his hands shaking on the cloth.

Ji said, "This is what we spoke about for so many years, you and me. Changing our world for the better. Painting true happiness for people with clear and true hearts." He made a sound of disgust. "But this is what we have become instead. Fleeing in the night from the dogs in the street."

Manoj lifted his head slowly. His left eyelid did not travel as far up. His voice was muffled. "My son, I am sorry." He turned and shuffled out of the door, leaning his hand against the wall as he went.

CHAPTER THIRTY-NINE

Kiran leant back in the chair. She said, "So I wasn't even trying to do a vision painting."

Elizabeth shook her head. "You were being you. It was just unfortunate that you ran into Devdar. He hated the idea of you."

"What happened to him?"

"Nothing. We were gone. I think Manoj became ill. He had a minor stroke but according to Dinesh he was never the same. He was still the leader of the Council but just in name. Ji did not talk to him again until we came back in 1992. Manoj was quite sick by then and I think they made their peace before Manoj died a few months later."

"So Dad went back to the Association after what had happened?"

Elizabeth nodded. "Many years had passed. Devdar was dead and there were all new men on the Council. Dinesh was the leader. Kiran, you should understand, your father was always a vision painter at heart. It is as natural to him as breathing."

Elizabeth tried to straighten up in the bed

"But how could he be a part of that group? After that? After they kicked him out for loving someone, for having a child?"

Ji's voice from the doorway was harsh. "There are things you cannot understand, Kiran. Things you have no right to judge."

Kiran looked up in surprise. Her father was standing with his hand on the handle of the door.

He didn't wait for a reply. "You have a visitor."

"Me? Here?" Kiran got to her feet.

"Yes." Her father's voice was tired and his face drawn with lines of exhaustion.

"Ji, come and sit with me." Elizabeth's hand patted the bed beside her.

Ji moved to the bed and sat down. He took Elizabeth's hand and slumped back against the wall.

Kiran hurried out of the room and down the stairs. There was no one in the living room. The front door was open and she poked her head out. The porch was empty.

Babu was wiping the dust off the Jeep. He looked up at her as she stepped out onto the porch. He gestured around the side of the house.

Kiran left the shade of the porch and felt the sweat spring out on her face. The thin blouse she was wearing was soaked by the time she rounded the corner of the house. She peered through the aisles between the banana trees at the back of the house. She could see the old shack leaning against the fence her father had built beside it. She knew now why he hadn't dismantled the structure. Kiran picked her way through the rough earth beside the trunks of the banana trees, the wide flat leaves brushing her hair as she passed.

The door was hanging from the top hinge and it groaned as she pushed it open and walked slowly into the dimness of the shack.

She had reached the centre when Rishi stepped out of the shadow at the back of the shack. Kiran felt her heart jump and then sink as rapidly. He was wearing neat grey slacks and a white Polo shirt but he looked strangely dishevelled. The sudden sour taste in her mouth made her gag. She started to back out and he held up his hand.

"Please, Kiran. Stand there if you want, just don't leave. Not yet."

She shook her head and took another step back.

His hand was still held up, its pale palm facing her. "You know I could stop you if you try to run. Just hear me out." His voice was an urgent whisper.

"Rishi, you attacked me. You told Vijay you were going to tell our fathers lies to cover what you did." Kiran tried to keep her voice steady but the anger was pushing it staggering across the room towards him.

He didn't take his eyes off her but she could see them narrow. The sun pushed a line of light through the damaged window and it fell across the earth floor between them. She could feel the sweat slithering down her back.

Rishi's forehead was glistening and he rubbed at it as he spoke. "That was a mistake. I don't know what happened to me."

Kiran heard herself snort and Rishi frowned. "I have never done anything remotely like that before. You have to believe me."

He moved forward but stopped as she flinched. "Kiran, I swear to you. I was married for many years and we fought a lot but I never was in any way physical with her, not even when she left me like that." He pushed his hand over his forehead and into his hair. His eyes were tortured. "That woman wrecked my life but I never would do anything like that. I don't know what happened to me in your friend's house. I just felt this cloud of red come over me and I couldn't see anything except the way you were throwing me aside like she had."

He stared at her. She didn't forgive him but she sensed he was telling the truth.

He must have seen the slight softening in her face because his shoulders slumped as he sighed. "You believe me."

She nodded. "It still doesn't excuse what you did."

"I know. I just needed you to know that was completely out of character for me. And that I am so sorry. There is nothing I can say to excuse my actions and I don't know where that leaves us."

Kiran said, "You just don't want me to tell my father. Or yours? Is that why you are here?"

Rishi shook his head. "I mean it. I wanted you to know. But that's not why I am here." He reached into his pocket and took out a packet of cigarettes. His fingers pinched the filter as he withdrew one. "Do you mind? You don't smoke, do you?" She shook her head and he lit the cigarette and drew the smoke deep into his lungs.

"I talked to my mother." The smoke swirled in the dense air between them as he breathed it out with the words.

Kiran felt her heart quicken.

He watched the patterns of smoke. "She told me you went to her house. I am glad my father did not know about your visit, he would have presumed you were looking favourably on the proposal." His smile was quick and tight. "So, why did you go to see my mother? We both know it was not to accept the proposal."

"I wanted to find out what happened here years ago that made my parents leave. I know that now. But I still don't know what made you leave."

He frowned. "So, it was not to tell my mother about what I did in Galway?"

Kiran shook her head. "No. Rishi, will you tell me what happened that made you leave? I am more concerned about helping my mother at the moment and if you know anything that might help her, just tell me." He was still looking confused and she added, "You owe me at least that."

"You think that has anything to do with what is happening to your mother now?"

"I don't know. Just tell me. Please."

She saw Rishi's gaze waver. He looked out of the window. His voice dropped to a whisper. "I was told that I could leave on the condition that I never spoke about it." His eyes had become dark pools rippling in a storm. "I was only 14 and she was my mother even though I was only meeting her for the first time."

He looked at her. "They can still get to her, even after all these years. I am still tied by the same ropes that strangled my voice then." He tried to straighten his shoulders but they suddenly seemed frail.

Kiran lowered her voice as well. "Rishi, I will not tell anyone you told me anything. No one will get to your mother because no one will know you spoke to me about it." He closed his eyes and she said, "You have been carrying a secret for over 30 years. To protect your mother?" He nodded and she continued, "I need to protect my mother too. She was once like a mother to you."

Rishi opened his eyes. She could see the memories flood back.

He whispered, "I was jealous of you. Your mother was there with you. And she was beautiful and funny and she loved you so much. She was so good to me but it made me want to meet my own mother. And then when I found out that they had threatened to kill you," his voice choked, "you, a little girl, my little kitten..." She could see his throat moving as he tried to speak. "I could not help you, I couldn't protect you. You were gone, all of you, you were gone that morning and I tried to find out what happened. No one would tell me but I overheard my father and my grandfather talking. My grandfather was trying to explain to my father that Ji had to leave in the night with both of you because it was not safe anymore for the two of you, that you would have been killed if your father had not run with you."

Rishi's body was trembling and his voice rose and fell in the shadowed sunlight. "How could they do that? Were they monsters? You were a child, a small girl. I ran. I ran away to where I had heard my mother lived. I found her and I begged her to let me stay with her. She was afraid. My mother was afraid and I didn't understand why. She told me then."

Rishi sank down onto his knees. He stared at the brown dirt as it settled around the grey of his slacks. His voice sounded like it had been dragged from deep in his stomach.

"She told me I had a sister once."

Kiran gasped and Rishi looked up, his eyes dull.

"Yes, a sister. My mother told me that the first baby she bore had been a little baby girl."

Kiran shook her head. "I don't understand..."

Rishi continued as if she hadn't spoken, his eyes fixed on an empty space inside him, "They took her away. They killed her. A little baby. Just because she was not a boy."

Kiran could feel her legs starting to give way and she clutched at the wall. The shack creaked as her weight rested on it.

"No! Who? Who would do that?"

"There are men who cannot let go of the past. Men who think that a baby girl is nothing. Worse than nothing. An abomination if born to a vision painter. An impossibility. If they are to remain with the illusion then the baby must not exist."

"Did your mother say who they were?"

Rishi shook his head. "My mother did not want to tell me any of it. She was frightened. But when I begged for us to go away, she went to speak with my father. He must have been very upset too at what was happening, at your father going away. He arranged everything. He sent us to London and sent us money when we needed it. I wanted to support us and I did not want to take his money. I put myself through college working wherever I could. She still took his money but I was able to support us eventually. I hated him. Hated that he did not try and find out who did these terrible things. He is a coward."

"The man who threatened me was called Devdar. Is he the one who took your sister?"

Rishi sighed. "I don't know. I wanted to leave all of this behind me. I don't know why I came back. My father wanted me back and there was a part of me that needed him to respect me. After my divorce, I needed some respect, even from a man I could not respect."

Kiran asked, "Rishi, did this happen to anyone else? Do you know?"

Rishi looked at her. She could see an awareness creep into his eyes, of her, the shack, where they were. He leant back and got to his feet. "You shouldn't know any of this. If anyone knew that I told you. I must..."

"Kiran!" Her father's voice was close and worried.

Kiran jerked upright. *Amma?* She pushed at the door and ran into the sunlight blinking at its harshness. Ji was standing in front of the shack, his face as pale as his beard.

His voice shook. "What are you doing in there? Come into the house."

Her father had already turned to go and Kiran did not look back as she followed him through the trees, the fronds waving into her face as they brushed off his shoulders.

"How is Amma? Is she ok?"

"She is the same. Come. I want you to stay inside with her. I need to go out."

Kiran glanced over her shoulder and saw Rishi's face at the window of the shack, the broken glass distorting his features. He pulled back into the shadows when he saw her looking.

CHAPTER FORTY

The Vision Painting Centre was dark but Kiran could see a hint of light through the window. Her breath came out in sharp bursts after her stumbling run from her parents' house. The streetlights were not working and her father had taken the lantern when he had left after he'd escorted Kiran back to the house. She knocked on the front door. Rishi's words rang in her ears, her mother was not getting any better, and Kiran could not bear to sit any longer and listen to her mother's laboured breathing.

She moved back to the window and placed her ear against the glass. She heard movement inside but could not see anyone coming to the door. Down the long corridor she could see the light flicker from the room at the back of the house.

She tried the handle of the front door and it moved down freely, the door swinging open as she pushed gently. The sun had almost disappeared, but she could feel its stagnant heat following her down the hallway, past the empty training room with the shelves of painting paraphernalia.

The voices were a murmur from the room at the back of the house where the only light was coming from what seemed to be a lantern. Shadows danced along the floor of the hallway, moving to the beat of the shivering flame. Kiran could make out her father's voice though she barely recognised it through the veil of anger.

"I tried for years to root out this evil. I searched wide and far, looking for our history, looking for reasons, and all the time it was here. My brother, my best friend, why did you not stop them?"

Dinesh's voice was subdued. "I was not as strong as you. Isn't that what my father said? When he chose you to be his son, to be leader."

"He loved you as a son. He did not think you wanted the role of leader. He thought that you were happy as you were. I did not mean to take anything from you, Dinesh. I had my life taken away from me when my father died and I never meant to take your father away from you."

Kiran reached the doorway. Both men were standing by the table and chairs at the top of the room where they had made their speeches. A lantern stood on the table and the room was full of empty chairs lined up facing the two men. Neither of them noticed Kiran in the darkness of the hall.

Ji said, "Your father wanted me to help him to continue the work my father had started. To chronicle our history. To expose our secrets. To remove the bad so that the good would be pure. My father tried but his life's path was cut short and it took time to find our way back. And I had so many diversions that the task was put aside."

Dinesh leaned against the lectern. "Why do we need to dig through the past to have a future? We have a long and proud history. As a profession, we have brought light into so many people's lives. We have made their visions come true, we have brought happiness."

Ji's voice grew louder. "That is what most of the Council wants. Men like Devdar could hide behind the positive and allow evil to sneak inside, in the folds of the cloak of good."

"My brother, you overreact as usual. It is not evil to keep the line pure, to adhere to the purity of the vision laid out by the first Guru."

Kiran could see her father's hands curl around the top of a chair. "Dinesh, if you can speak like that, if you can believe that, do not call me 'brother'. I am not your brother though I loved your father like my own."

Dinesh's body was mostly hidden behind the lectern and the light slid across his head as he waggled it. His voice was harsh "You always thought you were better than anyone else. You think you have been the best vision painter, the best leader of the Council, the best man. But the truth is that you are nothing. You have failed. You were weak and you broke the rules. You have produced no son. In fact, you have produced a girl." Dinesh laughed and the sound crackled through the room. "It gets even worse, does it not, Ji? You have produced a girl who has sex with other girls."

The gasp from Kiran was covered by the sound of the crash of wood breaking as Ji knocked over the chair he had been gripping.

"How dare you? Do not talk about my daughter like that." Ji's voice was hoarse.

"It is the truth, is it not? We are allowed to speak the truth, are we not? I am happy the girl that was born to Seeta is not alive to shame me like your girl child has done. You should not have been allowed to continue as a vision painter when you married Elizabeth, and you certainly should have been removed when she gave birth to a girl. Those are the rules that everyone else has had to live by, why do you get away with breaking them?"

Ji shook his head slowly.

Dinesh continued, "For every other vision painter, they have to produce a male child by the age of 25, otherwise they have to leave. What did you think? Did you believe in that myth that vision painters can only produce a boy? The eternal chain that just recreates itself? Well, sometimes, the myth needed a helping hand from us."

Kiran could see her father's hands clenching and unclenching as he spoke. "A helping hand? Did you kill that poor little baby because it was a girl? Were you the one who did that?"

Dinesh snorted. "I did not need to, Ji. There are men to do that. They do a job for those of us who have to live by the rules to remain in the profession. We are not all blessed with your good fortune to live exactly the life you want in exactly the way you want, to go against everything we believe in and still remain as one of us."

Ji staggered and put one hand against the wall to keep himself upright. Kiran rushed into the room. She put her hand on her father's arm and she could feel him recoil in surprise. His face was a moving patchwork of shadows and light as he looked up at her and she straightened up as he rested his weight on her.

Dinesh said, "You are like my father. Weak. He collapsed when you left. That night. Like a woman. And you support yourself on a girl. You look ill, my dear brother."

Kiran could feel her father trembling. His fingers were curled around her forearm. She looked at Dinesh and tried to keep her voice from cracking and screaming. "You are a monster. You and those men who would kill a defenceless baby because she was a girl. Are you so lost that you cannot see that?"

Dinesh snorted. "I hear the wind rustling through an empty can somewhere, Ji, do you hear it?"

Kiran felt the weight as her father straightened up to his full height. "My daughter is speaking and I hear her words. And she is right. You are a monster, a weak and pathetic creature that hides behind your misguided beliefs."

"And this from a man who threw away his son." Dinesh laughed. "Who is pathetic now?"

"My son?" Ji's voice was loud in the room. "What are you talking about? I have no son."

Dinesh came out from behind the lectern. The light of the lantern glinted in his eyes as he stared at Ji. "Your son. Who was born of the girl who was picked for you. Come on, Ji, don't tell me you never suspected?"

Kiran staggered as Ji jerked away, his hands coming to rest on the table. "I did not have a son. Somebody would have told me. My father would have told me." His shoulders slumped. "I would have taken him with us. If I had a child, I would have taken him with us."

There was a snigger in Dinesh's voice. "My father did not know. I did not tell him. Do you think I would have let him put you on an even higher pedestal? No, Ji, you were placed too high for your own good."

"Where is he? What did you do to him?" A look of satisfaction sauntered onto Dinesh's face at the fear in Ji's voice.

"I took care of everything for you, my brother. Is that not what brothers are for?" Dinesh held his hands over his heart with a mocking smile and Kiran could feel the shock of hatred curl and sizzle through her.

"What did you do to my brother?" Kiran knew he would ignore her but she couldn't stop the words.

Dinesh continued, addressing Ji, "I had a client who came to me for help. A rich man but with troubles. A widower. It was quite clever of me actually. I painted him with a beautiful woman and a child. And when I took the girl to him, he was very grateful. The baby boy was born 8 months later."

"I would have stood by him. He was my child, my son." All the energy seemed to have seeped out of Ji.

Dinesh said, "I took care of it. You had no son, and I had Rishi. And everything would have been fine if your girl child did not cause problems by painting. It was bad enough that she existed and you were not removed from us, but to flaunt the abomination in our faces. What did you expect, Ji?" For the first time, there was distress in Dinesh's voice. He walked over to the chairs as he talked. "If we did not have to deal with that abomination, my son would have remained with me. He would have been a great vision painter and leader of the Council now. He would have continued in our ways, kept the line pure. But instead he became infected by the need for a mother and he ran like a snivelling child to his mother. What was I to do? He would not stay and when he found out about the first baby, he became even more deranged. I had to take care of his mother too. They were sent away to England and I lost my son too." Dinesh sat down on a chair in the front row.

Ji said, "Where is my son?"

Dinesh looked up. "He did not have a good life, your son. I kept an eye on him but there was nothing I could do. His father, well, his step-father, was a beast of a man." He smiled at the sound of pain that emerged from Ji's mouth. "Yes, the man used his newly gained family to demonstrate his strength. Years of physical and mental brutality for the boy and his mother. Things did not end well for the stepfather though. His so-called son proved to have the gift of his real father, one of the greatest vision painters, and the boy did not have the training to restrict it to the positive."

"Why are you telling them these things? You promised me." The voice from the door behind them was familiar and strange at the same time. It carried years of pain and betrayal in its tone.

Kiran spun around. Vijay's face was a portrait of confusion that matched hers. Ji had turned as well at the sound of the voice from the doorway. Kiran could feel him gripping her arm. He moved her back slightly so that he was between her and Vijay.

Dinesh stood up. "Vijay, what are you doing here? I thought you were in Ireland."

"Why are you talking to them?" Vijay took a few steps into the room. His eyes were bloodshot, his hair unruly. He was staring at Dinesh but his eyes flicked to Ji and Kiran and away just as quickly.

Dinesh sounded uneasy. "I was not saying anything that needs to concern you."

Vijay's voice rose. "How can it not concern me? You are telling them my secrets. You promised never to tell anyone. You made me do all those paintings so that no one would ever know. Why are you not telling them your secrets?" He moved further into the room.

"Vijay, I told them nothing." Dinesh moved forward, his voice pleading.

Kiran fought the confusion and found her voice as she saw Vijay's hesitation. She said, "Except that you are my father's son and that you painted your step-father into what, death?"

Dinesh took a step back at the fear and rage in Vijay's face. Ji put his hand up and Kiran could see the shake in it. "*You* are my son?"

Vijay took his eyes off Dinesh and looked at Ji. He looked away again, this time his eyes met Kiran's. She thought she could see sorrow in the deep brown of his eyes.

Ji said, his voice growing firmer, "And you did that to Elizabeth? You painted her into this sickness?" He was drawing himself up to his full height and Kiran could see Vijay shrinking.

"She knew about me and did not tell you." Vijay blurted the words out.

"What? No!" Both Ji and Kiran spat out the words at the same time.

Vijay said, "Yes, she knew my mother was pregnant with me and did not tell you. She let us go and we suffered so much. My mother suffered and I had to watch. Until I could do something. Something I did not even know I had the power to do. I tried to protect her but he was too strong physically." His eyes were burning reflections of the flame of the lantern.

"Elizabeth never would have done that." There was a certainty in Ji's voice that made Vijay stall.

Vijay turned to Dinesh. "You told me that. You told me she was the one who asked you to get rid of us."

Dinesh's eyes seemed to search the room for a way out as Ji turned to him.

"I know Elizabeth and she would never do that. She would have done everything to give my son the best chance in life. With us if he wanted. We can go and ask her now but I have no doubt."

Dinesh shook his head.

Vijay's voice was a cry, "I would never have painted her if you had not told me that." He gripped his own head with clawed hands.

Dinesh said, "You did what I wanted because you were angry at your father. Do not try and excuse your actions now."

Vijay's voice was muffled. "I was angry at him but I would not have done anything to her."

Kiran said, "And what about Ashley? Why did you do that to Ashley? You did, didn't you?

Vijay nodded slowly, his head still in his hands. "I am sorry. I am sorry. He made me do all the paintings. He said he knew what I had done to my step-father and that he would tell everyone if I did not help him. Then when I met my real father and I knew he did not know about me, Dinesh told me that it was Elizabeth's fault. I could not get away. He told me I had to paint you and cause you the same pain. I tried but I could not for some reason and then I heard Ashley say that she had so much guilt for what she had done to some Jennifer and I knew I could paint her instead. But I did not want to paint the baby. I really did not want to paint the baby. I do not understand how he could demand that."

Kiran's hands flew to her belly. "No!"

Vijay looked at her and held out his hand towards her stomach. He stopped when she flinched. His voice was shaking. "I am so sorry. It will not work anyway. The baby has no negative energy. I could only paint your fears. If you remain positive and believe in your baby, it will be safe. I hope. I hope so much. Kiran, I never meant to hurt you or Ashley. But I was afraid of what Dinesh would do. I was all that my mother had. When she died last year, he told me all these things. I was filled with so much hate and anger." The tears were running down his face.

Dinesh's voice was harsh. "Another weak one. What is it, Ji, that your offspring are a weak man and a girl?" He walked towards Vijay. "You are so weak that you did not even have the power to finish your step-father off with that painting." He laughed as Vijay's hands fell from his face.

"What? You think you have the power to kill someone with your painting?" Dinesh was still talking as he walked past Vijay and to a cupboard in the hallway. He reached in and his hand emerged gripping a machete. His voice got louder as he walked back into the room. "Though you undoubtedly have a powerful gift. You painted your step-father in horrible pain with red across his chest and you were obviously in a fury. You probably would have killed him with your bare hands if your mother had not done it first. She wanted to protect you because she thought you would kill him and your life would be over. An 18-year-old man and your mother had to do the job for you. She had to get me to clean up your mess. But when I saw the painting and the matching state of the man I realised you did have your real father's gift."

There was a noise as Ji pulled Kiran behind him. Dinesh turned away from Vijay's shocked face and stared at Ji. "It is over. And you can do nothing about it. Who will believe I did this? Vijay is practically a stranger here. He will get the blame for going mad and killing his father and half-sister. And when the police hear about his history..." Dinesh smiled as he shook his head. "It is over, Ji. And I can finally say words to you that I have wanted to say since I was a 17-year-old boy. This long battle to make my mark on this world without your interference. Everything has always been about you, has it not? You lose your father and your way and I suffer as a result. It was always me that suffered, that lost. My father, Elizabeth, my leadership, my son."

Ji said, "Elizabeth?"

Dinesh said, "Your father was searching for answers in our history as well. He did not believe that the vision painters could only produce a boy child and he was right. Your father found the ancient scripts and translated them. He found out why we were only men with this gift. And he was going to use that knowledge to expose those who would protect it." He sighed. "That knowledge would have remained hidden after your father died but my father insisted on searching for it and you were helping him. I may have helped your father on his way but I did not even have to help you off the cliff. You were more than capable of walking off it yourself. And Elizabeth never noticed me but she at least got you out of my life for a time. I could not believe my father would let you back in again and even the birth of a girl could not seem to remove you from this place. But there were men who believed as I did in the purity of our faith and they were as disgusted by the abomination of your girl child living amongst us."

Dinesh continued, his words falling into the hush that had descended on the room. He seemed oblivious of Vijay and Kiran, his eyes fixed on Ji as he spoke. "You would have discovered the knowledge very soon anyway. You have the papers and I would not be able to stop you reading them though I tried to distract you." Dinesh sighed. "I do not understand why it mattered to your father or mine. We live good lives, we help people. Our vision painters need to believe in the rules. They need a shared history, a sense that they are chosen, born into their gift. That is all that I have done. Continued to provide them a structure and a belief that helps them to feel their superiority and translate that power into helping others."

Vijay blurted out, "It was built on a lie. I have read the script too. The first Guru did not just have a son, he had twins, and one of them was a girl."

Dinesh smiled. "So you got the papers as well. Yes, that is what was written."

Ji said, "What are you talking about? Guru had one son and the boy had the same gift. There were no girl children. The Guru was very clear that the gift only came through men. That the purity of their thinking and the focus they could bring to their gift was crucial. We grew up with no mothers, no female influence for that reason. No weakness or distraction was allowed."

Vijay wiped roughly at his face. "They took out the part where it showed that the girl had as much of a gift as the boy. She was more interested, in fact. But she was brought down by her empathy. She made a mistake when she painted for the wrong person. She did not agree with the customs of the time and she stopped a young woman being burned to death because her husband had died."

Kiran moved so she was standing beside her father and asked, "What happened to her?"

Vijay said, his voice betraying his shock, "The young woman escaped and the husband's family found out about it because they found the painting in her possessions and accused the twin boy but he confessed that it was his sister and she was burned instead. On the same pyre that was still flaming with the fire of the husband's body."

Kiran felt her stomach churning.

Vijay whispered, "The Guru was heartbroken. He believed until then that the gift was open to anyone with empathy, with pure love in their hearts. He hardened his heart after that. He let his son continue and the son was so filled with shame that he changed the story until the girl did not exist anymore in the scripts and the myth was started and sustained for years. That only men could be vision painters." Vijay's voice strengthened. "That women were dispensable and that a vision painter was not fully a man if he needed his mother and could not fit in with the beliefs of the group. They kept the myth going by getting rid of any baby girls in secret. They did this in secret because part of the myth was that the vision painters could only produce a son. If they did not, they had to leave. Who would want to leave, to lose this gift, this power, this brotherhood? Some did what they had to do to remain." Vijay looked at Ji. "But the majority of them were good men who knew nothing of this."

The lantern flickered and the shadows jumped and receded. Dinesh looked around. "Why are we in the dark?" He walked over to the door and switched on the light. The shadows shrank away and disappeared. All except Dinesh blinked in the sudden brightness.

Dinesh said, "The history lesson is over." He hefted the machete and ran his finger along the edge. The fear in his eyes was mixed with regret and hatred.

Kiran felt Ji push her behind him again and she felt the edge of the table bite into her back. Her hands reached behind her for support and jerked back as they came into contact with the heated glass of the lantern.

Dinesh moved with care, almost reluctance, as he approached them. The machete flashed silver as Vijay took a step to block his path. Dinesh smiled as Vijay stopped. He gestured with the machete towards the left but Vijay remained where he was, too far away to stop Dinesh's progress towards Ji and Kiran.

Dinesh said, "You did not see your step-father die but you will see your real father finally get out of my way. And you cannot even protect your sister like..."

Dinesh's scream rang through the room as the glass shattered and hot oil sprayed his face and chest. Kiran did not even feel the burn in her hand as she grabbed the machete from his hand and backed away. She dropped the machete at her father's feet. Ji was still staring in shock at Dinesh writhing on the ground. Kiran dragged Dinesh onto his back and tore at the burning shirt but it was stuck to skin.

Vijay and Ji both jerked forward as if out of a dream and Ji tore off his mundu and used the cloth to smother the flames. The sound of Dinesh's screams was muffled by their efforts but as the flames died out, the screams rose again until they filled the room.

CHAPTER FORTY-ONE

Kiran woke up with a start. She grimaced as she tried to work her neck back into shape. The light bandages on her hands were streaked with paint and she picked a few specks of brown and red off before giving up.

The right side of her body felt hot as it lay in the direct path of the sun which sneaked in under the half-open blinds. She could hear the faint trickle from the water feature outside the window. The wind rustled through the dried fronds on its passage through the banana trees. She was grateful for the relief it brought slipping in the open window onto her damp forehead.

The canvas rested where she had leant it against the wall the previous night. She had finally been able to paint again, the heavy bandages she had sported on her hands for a month having been replaced with the now stained but lighter ones.

Kiran tilted her head against the wicker of the chair as she examined the face of the man who smiled back at her in painted hues of ochre and sienna, the smile a brilliant flash of pale white against brown. She had not painted in the anguish in his eyes as he had begged for her forgiveness or the caged hurt of a wounded animal as he watched his father walk away. She had instead used the colours of his future happiness and poured the love she could not express into the pigmented shades of her lost brother. She had not even needed to see his eyes at her words of forgiveness to know that he would let the painting work when he saw it.

As for her father, she could only hope that he would see past the pain inflicted on her mother to see a betrayed child begging for his love.

"Kiran? Come." Her mother's voice sounded bemused through the thick carved door of the studio. It trailed off as her mother walked past the studio towards the kitchen.

Kiran got out of the chair, stretching her cramped muscles. She found her slippers and unlocked the door and stumbled into the hall.

"Thank you. That was very nice. A bit on the milky side but very nice." The voice was loud and familiar but so out of place that Kiran did not recognise it for a few seconds.

Delilah?

"I don't think he understands. No, saying it louder won't help either." Kiran heard Ron's quiet voice as she reached the living room door.

She hurried into the living room, bumping into Babu who was coming out carrying a tray of empty chai cups. He seemed relieved to see her. Ron was standing by the door and Delilah was sitting beside Ashley on the wicker couch. Kiran stopped.

The halo of red outlined Ashley's face which was almost invisible against the white walls. The light in Ashley's eyes was dimmer than she could remember seeing and Kiran knew it was her hand that had shielded the flame of that candle.

Delilah jumped up from the couch and enveloped Kiran's frozen figure in a hug. "I'm sorry I'm wringing here. Good Lord, how do you do it?" She squeezed before releasing Kiran who still couldn't seem to find her voice.

Ron smiled. "Sorry to just arrive like this. I think we might have upset your mother. She has gone to get a feast together I think"

"You are very welcome." Ji's voice came close to booming in Kiran's ear as he entered the room. "You are our first visitors from Ireland. This is an unexpected pleasure."

Ji shook hands with Delilah and Ron. Ashley got to her feet and Ji paused before taking her hand and examining her pale face and luminous brown eyes.

"Ashley, you are very welcome. I hope you are feeling better." Ji nudged her back to the couch and Ashley sank down on it. Ji sat beside her and gestured to the other chairs with a smile. Ron and an unusually subdued Delilah took their seats.

Ashley smiled at Ji and Kiran felt her heart jump as she watched the sparkle flick back into Ashley's eyes with the smile. Ashley's voice was weaker than usual. "I am feeling a lot better, thank you. The pain finally went away completely a week ago and I'm just getting used to moving around freely again."

Ji said, "I am truly sorry you had to experience that. I hope you had the good experience of vision painting as well as the bad. None of us have had to suffer the negative side in such a way before." He sighed. "History has a way of reaching from the past and colouring our future. And even when we do not know the details, we must take some responsibility for not searching hard enough and stopping the negative."

Ji shook his head and looked up. "Kiran, are you going to stand there like a tree or are you going to talk to our guests?"

Delilah found her voice. "It is lovely in here. It is a furnace out there. May I call you Ji? Thank you. Did you find it hard to re-adjust jumping from a fridge to an oven after you got back here from Ireland?"

Ji smiled. "That is why I installed air conditioners in every room." He waved both hands. "I modernised this house when we got back. They did not even have a proper kitchen. I designed an excellent kitchen. Do you want to see the house? And I can show you the retirement complex I built. Not with my own two hands, of course, but I designed it and the builder was a client of mine. Top builder in Kerala. He was a very busy man but he would do anything for me. I did a vision painting for him years ago."

Delilah jumped up. "We would love to see the house and the complex. Wouldn't we, Ron? Ashley, you should stay here. You still need to rest, that was one hell of a crazy journey. Ji, do they have driving licences or driving tests here?"

Ron made a sound of protest aimed in Delilah's direction, but Ji ushered them out of the room with a laugh. Kiran could hear him describing the road and rail network in Kerala as his voice receded down the hallway towards the kitchen. She leaned against the armchair and drank in the sight of Ashley then slid into the seat as she felt her legs weakening.

Kiran said, "This is a lovely surprise." She tried a weak smile in Ashley's direction and was rewarded with a frown. Her voice caught in her throat.

Ashley's voice was still weak but there was a thread of steel through it. "Kiran, I would not be here if my father and Delilah had not insisted that they wouldn't leave me on my own in the house."

Kiran felt the hope she had felt seeing Ashley sitting on the couch sizzle and fade as it sank. Ashley's face was remote and unforgiving.

Kiran whispered, "I had to do it, Ashley. I had no choice. If I had a choice do you think I would have done it?"

Ashley said, "There are always choices, Kiran. You made a choice. A choice to throw me away, to throw my love away."

"But if I hadn't you could have died, or had to be kept in a coma for who knows how long. I had to paint you out of my life. I had to paint a positive vision of your future to counteract the negative painting Vijay did. And it worked, didn't it? And what was holding you in that negative, Ashley? You haven't told me that. How Vijay could paint you into that pain unless you carried such guilt. Guilt over what, Ashley? Did you love Jennifer so much that you could not let go of her? Did you have an affair with her?" Kiran found the words rushing past her lips like a torrent that she could not hold back.

Ashley looked surprised at the outburst. She shook her head. "No, Kiran, if you'd stayed around to ask, you would have known that I didn't have an affair. I spent a little time with Jenny to discuss my new job but it was totally innocent. On my part, anyway. I cannot speak for Jenny and I can't make her stop having feelings for me but I never encouraged those feelings. In fact, I was very clear with her that we could try to be friends only if she was able to do that without hurting. And yes, I felt extreme guilt at what I had done to her. It was not easy for her to spend years believing she was with the person that she was going to marry, that her life was going to follow a particular route, and then have that person leave her. Not just leave her, but come back to her and then leave her again in a few weeks. You know, that is what I feel guilty over. The first time I left her was because I fell in love with you and I knew I had never been in love with Jenny, I just went with what she and everyone else wanted for us. But the second time, Kiran, I only went back to Jenny because my mother threatened to destroy you. That was my mother's fault and not Jenny's. But Jenny ended up suffering."

Ashley paused and slowly unclenched her fists. She continued in a softer voice, "I spent the time after you left as you told me to. I went over everything with Jenny and I came to terms with it and with what my mother had done to me. How she played on my guilt over Sarah. How she used my need for her forgiveness and her love to control me, to control everything about my life." She looked up at Kiran and her eyes were wet with tears. "I decided to stop living with guilt, to stop begging for love, to be satisfied with who I am and what I have in my life."

There was a certainty in Ashley's voice and Kiran's heart sank at her words. She'd known what the painting would mean but she realised that most of her had lived in hope. She was deafened by the dying screams of that hope.

Kiran struggled to her feet. She kept her voice steady. "It sounds like you have found the happiness I hoped for you. That makes me happy, Ashley. Will I get Shalini to make up a room for you and Ron and Delilah?" She managed a smile and wondered if it looked as false as it felt. "Is that three singles or have the two of them finally figured out that they're meant for each other?"

Ashley shook her head. "They've already booked a double room for themselves in a hotel in the next town." She smiled. "They have finally figured it out. It seems age brings the benefit of sense at some point."

Kiran stared at Ashley's smile and searched for words but her vocabulary had deserted her.

Ashley stood up. There was a glimmer of mischief in her eyes. "I, however, don't have a room. I thought I might sleep in yours. Unless of course your parents would object to such crazy Western practices."

"I thought..." Kiran stopped.

"Perhaps you should take a break from that. You've been doing too much of that and coming up with the daftest things." Ashley smiled again.

Kiran felt her breath slow down as Ashley ran her finger along Kiran's bottom lip. She could see the flecks and ridges, the familiar terrain of Ashley's eyes as Ashley leaned in close to Kiran's face.

Ashley whispered, "If I didn't know your defence mechanism by now, I might have walked away. But I know you love me and you live in fear of losing what you love. Don't worry, I'll get you to say it later, I'm not letting you get away that easily. And by the way, you can add Delilah to the list of terrible liars that you occupy with my dad. How is the miniature Dane doing, making you very sick every morning I hope? Speaking of Danes, I've decided we're getting a dog. Or maybe two or three. I've always wanted a lot of animals around the house."

"I thought..." Kiran stopped again. She couldn't find any other two words despite a desperate search through her brain.

Ashley sighed and shook her head.

Kiran felt her blood slow before making a heated dash into her face. Ashley's finger moved along the line of her jaw. Hope resurrected sang like a choir in her ears. She closed her eyes but they sprang open again, defying her, and she realised she could not bear to shut Ashley out anymore. She had made the sacrifice saying it was for Ashley's sake, but there had been greys thrown onto the palette. The greyness of fear and doubt, the fog that surrounded Kiran, the constant need to run in case she was responsible for the changes and losses that inevitably followed her laughter and happiness.

Ashley whispered, "So, what will it be?"

Kiran felt her hands tangle in Ashley's hair. She pulled gently until Ashley's lips were a breath away from hers. "I love you. I have loved you from the moment I first looked into your eyes. I will love you even after the colours have slipped from our lives and moved onto the canvas of our future."

She moved until their lips touched and the need for words ceased and all she could feel was the woman who fit her soul.

She could feel the curve of lips after a few moments as Ashley smiled. Ashley's voice was breathy. "I just wanted to know if you were okay with us having dogs."

Kiran giggled. "I thought I was the one who never took anything seriously." She hugged Ashley. "Now, I've to figure out how to get my parents to let us sleep in the same room. Because, crazy Western ways or not, I'm never sleeping apart from you again."

EPILOGUE

Ji stared at the man across the waiting room and the man lowered his eyes. Ji looked down at his clothes, very smart trousers and shirt. It must be the thick white beard. It was close to Christmas in Ireland, but he did not think he looked that much like Santa Claus. He was much more distinguished looking, and he was brown.

He picked up a magazine and scanned the articles as they flew past on the pages. Crazy Westerners. What was an X factor? He put the magazine down and picked up a newspaper. He should have gone in. They would have let him. Though he might have talked in very long words to that nurse who had asked Kiran if she spoke English. Ji snorted. He had begged Kiran to have the baby in Kerala where he had the inside track to the best hospital. She had laughed on the phone and insisted he and Amma make it to Galway for the delivery. They were staying in Ron's house. Ji's allergies extended to dog hair it seemed and with three dogs the house in Connemara was difficult for him.

Ji sneezed at the memory and the man said, "Bless you."

Ji nodded politely. "Thank you." *What was going on in there? Was the baby alright? If someone didn't come out soon with a baby, he was going to...*

Elizabeth's voice broke through his thoughts. "Ji, come." She turned and walked back to the delivery room before he could ask.

Ji got to his feet and the man smiled. "First grandchild?"

Ji nodded. A beaming smile split his face. He walked towards the delivery room doors remembering his fear so many years ago.

Elizabeth stuck her head out. "It's a boy."

Ji felt a strange sense of disappointment. He had been so sure.

Elizabeth smiled at his expression. "You might want to wait outside, there's another one on the way. And it's a girl."

"Twins!?" Ji stopped. "How are they going to manage? I told them not to get those dogs."

Elizabeth looked guilty and he said, "You did not promise we would stay, did you?"

She nodded. "Just for a few months. It will do you good to get away from the Council work for a while. It has been too much for you. Let Vijay take care of things there until you get back."

"But I have a lot of work to do. I have to write the history of our profession. It is even more vital now to show all the good we have achieved. I have to find all the men involved and make sure they are brought to justice, and there is the court case against Dinesh. I cannot just, what do they say, 'hang out' here."

Elizabeth came out of the room and stood in front of him. Her eyes were determined. "All those years that you gave to your profession and that Association and especially that Council. It is time to give some to Kiran, and Ashley, and little Sarah Elizabeth Delilah and Jamie Ji Ron."

Ji smiled. They are calling him after me?"

Elizabeth smiled. "Yes, and Ashley's father too."

"Of course, of course. But who will ever say all three names?" Ji chuckled as he followed Elizabeth through the delivery room doors.

He came back out quickly as the sound of one baby's wail was duplicated a few seconds later by another twin cry.

THE END

ABOUT THE AUTHOR

R J SAMUEL was born in Nigeria to Indian parents, moved to Ireland where she lived for thirty years, had a few years sojourn in France, and now lives in America. Her novels reflect her varied life with settings from Galway to Kerala and a compelling mix of genres.

BOOKS BY R J SAMUEL

HEART STOPPER

THE VISION PAINTER SERIES:

> **FALLING COLOURS** – The Misadventures of a Vision Painter
>
> **CASTING SHADOWS** – The Further Misadventures of a Vision Painter

A PLACE SOMEWHERE – (See excerpt that follows)

Social Media

Website : www.rjsamuel.com

Blog: www.rjsamuel.com/blog

Twitter: www.twitter.com/r_j_samuel

Facebook Author Page: http://www.facebook.com/RJSamuelAuthor

Check out the extract of A Place Somewhere that follows...

A PLACE SOMEWHERE

PROLOGUE

There are so many steps I took along the way that felt wrong. My feet landed, but there was no earth beneath them. It is too late to say I wish I had picked my way more carefully, that I had not listened to the wrong voices, that I had been able to hear my own voice, the little voice that spoke to me in the moments between the closing and opening of my eyes.

Will my life have meant anything to anyone except for me? Or even to me? I did the wrong things for the right reasons. Now, I am about to do the right thing for the wrong reason.

I should be able to live for myself, but I can't. So this is the right thing to do. I have lost the one I would have lived for. This is the wrong reason to die.

But what is one more wrong to add to the wrongs I have done.

The loss of hope, of belief, of innocence. That to me is the death of a soul. This is just making it real for the body.

I wish I had never gone to that place.

1

The woman lay on her back in the lifeless room. A breeze trickled through the window and along the walls, caressing the lock of hair that fell across her forehead and battling to wrest the piece of paper from under her hand, but the paper rested, weighted down, agitated only at the corners.

Outside, the wind raged at its loss.

CHAPTER ONE

Alex pushed the hangers of red T-shirts apart and stared at the woman she had pursued for weeks through an online maze. The woman was a cheap imitation of the blonde in the photographs. Her clothes matched some of those on the racks that sheltered Alex; a leopard-print blouse hugged tight black leggings. An employee name badge that proclaimed her true name hung lopsided in black and white against the jungle print.

Alex knew she was avoiding the inevitable, taking refuge in the solace of the assembled clothes and in their colour changes over the full spectrum from reds to blues to greens, every shade provided in a department store in one of the busiest malls in the U.S. The air-conditioning chilled the sweat on her forehead that was due in part to the sweltering heat outside on Queens Boulevard and in part to her nearing the end of the chase, to the discovery of the quarry, and the imminent confrontation. She wondered if she would ever get blasé about this part, no matter how much she tried.

The woman had finished folding the T-shirts back onto the display shelves. Her skin was pale against the vivid colours, her hands mottled with sun stains. She looked like she was going to leave Oversize and Alex straightened herself out of the clothes rack and walked in a diagonal line towards Petites. She had watched the woman for an hour. She knew this was the right one.

3

The woman reached the aisle before her and Alex picked up her pace as she followed the scrape of sandals on shiny floors. She was not sure how she was going to play out the end of this search. Judith just wanted the truth, good or bad. Alex wanted more. She wanted answers. And something else. She wanted some release from the anger and pain, and this woman did not deserve gentleness.

It was almost lunchtime. The woman grabbed a blue leather handbag from behind a counter and waved at another employee before walking out of the exit to the store and into the stream of shoppers. Alex followed dodging the knapsacks and shopping bags, keeping out of sight behind the teenagers glued to their smartphones. The two women were separated by an escalator of people as they descended into the food court and Alex used the slow ride down to pick what food she would get to hide behind. She wasn't hungry though she hadn't eaten since she had booked the flight from Orlando. That had been yesterday and she'd flown in to New York this morning. She probably wouldn't be able to eat until tomorrow morning, when she had slept a night in Boston. After this job was over.

The Food Court was busy and Alex tracked the woman's movements with tired eyes. The journey had been hot and awkward. Everything here seemed hot and awkward to her. The crowds of people, the noise, the humidity. She felt the longing for her old home of Ireland the most at these times. For the uncrowded quiet, the cool dampness of air.

She aimed for an outlet that offered salads and watched the leopard-print join the queue at the Chinese counter. Alex bought a salad and waited until the woman was seated at a table. A bamboo plant fanned out of a pot right beside the table and shaded it from the ring of lights suspended from the ceiling. Alex sat at the next table, edging her chair closer, angling it so that she could see and now, could be seen.

4

The woman was on her phone. Her voice was loud but it barely made a dent in the hall of echoed conversations. She teased at her yellow hair, straightening reluctant strands between pincers of blue fingernails.

"I told you not to pull your sister's hair. Brittany, how many times I told you? And you're supposed to be taking care of Ethan, not bullying your sister." The words were muffled by the noodles she was pulling into her mouth with the plastic fork in her other hand. "I don't care. I don't know why I do this. Your father can take care of it when he gets home. Don't screw with my computer. I need it tonight and if I find your dirty paw prints all over it I'm going to make sure you don't get to use Facebook again for a very long time, you hear me?"

The sound of teenage angst was still coming from the phone as she placed it down on the linoleum surface and jabbed at it to put it off.

Alex kept her voice soft. "Kids, huh. Aren't they such a pain when you need to work on your stuff?" She gave a smile as the woman looked up from her food. The smile she knew worked on straight men as well as lesbian women, and on women who'd ever thought about other women in ways they had never expected.

It worked on this woman. Alex saw the slight widening of her eyes and the wipe of fingers over her mouth.

"Yes, kids can be such a pain. You'd think I was asking for world peace." This time a stroke of her lips with a napkin. "That's such a beautiful accent. Irish, isn't it? I love that accent. My husband's ancestors are from Ireland."

Alex nodded and forced more of a brogue. "I'm just visiting, a bit lost really. Everything is so much bigger here in the States." She moved in her seat and gestured around in as helpless a manner as she could.

"I hear Ireland is wonderful. My husband always wanted to go back to visit there. Me, I was born and bred here and I don't know if I'll ever get to travel so far away."

Alex said, "You should visit. It takes less time than you think. About the time it would take to get from here to California."

"Maybe one day, maybe, who knows. Welcome to New York. I'm Pam." Pam ran a finger along her name badge which pronounced the full version.

"Hi Pam, thanks. I'm Alex."

"Not a very Irish name. I thought it would be something unpronounceable, you know like that kid actress, you know the one who has a name that is said completely different from how it is written. Or else something like Mary."

"It's short for Alyson." Alex smiled again and watched an answering smile grow on Pam's lips.

"Very nice." There was a slight huskiness to Pam's voice. "So, what brings you to New York, Alex?" She gestured with her fork at her noodles before digging in again.

"Just a visit." Alex played with her lettuce. The smell of the food all around them was making her feel sick. Or it might have been the residual effects of the sun on her black hair leaving her with a headache. "So, are you from Queens then?"

A strand of noodle drooped before being sucked in. "Yes. Grew up here and married and had my kids. Three of them, a boy and two girls."

"Have you ever lived anywhere else?" Alex asked without enthusiasm. She knew the answer. And despite the job she was doing, she hated the lies. She stuck as close to the truth as possible in everything she said.

Pam shook her head. "Never been out of the state. Well, unless you count Atlantic City. That's New Jersey."

6

Suddenly, Alex just wanted this to end. She wondered how jaded she could get before disappearing? After only four chases? Three of which ended like this. She could barely bring herself to be charming, to work her way into another woman's life, especially another one like this. Alex did not need these questions answered, she knew what this woman was; she just wanted to know why.

She said, "Trish?" and saw the blood drain under the tanned skin and makeup. Pam's lips struggled to decide on a position. They finally settled on open.

Alex got up from her table and moved the few feet over to Pam's. Pam's eyes darted from the abandoned salad and back to Alex.

Alex said, "Judith sent me."

"Sent you?" The words finally dropped out of Pam's mouth. "Judith? I don't know any Judith. Or any Trish." She pushed away the half-eaten Chinese food and shifted her weight to get up.

Alex didn't move. "Would you rather do this here or at your home? In front of your husband and children?"

It took a few seconds for Pam to slump back into the chair.

Alex picked up the phone that lay on the table between them. "I assume you have Judith's number on this?"

Pam mumbled something that sounded affirmative.

Alex sat down. "And I assume since you didn't tell her you were married and have three children you don't have any intention of following through on any of the promises you made to her?"

Pam crept further back in her chair and closed her eyes. The shake of her head was so slight that Alex would have missed it if not for the jangle of frizzy blonde hair against the patterned top.

7

"Was it even your photograph?" Alex examined the woman. "Actually, yes, it was. Photoshop?"

Pam opened her eyes, sparkling blue in the photo, a washed out grey in life. "I only sent her one photo of me. Maybe I was a little younger in it. And okay, Brittany had messed around with it a little before I gave it to them at work." Her hand was smoothing at her hair. "How did you find me?"

"That picture actually. After I checked your IP address and it wasn't in California like you said you were. I did an image search. Found that photo on your store website. Traced you through Facebook."

"But I don't use that Facebook account much."

"It was on your colleague Sandra's page. You were at her party, with your husband and kids."

Pam pursed her lips. She asked, "What does Judith want? What did she ask you to do if you found me?"

"Just to get the truth."

"You're not going to tell my husband, are you?"

Alex didn't reply, but she could feel the muscles in her jaw tense.

Pam rushed on, "Judith will be better off without me. I wish I was all that, you know, what I wrote. That I had the glamorous PA job I told her I had, but I just work in a department store. She wouldn't have wanted me anyway, would she? Not in real life. A rich widow? She has a nice life. All the Art stuff she's into, the galleries."

"She believed you, all your emails, phone calls, your protestations of love. She thinks you are someone special in her life. She just wanted me to check after you kept avoiding her invitations to the cottage in Cape Cod." A beep sounded and Alex looked down at her clenched hand. She put Pam's phone back on the table. "That's going to be the hard part. Telling her you were lying the whole time. I don't think she

8

would care what you really work at or that you're not any of the things you said you were. You aren't, are you?"

Pam shook her head.

Alex frowned. "You went to a lot of trouble to be this other person, this perfect partner for Judith. But I guess a year is a long time and you had to fill it."

Pam said. "I found a lot of stuff online."

"Art exhibitions, galleries, a job as a PA to a famous actor."

Pam's face in person showed lines that seemed deeper, her flesh looser on her cheeks and jaws than in the posed and airbrushed photo.

Alex leaned forward. She was close enough to smell the sweat that trickled down Pam's temple.

Alex whispered. "You're a coward who hides behind her computer screen and hurts people, decent truthful women who just make the mistake of believing in you. What kind of person needs to do that to have her fun?" The words felt like acid dripping from her lips, but they brought no relief. She had a well of acid in her now.

Pam shook her head, but her eyes betrayed her guilt, and her fear. She closed them, tilting her face away.

Alex sank back. "I should let you face Judith, look her in the eyes and tell her yourself. You wouldn't have the guts to do that though, would you?"

Pam opened her eyes.

"Don't tell her anything then." There was a flicker of something like hope in Pam's eyes as they rushed to Alex's face. "Just say you couldn't find me. I'll end it with her online. I will. I'll tell her that I meant everything I said, but that we were not meant to be together. I'll find something, some kind way of letting her down easy. There's no need for her to know. Please. Alex. That is your name, isn't it?"

"Yes. I don't lie about things like that." Alex looked around at the people eating around them. How many were like her, how many like Pam? She leant back and felt the exhaustion settle around her shoulders. It would be so much easier if she didn't have to make the trip to Boston, didn't have to face another broken heart crying tears for an unknown loved one. Maybe one less cynic could actually be a good thing, pacified by the sad yet romantic words of fate. Let Pam do it her way.

Alex sighed. There were rules. She had written them for herself, guidelines on this strange path upon which she had been forced. And one of them was that she would see all cases through. She would be the truth that the women could cling to, could trust. They needed that anchor after they swam the depths of betrayal. And she needed to be real for them.

"No can do. I'm sorry," Alex said. "However, I won't tell your husband." She waited until the words registered and the look of hope was firmly installed in Pam's eyes. "But you have to answer my questions. With the truth, if you know what that is."

Pam nodded, her hair bouncing vigorously.

Alex said the words that now felt permanently etched on her lips. "Why did you do it?"

Pam frowned. She seemed to be searching for her thoughts on the matter. Like she had never considered the question before. The look was so familiar to Alex that she had named it the 'Hell if I know' look.

"I guess I wanted to have a different life for a while. You know, have someone different but not have an affair. Yes, that's it. I didn't want to cheat on my husband, but things can get a little settled after a while." Pam paused and Alex could sense her picking the words that would elicit sympathy. "See, I didn't really have an affair, did I? No one really got hurt here. Judith and I had some chats and she felt

10

good with a girlfriend like me. Yes, you see she was lonely and she fell for me and I didn't want to hurt her by telling her I wasn't really like the person she got to know. I mean, what good would it have done? And it isn't like I took anything of hers. I just gave her a dream. What's so wrong with that? We all need something to dream about." Pam's voice had strengthened from a whisper and was now convincing.

Alex shook her head. She tried to control her voice. It came out in a low hiss. "And you really don't think what you did was wrong? Lying about loving her, lying about the interests you shared, not telling her about the family you had, building a future with someone who right now is waiting for you, waiting for what she thinks is a true love? Did you ever have any intention of going to her?"

There was a whine in Pam's voice. "What do you want me to say? Why are you so angry? It was just an online fling. It's not like this is going to break Judith's heart or anything. I mean, we never met. Just emails and phone conversations. How can she have loved someone she never met? I thought she was doing the same thing I was, you know, having a little fun."

Alex realised she was gripping the table top. She loosened her fingers and rubbed the blood back into them. Each confrontation seemed to be adding to the anger in her, rather than releasing it. The role of avenger she had taken on was taking its toll, especially when she could do nothing. No, not nothing. She could at least stop the deceit from continuing for the innocent.

Pam stood up, "I gotta get back to work. I answered your questions. You don't need to tell my husband. Besides, I didn't do nothing wrong. Not really. He would see that too. He'd probably want in on it." She grabbed her phone.

"Is there anything you want me to tell Judith?" Alex didn't know why she always asked this question. Was there another lie that could make all the other lies better?

"No. Just tell her... I mean, I don't know. I gotta go, really. Can't afford to lose this job. Tell her I said I was sorry. Yes, tell her that for me." Pam put her phone back into her handbag and wiped her palms on her leggings. "She'll find someone else."

Alex stood up. She could see the grey hairs that edged the parting of yellow at the top of Pam's scalp.

"Actually, she thought she had found her someone else. Judith is a decent woman. She is going to be devastated because she seems to love you. Or at least the 'you' that you fed her. It isn't a crime to be lonely, she doesn't deserve this." Alex felt the words were sliding off Pam's ears, dangling from her earrings. The woman was partially turned, almost fully gone.

Pam nodded. "I know, I know. No one deserves to be hurt. Tell her I'm sorry."

Alex watched as Pam clutched her handbag close and hurried into the open centre of the mall. She stood until the woman rode the escalator out of view and then sat down heavily, her legs shaking with tiredness, the familiar acid taste of anger in her mouth.

A PLACE SOMEWHERE is available on Amazon as a paperback and at online retailers as an eBook.